THE MASTER OF DREAMS

THE
MASTER OF
DREAMS

BOOK ONE OF THE
DREAMSCAPE TRILOGY

MIKE RESNICK

DAW BOOKS, INC.

DONALD A. WOLLHEIM, FOUNDER
1745 Broadway, New York, NY 10019
ELIZABETH R. WOLLHEIM
SHEILA E. GILBERT
PUBLISHERS
www.dawbooks.com

To Carol, as always.

And to Sheila Gilbert,
Friend and editor of half a lifetime.

What am I doing here? thought Eddie Raven. *I could be watching the ballgame, or losing less money at Belmont Park than this afternoon is gonna cost me.*

Then he looked at the lovely girl holding on to his arm as she inspected every window of every shop up and down Fifth Avenue, and he remembered.

"Oh, isn't that a gorgeous hat?" said Lisa, pointing to a window.

"Do women still wear hats?" asked Eddie.

"Of course we do!"

"I've never seen you wear one," he noted.

"I haven't found the right one," she answered.

"And you've been looking for how many years?" asked Eddie with a smile.

She made a face at him and led him to the next store on the block. And the next after that. And after that.

"You ready to eat?" asked Eddie.

"It's only midafternoon," replied Lisa, taking his arm and leading him across the street. "If you're tired of looking at shops, you can look at ladies' legs while I window-shop."

"That day is gone forever, alas," replied Eddie.

She frowned. "What are you talking about?"

He looked up the sidewalk. "Women don't wear skirts anymore," he said. "I see twenty—no, make that twenty-one—walking toward us. Nineteen are wearing slacks, and one of the other two has got to be a great-grandmother."

Lisa chuckled. "Slacks are comfortable," she said. "And comforting."

He looked puzzled. "Comforting?"

"It's comforting to know that dirty old men aren't trying to look up your skirt when you're sitting in the subway," she answered.

Eddie shrugged. "Never occurred to me."

"It wouldn't," she said, then stopped suddenly and peered into a window. "Isn't that the loveliest sweater?"

"It's ninety degrees," he said.

"It's not ninety year round."

"If you want it, let's go in and buy it," said Eddie.

"If I don't find something better," said Lisa, "I just may do that."

"Right," said Eddie grimly. "There are only nine hundred more stores on Fifth Avenue. Then we can hit Sixth, and then Broadway, and then—"

"Oh, stop complaining," she said. "It's a beautiful day. Why not try to enjoy it?"

"You've got a point," he admitted.

They walked another block, and as they were crossing the street they looked off to their left at a movie theater marquee.

"Another film aimed at teens who'll never graduate from high school," he said.

"When I was a little girl," said Lisa, "the local theater had a special show for kids every Saturday afternoon." She smiled wistfully. "I can't tell you how many times I saw *The Wizard of Oz*. I knew every word, every note of every song. I could even do some of Ray Bolger's dances."

"With me it was *Casablanca*," replied Eddie. "A man with no country, no past—at least none he's willing to talk about—and no woman, takes on the Nazis in his own way and wins a limited war that no one will ever know about. I must have seen it on television a hundred times before I bought a video player—and of course it was the first DVD I bought." He sighed deeply. "Hard to believe they made it seventy-five years ago."

"Why *don't* they make films like that anymore?" asked Lisa.

"Beats me. The moviemakers have dumbed down just like the audiences have. They think that bigger is better." He paused, searching for the right word. "Hell, bigger is just *more*. Take *that* film," he said, nodding his head toward the theater. "One corpse was enough for Sam Spade, but if that's a mystery or an action-adventure, it's probably got five hundred of them."

"Or five hundred aliens," she agreed.

"Or five hundred nudes," he concluded. "I wonder how one of those teenage protagonists would have fared in Casablanca?"

"Or even against the Wicked Witch of the West," she added with a sad smile.

"Welcome to the mature world of today," he said.

She made a face, he grimaced, and they began looking into shop windows again.

Suddenly Lisa came to a stop.

"What is it?" asked Raven.

"Across the street," she said. "Look!"

He turned and looked to his left. "Bunch of shops," he said without much enthusiasm.

"I've never seen that one before," said Lisa.

"It's just another clothing store," said Raven in bored tones. "Clearly that's exactly what Fifth Avenue was lacking."

"No!" said Lisa, pointing. "Right there! It's a fortune-teller!"

Raven looked where she indicated. "Fifty bucks for a reading," he said, frowning. "You can get it for free just by reading the horoscope column in the paper."

"Oh, come on, Eddie!" she said, grasping his hand and starting to pull on it. "I haven't been to a fortune-teller since my dad took me to a carnival when I was eight years old."

"And I'll bet he said you'd grow up to be prettier than Marilyn Monroe and smarter than Albert Einstein." *Well, he was half right, anyway,* added Raven mentally.

"Please!" said Lisa. Suddenly she smiled. "I'll pay for it myself! If we have our fortunes read, I promise I'm through window-shopping for the day. We'll have an early dinner and we can spend the evening any way you want." Another smile. "Within reason."

Raven noticed that they'd drawn a crowd of five or six onlookers. "Okay," he said with a shrug. "Let's go be eight-year-olds again."

"Thanks," she said, giving him a quick kiss, then grabbing his hand and leading him through the honking traffic at midblock.

"We could have gone to the corner and waited for a green light," commented Raven. "I seriously doubt that he's closing up shop and moving in the extra minute it would have taken."

"Where's your sense of adventure?" she asked with a laugh.

"I left it in my other suit."

They made it to the other side of the street and approached the little storefront.

"Now *that's* interesting," remarked Raven, staring at the window. "What kind of business does he think he's going to draw with a bunch of skulls on display right here where everyone can see them?"

"They look phony to me," said Lisa.

"You've seen a lot of human skulls, have you?"

"In films and museums," she answered.

"Take a closer look," said Raven. "These skulls have fractures, and the one in the back on the left looks for all the world like it has a bullet hole in it."

She laughed. "That's just to make them look real, Eddie."

Raven grimaced. "Okay, let's get this over with." He reached out and opened the door for her, then followed her in.

She took a deep breath and wrinkled her nose. "What is that?"

"Incense," said Raven.

"So where's the owner, or the fortune-teller?" asked Lisa.

"Probably scouting a less expensive location," replied Raven.

"Look at those gorgeous tapestries!" she said, pointing to a trio of tapestries with strange scenes and stranger letters woven into them. "What language is that—Chinese? Or maybe some Indian one? Asian Indian, I mean, not American Indian."

Raven frowned and shook his head. "No, it's not either."

"What is it, then?" asked Lisa.

He stared at the tapestries. "I have a feeling I knew once." Then he shrugged. "Must have been in college."

"They're so exotic!" she enthused.

"They must cost a bundle," replied Raven. "Even *I* think they're stunning." He looked around. "So are those little statues, though I hope I never run into anyone who looks like that."

Suddenly a small man clad in a black robe with a black ponytail, arching eyebrows, and exotic tattoos all over his arms and neck emerged from behind a curtain.

"Welcome," he said to Lisa with an accent that neither she nor Raven could place. "And how may I be of service to you?"

"Your sign says that you read fortunes," replied Lisa.

"So I do," said the man. "And since our hands will be touching each other, it is only fair that we know each other's names. I am Mako."

"And I am—"

"Lisa," he said with a smile. "I know."

"What now?" asked Lisa, wondering how he knew her name—but that just made him all the more exotic and mysterious. "Do we sit at a table, or—?"

"Whatever makes you comfortable," replied Mako. "I can do it right here if you like."

"How much is this going to cost?" asked Raven.

"For someone as beautiful as Lisa, ten dollars."

"You must read a lot of fortunes to pay for this place," said Raven.

"Sometimes all it takes is the correct hand," answered Mako as another customer entered the store.

Raven turned to look at the newcomer. He was a large bald man, much closer to seven feet than six, and it was clear that his burly physique came from muscles, not fat. He wore a light colored trench coat, and for all Raven knew he was naked beneath it, because except for sandals his legs were bare at least from the bottom of the coat to his knees, and his hands and wrists were the same. His eyes were the deepest black. Raven decided that he looked right at home in a shop that was selling the supernatural.

"Have we met?" asked Raven.

"Why should you think so?" asked the man.

Raven shrugged. "I don't know. I just have a feeling that I've seen you before."

The customer half smiled and half grimaced, and Raven turned his attention back to Lisa and Mako.

"You are twenty-three years old," said Mako, staring at her open palm. "You were born in February. You like Sondheim musicals. You adore Agatha Christie's mystery novels. You—" Suddenly he froze.

"What is it?" asked Lisa.

"You will die in seconds!" he whispered. He stared at her. "But why?" He turned to Raven. "It's got to be *you*! Why did you come here? You know better!"

"What are you talking about?" demanded Raven. "Or is it that you'll charge ten dollars to read her palm and ninety bucks to save her from a nonexistent—"

Before he could finish the sentence a gunman entered the shop and started blazing away. Lisa fell to the floor with two bullets buried in her chest. Mako followed an instant later with a bullet to his head.

The gunman frowned, turned, aimed at Raven, and pulled the trigger again, but the tall customer dove between them and took the bullet meant for Raven.

Raven could hear nearby sirens and people screaming. He spun around, looking for the shooter, but the man had fled into the gathering crowd. He stood where he was, numbly surveying the scene, then knelt down to see if any life remained in Lisa.

And as he did so, before he could determine if she was still breathing, he heard a voice that seemed to emanate from the empty air surrounding him. *Run, Eddie Raven! You knew better than to come here! Nothing can save you if you don't flee!*

And, almost without thinking, Raven opened the door and ran.

2

By the time he'd gone a block, Raven's brain started working again, and he skidded to a stop. All he could think was *She's dead, and I didn't do a thing to save her.* He had no idea how long he stood there, attracting stares from passersby, but finally he made his way back to the shop, just as the police mortuary van was driving away.

Eddie approached one of the two cops who had been left behind.

"Where are they?" asked Raven.

"Who wants to know?" demanded the nearer cop.

"One of them is a friend," said Raven. "A very good friend."

The cop stared at him for a moment, then shrugged. "The hospital over Ninth Avenue, just north of here."

"Thanks," said Raven.

He turned and began walking away before the cops thought to ask him any questions, and in another twenty minutes he entered the hospital and walked right up to the reception desk.

"May I help you?" asked a receptionist who was clad all in white.

"There was a shooting over on Fifth Avenue close to an hour ago," he began.

"Yes," said the receptionist. "It was quite a tragedy. I'm afraid one of the men was dead on arrival."

"What about the woman?"

She frowned. "What woman?"

"Two men and a woman were shot," said Raven. "I'm interested in the woman."

She shook her head and stared at him strangely. "There was no woman. There were just two men."

"There *had* to be!" said Raven. "I was there!"

She checked some papers on her desk. "I'm sorry, sir. There were two men and no one else. And, as I said, one of them was dead." She looked at the papers. "His name was Mako."

"May I speak to the other one?"

"I'm afraid not, sir," she replied. "He's in surgery even as we speak."

"Has he got a name?"

She frowned again. "I thought he was your friend."

"The *woman* was my friend," said Raven.

"I told you, sir," she said irritably, "we have no record of a woman."

Don't keep mentioning her, Raven told himself, *or they'll think* you're *the nut who shot the other two.*

"Right," said Raven. "My mistake. Can you tell me the name of the survivor?"

"Rofocale," she said.

He frowned. "Is that a first name or a last name?"

She shrugged. "Beats me."

"Can you tell me what room he's in? I'd like to speak to him when he's out of surgery."

"He'll be heavily sedated," she said.

Cool it, Eddie, he told himself. *She already thinks you're only operating on one or two cylinders. Nag any more about this Rofocale and she'll think you shot him—and there are cops bringing in druggies and crash victims to the hospital every couple of minutes.*

"Thank you, ma'am," said Raven. "Take good care of him."

"According to these reports he was in a bad way," she said. She stared at him for a long moment. "You weren't really there, were you?"

"No, ma'am," he answered. "I'm a reporter. Just trying to get my story before all my rivals descend upon you."

She smiled and nodded her head. "I thought so," she said in a self-satisfied tone.

And suddenly Raven saw a tiny opening. He pulled out his tablet, activated it, and asked for her name.

"My name?" she responded.

He nodded. "If you can let me see him before the rest of the press gets here, the least I can do is mention your name in the article."

"How very thoughtful of you," she said. "It's Mildred."

"Just Mildred?"

"You'll never be able to spell the last name." She scribbled it down on a piece of paper and handed it to him. "Here you are."

"Thanks, Mildred," said Raven, tucking the paper into a pants pocket.

He was about to turn and leave, and try again when she was off duty, but she crooked an index finger, gesturing him to lean forward. "He's in critical care," she whispered.

"Thank you."

"He'll probably be sedated for the next few hours, maybe longer," she warned him. "So just look at him long enough to satisfy yourself that he's alive—if indeed he *is* still alive—and then leave."

"Right," said Raven, heading off to the elevator.

He was joined by a doctor and a pair of nurses as he ascended to the sixth floor, got off with one of the nurses, waited until she had disappeared into one of the rooms, and then hunted up critical care.

He opened the door, stepped inside, and closed it quickly behind him. There was only one other person in the room, the man named Rofocale, who was swathed in bandages from his neck to his hip and attached to half a dozen tubes and monitors.

"You awake?" asked Raven, staring at the huge man.

No answer.

"Hello?" he said.

Still no answer.

Suddenly the door opened and a balding doctor entered the room.

"May I help you?" he asked. "One of the interns told me someone had entered the room here."

"Just checking up on my friend," said Raven.

"He's in a bad way," said the doctor. "Truth to tell, I'll be surprised if he's still with us tomorrow morning."

Raven grimaced, but made no comment.

"You a friend of his?"

Better say yes, Eddie, thought Raven. "Yeah," he said aloud.

"We'll do our best, but don't expect miracles."

"I appreciate that," said Raven.

The doctor frowned. "As long as you know him, perhaps you can tell me where he comes from."

"Where he comes from?" repeated Raven.

"Yes," answered the doctor. "What kind of name is Rofocale? I suppose it's Eastern European, but it could be Asian."

"I never asked him," said Raven truthfully.

"Oh, well," said the doctor. "If we have to run him through a mortuary and then deliver him to a church, it would have been helpful to know." He walked to the door. "If he wakes up, and the odds are about fifty-to-one against, stick your head out the door and holler for a nurse."

Then he was gone.

Raven walked over to a table and considered picking up a magazine when he heard a voice. *They're after you, Eddie. Why were you so foolish as to visit Mako? You should have known they'd be watching him. Now they know who you are, and you're no longer safe.*

Raven whirled around. "Who's talking to me?" he demanded.

I am, said the disembodied voice.

"Where are you?"

Right here on the hospital bed, attached to all these tubes.

"What happened to the girl who was with me?" said Eddie. "Nobody seems to have seen her."

Why should that surprise you?

Raven stared at the bandaged body and the motionless face.

"What the hell is going on? I'm no telepath, and you're ninety-five-percent dead. How are you communicating with me, and where is Lisa, and *who* am I not safe from?"

There's no time. They're in the hospital right now. They're on this floor! They know what room we're in. You must leave, Eddie. I'm in no position to save you again.

Raven began backing away toward the door.

NOT THAT WAY! screamed the voice within his head.

"Then how . . . ?" began Raven.

You know what to do! Make the sign! Say the words! I'll guide you as best I can.

"What sign? What words?" demanded Raven—but suddenly, instinctively, without thinking, his hands made a mystic sign in the air and he recited words that made no sense to him.

The last two words were uttered as the doorknob began turning.

And Eddie Raven vanished just as someone or something opened the door.

3

Raven overcame a sudden wave of dizziness and straightened up, waiting to feel bullets thudding home in his body. Instead he found himself in what looked like a nightclub. Not a modern one, but something that might have been popular in the 1930s or 1940s.

He looked down to see that he was wearing a white dinner jacket and a black bow tie. He held a lit cigarette between his forefinger and middle finger, and he was seated at a table, staring at a chessboard. The empty chair facing him indicated that he'd been working out a chess problem, not playing against an opponent.

He shook his head to clear it. *What the hell happened to the hospital?* he thought. *And where am I?*

He took another look at his surroundings. *Lot of robes, lot of fezzes. Every woman's in a dress or a skirt; not a single one in trousers.*

There was a shot glass and a bottle of bourbon sitting right next to the chessboard. He poured himself a drink, finished it in a single swallow, and continued trying to make sense of his surroundings.

There was a black man singing songs and accompanying

himself on the piano, and both he and the songs seemed familiar to Raven.

If I didn't know better, I'd think I'd stumbled onto the set of Casablanca. He shook his head vigorously. *But they made that film before I was born. So where am I?*

Suddenly there was a commotion at the bar. A small, pudgy man and a tall, lean one were yelling at each other and making angry gestures—but before they could come to blows, a burly ogre with mottled green skin grabbed each by the scruff of the neck, held them aloft, growled something Raven couldn't hear from where he sat, and put them back down. They remained motionless until the ogre glared at the taller one, who immediately slapped a bill on the bar, made his way to the door, and left.

It was obvious that the small man was thanking the ogre. He got a roar for his trouble and scurried back to a table, where a medusa was waiting to throw her arms lovingly around him.

Well, at least it's not Casablanca, thought Raven. *Not with an ogre and a medusa in it.* Suddenly he frowned. *I'm not thinking straight since the hospital. Where on Earth* is *there a place with ogres and medusas?*

Raven resisted the urge to ask a waiter or one of the patrons just where the hell he was. There was no sense, he felt, advertising his ignorance. He'd just stay seated, move an occasional piece on the chessboard to convince any onlookers that he wasn't as confused as he felt, and try to search the room and the crowd for cues.

After a few moments had passed, he noticed a man staring at him from the doorway. Finally he began approaching, and Raven saw that he had three eyes, two on the left side of his head, and three arms, two on the right side of his body. The man walked with a discernible limp, but finally he reached Raven's table and came to a stop.

"The letters," said the man with a thick accent Raven couldn't identify. "Are they safeguarded?"

"What letters?" asked Raven.

The man lowered his voice to little more than a hiss. "The letters of transit, of course!"

"What the hell are you talking about?" demanded Raven.

"Don't play games with me!" growled the man.

"This is someone's idea of a bad joke," muttered Raven. "I don't know what's going on here, but I'm not participating in a bad remake."

The man frowned. "What are you talking about?"

"I might ask you the same question," said Raven.

"I risked my life for those letters!"

"Yeah," said Raven. "And they cost you an arm and an eye, right?"

"I will not put up with this abuse!" snapped the man.

"Fine," said Raven. "Leave."

"Damn it, Eddie!"

Raven was about to reply when there was another commotion at the door and half a dozen men burst in, wearing what looked like a B movie's notion of futuristic police or military uniforms. Finally another man entered and stepped around them, dressed in such a dapper, elegant version of the uniforms that he seemed to be in a totally different movie, or perhaps a nineteenth-century operetta on which the other uniforms were poorly based.

Raven noticed that the three-armed man or creature had

gone, and the newcomer walked right up to Raven's table and sat down opposite him.

"Knight to king's bishop five," he said. "Good evening, Eddie."

"Queen to queen's knight three," replied Raven. "Do I know you?"

The man smiled in amusement. "Drinking again? I should have thought you'd learned your lesson."

"I don't need any lessons on how to drink," said Raven. He stared at the man. "Do I know you?"

"Stop kidding around, Eddie," said the man. "I'm here on business."

"With those clowns?" asked Raven, indicating the men who had entered with him.

"You seem to have forgotten that those clowns saved your life three weeks ago."

Raven stared at the men, found their uniforms slightly less laughable, and shrugged. "Okay, so what can I do for you?"

"Two things," answered the man. "We're going to make a major arrest here tonight or tomorrow. I would appreciate no interference. Keep your hands and your hired help off the situation, and I'll make sure it makes all the papers. Probably triple your business for at least a week."

"Does it need tripling?"

The man chuckled. "Does Joe DiMaggio need two more infield hits? And yet he runs his ass off trying to get them. Anyway, when the press shows up, make sure they spell my name right this time: P-E-U-G-E-O-T."

"Not Renault?" asked Raven, only half kidding.

"Certainly not," replied Peugeot. "I have class, and I run on more than four cylinders."

Raven couldn't help chuckling at that. "Okay, that's one thing. What's the other?"

"You've heard of Paul Brff?"

"Heard of him?" repeated Raven. "I can't even pronounce it."

"No jokes, Eddie. We know he's on his way to town if he's not here already." Peugeot learned forward. "He must never leave."

"Why not?" asked Raven, wondering idly if Brff looked anything like Paul Henreid. "What's he done?"

"Oh, come on, Eddie," said Peugeot. "He's one of the three or four most famous men alive."

"One of the three or four most famous men?" repeated Raven. "What position does he play?"

Peugeot threw back his head and laughed. "You always had a great sense of humor, Eddie. I'll give you that much."

"How will I know this Brff if he shows up?"

"His picture's in all the papers."

"I only read the sports section," said Raven.

"Normal height, normal weight, normal facial features, no physical aberrations. He used to have a mustache, but he shaved it off." Peugeot shook his head. "Pity. It was a really distinctive handlebar."

"So how do you expect me to spot him?"

"You always had an eye for the ladies, Eddie," said Peugeot.

"He's a drag queen?" asked Raven.

Peugeot chuckled. "No," he answered. "I wish he was. It would make him much easier to spot." He paused and leaned forward. "He travels with a lady. I know your tastes, Eddie. This is not a woman you can ignore."

"So I'm on the lookout for a nondescript man with a

good-looking woman on his arm?" said Raven. "That lowers it to twenty or thirty couples just in the saloon here."

"It's a nightclub, not a saloon, and believe me, you'll know them when you see them."

Peugeot got to his feet, saluted, moved his queen's rook, and returned to where his men were standing. He uttered a brief command, headed to the door, and they followed him out.

Raven was still trying to dope out which of his surroundings he believed in and which he was sure he was fantasizing, when a tall black man, who looked like a cross between Michael Jordan and Kobe Bryant walked over and sat down at his table.

"Break time," he announced. "Damn, but I hate that Martian music. Wish you'd get a clientele that liked the songs from Jupiter's moons." Suddenly he smiled. "Of course, I'd need two or three more hands to play 'em, but what the hell."

"You're doing just fine as it is," said Raven, who hadn't even been aware of the music until it had stopped a moment ago.

"Thanks, Boss," said the man. "I see Peugeot was here again. Hasn't he got a home?"

"Beats me," said Raven. "Tell me, Sam . . . it *is* Sam, isn't it?"

The man chuckled. "We've been together five years and you have to ask? Better lay off the booze, Boss."

"Tell me, Sam," continued Raven. "How long have we been at this joint?"

"You bought it two years ago and changed its name to Eddie's," answered Sam. "You know what they say nowadays: In Casablanca, everyone comes to Eddie's Place."

"Casablanca?" repeated Raven. "For sure?"

Sam laughed again. "You really better start going a little

easier on the booze, Boss." He paused for a moment. "Tell you what. Give me another minute or two to rest my fingers, and I'll play the song for you. Maybe it'll help you remember."

"The song?" repeated Raven, frowning.

"You know," said Sam. "The one I used to play for you and *her*."

"What was the name of it?"

Sam shrugged. "I suppose it had one. I just call it 'The Boss's Song.'"

"Some other time," said Raven. "I'm trying to clear my mind tonight, not clutter it."

"I don't blame you," said Sam. "We've already got a medusa and three trolls over at the bar, and it's late enough for the vampires to start showing up." He stared at Raven. "I do wish I knew what it was that keeps you in a place like this."

"Maybe I don't want to go back to where I started," said Raven, and thought *First honest thing I've said since I got here.*

Sam grinned. "You and me both." He got up and stretched. "Okay, off to the little boys' room now that the zombie and the huge troll have left it, and then I'll go back to work. I'd rather play the piano than talk to most of our customers anyway."

He walked off to where Raven assumed the bathrooms were, and Raven waited a moment, then got up and decided he might as well explore Eddie's Place.

The bar was very long, once a fine, polished hardwood, now notched and scarred from too many drunks and too little supervision. Off to his left, toward the back of the place, was a large roulette table with perhaps fifteen men, women, trolls, and ghouls laying their bets, most in a currency he had never seen before but which seemed acceptable to everyone at the table. There were about twenty tables spread throughout the main part of the building, and Sam's piano was located right in the middle of them.

He heard music, but the piano bench was empty. He turned and saw Sam, working an accordion that sounded exactly like a piano, walking from table to table. Mostly he played show tunes from plays Raven had seen, plus a few that Raven was sure nobody in his New York had ever seen or heard . . . and then came a sweet, bittersweet melody that seemed to fill him with an infinite sorrow, and he knew instinctively that Sam was playing "The Boss's Song."

"Hope you like it, Boss," said Sam, walking over to him.

"It's lovely," replied Raven. "But you don't have to play it. Just do what the paying customers request—always assuming some of these men and critters eventually get around to paying for their drinks."

"I will, Boss," said Sam. "But I thought it was appropriate to play it now."

"Because I'm finally on my feet?" asked Raven with a smile.

Sam shook his head. "Because *she's* on her way here."

"She?"

"You know who," said Sam.

The hell I do, thought Raven. *The only "she" I care about these days is lying dead somewhere with a couple of slugs in her heart.*

He stood absolutely still for a moment, his mind racing back to the shooting at Mako's store. *All right, I might as well stick around and see who "she" is.* He grimaced. *Hell, I've got no place to go anyway.*

"Play whatever makes you happy," he told Sam, heading off to his right and continuing the tour of Eddie's Place. A swinging door led to a kitchen he hadn't realized existed, and indeed there was only one chef, a misshapen reddish creature with one eye in the middle of its face and a pair of fangs protruding from its mouth. It saw Raven, contorted its face into a smile, and went back to frying some eggs that were far too big to have come from any chicken that ever lived.

Raven opened the oversize refrigerator, decided that no refrigerator in his—or his world's—experience had ever held food like that, nodded pleasantly to the chef who growled an acknowledgment, and went back into the main body of the club.

He made his way to his table, sat down, poured himself another drink, grateful that this world's whiskey still tasted like whiskey, and downed it in a single swallow.

Sam, who had set the accordion aside and returned to the piano, began to play "The Boss's Song" yet again, and he got to his feet, walked over, and tapped him on the shoulder. Sam turned around without missing a note.

"I thought I told you to play what the customers requested," said Raven.

"This is the favorite song of a customer who just walked in," replied Sam, nodding his head toward the front door.

Raven looked across the room and saw Lisa entering on the arm of a totally nondescript man without a single distinctive feature.

"Who the hell is he?" said Raven.

"I recognize him from his pictures in the papers," said Sam. "That's Paul Brff."

"What's she doing with *him*?" said Raven, staring at them.

"Beats me," said Sam. "He should be dead half a dozen times over."

"And she *is* dead," said Raven. "Or at least she was, the last time I saw her."

"She don't look like no zombie to me," said Sam. "Just between you and me and every other guy who's staring at her, she's drop-dead gorgeous."

"Especially the drop-dead part," said Raven, frowning. "What the hell is going on?"

"Go ask her," said Sam. "It's the best way to get answers."

"If she's with him, will she even want to speak to me?" said Raven.

"If she's with him, she'll know you're not trying to romance her," answered Sam. "That probably makes her *more* likely to speak with you."

"Point taken," said Raven, nodding his head. He waited until the gnome that appeared to be his maître d' seated them, and then he braced himself, still not totally convinced that he wasn't hallucinating after catching a bullet back at the hospital, and walked over.

"Good evening," he said in his best Bogart manner. "Welcome to Eddie's."

"Thank you," said Brff. "We've heard wonderful things about it. Maybe I introduce my wife? Her name is—"

"I know," said Raven. He turned to her. "Hello, Lisa."

"My name is Ilsa," she corrected him.

It was everything he could do not to rip her blouse off and hunt for bullet holes. "My mistake," he replied. "Ilsa."

"The gentleman at the piano looks familiar," she said.

"Perhaps his song reminds you of happier times," said Raven.

"It's a sad melody," she remarked.

It's odd, thought Raven. *I think I love you. I didn't realize it back in New York. But seeing you come in with another man brings it home to me. I'd like to punch him out and run off with you—but I haven't set foot outside this place since I woke up here, and I don't even know what town or country we're in. I mean, parts of it look and seem like Casablanca, but neither Casablanca the city nor* Casablanca *the movie is filled with trolls and medusas and gnomes and the like. And you're no more Ilsa than Ingrid Bergman was Lisa. I saw you shot and killed, and if dying isn't permanent in this world, then why don't you look like the zombies at the bar? Why are you still so beautiful?*

"Are you all right, Mr. Raven?" asked Ilsa.

"Call me Eddie," said Raven. "Is something wrong?"

"You seemed to be in a trance for a minute there."

He forced a self-deprecating smile to his lips. "Watch out for the whiskey," he said.

"We thought we'd stop off for a drink on our way to the hotel," said Brff. "But if the owner warns us against . . ."

"I'm sure one drink won't hurt us," said Ilsa.

"Whatever you say, my dear," replied Brff, getting to his feet. "If you'll excuse me for a moment, I'd like to pay a visit to the restroom."

Raven pointed in the direction of the men's room, and Brff walked off. The moment he did so, Raven sat down on Brff's abandoned chair, leaned over, and whispered, "What the hell is going on here, Lisa?"

"I don't understand," she replied. "My name is Ilsa, I'm here with my husband, and—"

"You were dead!" he said in a harsh whisper. "I saw them shoot you. I saw you fall. I saw the blood."

She frowned. "Maybe one drink *is* too many, Mr. Raven."

"Call me Eddie," he said. "Something very strange is going on."

"Strange is an understatement," she said, staring at him.

"You say you've never seen me before?"

"No, I haven't."

"Let me take a guess," said Raven. "You and your husband are hoping to catch the next plane out of here."

"Well, the next ship, anyway," said Ilsa.

"Sailing to where?"

She stared at him for a long moment. "Not sailing. *Flying*."

"Flying where?"

"To Europa."

"Europe?" said Raven. "Didn't you just come from there?"

"Not Europe," she corrected him. *"Europa."*

Raven shrugged. "Difference of pronunciation."

"No, Eddie," said Ilsa. "Europa is a moon of Jupiter."

"And *that's* where you're heading?"

She nodded her head. "At least we'll be safe there."

"Safe from who?" he asked.

"Don't be naïve," she said.

"All right," he said, standing up as Brff began walking back to the table. "I'd like to speak with you later."

"About what?" she asked.

"If I told you now, I wouldn't have to speak to you later."

"All right," she said. "Paul's had a long tiring day. I'll meet you in my hotel's lobby once he's asleep."

"Thanks," said Raven. He turned to Brff. "She's all yours."

"Thank you," said Brff. "I think."

He and Ilsa each ordered a drink—his was whiskey, hers was wine—and fifteen minutes later they took their leave of the place.

Raven walked over to where Sam sat at the piano.

"Did you recognize her?" he asked.

"Of course," replied Sam. "It was Ilsa."

"Not Lisa?"

Sam shrugged. "Who knows how many names she's got? The one I know is Ilsa."

"And we were together where?" persisted Raven.

"Dining rooms. Bars. Probably a bedroom, though"—Sam smiled—"that's just guesswork, since nobody was ever thoughtful enough to ask me to join in the fun."

"You know what I mean," said Raven. "Where did I meet her?"

"The bar, probably. You spent most of your time there."

"What country, damn it?" snapped Raven.

Sam stared at him. "Don't ask questions like that, Boss. You make me really start worrying about you. Next thing I know you're gonna ask me what year it is."

Raven realized that *was* the very next question he planned to ask, but before he could voice it, Sam nodded toward the doorway. "Ah!" he said. "The competition comes calling."

Raven looked, and saw a corpulent woman dressed all in white entering the nightclub. She looked around, spotted Raven, shot him a smile, and began approaching him.

"What's her name?" asked Raven softly.

"Aw, come on, Boss," said Sam irritably. "No more pretend stuff."

"Her name, damn it!" snapped Raven.

"Ms. Maserati," answered Sam.

That figures, thought Raven. *Half the people in the damned movie were named for cars.*

"Good evening, Eddie," said Ms. Maserati with an accent that sounded like she was just out of finishing school.

"Welcome," said Raven. "What can I do for you?"

"The same as usual."

"Bartender!" called Raven. "The usual for Ms. Maserati."

The troll behind the bar gave him a puzzled look, while the woman chuckled deep in her massive throat. "I don't drink, Eddie. You know that."

"I forgot," said Raven. "The chef's still on duty," he added, "so what *is* the usual?"

"I want to buy Eddie's Place, of course."

"Of course," said Raven.

"I'm prepared to up my weekly offer," she continued.

"It's not for sale."

"Still?" she said. "I know it's operating at a loss. You must be running short of cash."

"Let me hit a few fifty-to-one shots at the track and I'll give you the damned place," replied Raven. "But not tonight."

She shrugged. "Can't blame a girl for trying."

Show me a girl and we'll talk about it, thought Raven. Aloud he said, "Find yourself a table and get comfortable. Whatever you order is on the house."

"Including Sam?" she asked with a smile.

Raven looked at Sam, whose face wore a thanks-a-heap-Boss expression.

"I don't buy or sell people," said Raven.

"That's a pity," said Ms. Maserati. "A lot of people in this town have made their fortunes doing just that."

"I'll meet you halfway," said Sam. "I'll sell you the piano."

She chuckled again and went across the room to sit at a small table, where a troll immediately walked up to her.

"Same as always," she said.

"Fried or poached?" he asked.

"Yes," she said.

"Busy night," remarked Sam to Raven.

"Yeah, I think I'll get a breath of fresh air," said Raven, walking toward the door.

He opened it and stepped out into the street, staring off to his left, then to his right. It *could* have been a street in Casablanca in 1942, but there were a few anomalies. Parked in among the rows of 1930s jalopies were a pair of cargo ships that looked like they were pointing up at the stars. In among the bars and brothels was a shop specializing in laptop computers, and another offering self-repairing washers and dryers.

"I don't know what the hell is going on," muttered Raven to himself, "but I'm not going back into the saloon until I figure it out."

He heard a sound off to his right, and an instant later a red-skinned pointed-eared demon holding a bright red pitchfork in his hand burst out of a nearby alley, growling hideously, and ran straight for Raven.

Now the town—or whatever it is—is trying to scare me to death. Raven resisted an urge to run and simply stared at the demon.

And then he seemed to hear a voice inside his head: *Trust*

your senses, Eddie. No matter what you think, everything you've experienced is real, including the demon.

Raven pivoted at the last second, stuck out a foot to trip the oncoming demon, and grabbed his pitchfork as the creature went flying forward. The demon picked himself up, snarling and growling, and began approaching Raven.

"Stay back," said Raven ominously. He stuck the pitchfork out. "I've got *this.*"

The demon continued approaching, and when he was almost within reach he screamed again, faked left, and charged straight at Raven, who braced himself, held out the pitchfork, and impaled the demon on it. Most creatures would have died once the points of the pitchfork went all the way through them, but the demon screamed and cursed at the top of his lungs for the next five minutes, drawing quite a crowd, until he finally succumbed.

NOW will you believe me? said the voice inside his head.

I might, thought Raven, *but nobody else will.* He nodded toward the street. *The damned thing just vanished.*

4

R aven went back inside the nightclub, had a stiff drink to calm his nerves, then left and made his way down the street—unmolested this time—to the hotel. He walked over to one side of the lobby, picked up a newspaper someone had left on a table, sat down on a worn, scuffed leather couch, and started reading, hoping he could learn a little more about this venue in which he found himself.

"LBJ Wins!" screamed the headline—but just as he was sure it was November of 1964, he read further and learned that Lover Boy Jake, affectionately known as LBJ, had won a major stakes race at Casablanca Downs. A quick glance at the photo told him that LBJ was not a racehorse, but a six-legged dragon. The winning margin was a neck, but that was a little misleading, as his neck appeared to be about ten feet long.

Raven thumbed through the paper, trying to find something a little more meaningful. It didn't help. Rodgers and Hammerstein had written a hit musical about farmers opening up a new territory, but the territory was Pluto, not Oklahoma. The top-grossing movie was *Gone With the Winnebago*, about a family that is unable to defend its farm during the Third Civil War. The Chicago Bears were unable to take the field against the Detroit Lions because all but three of them were still hibernating.

He tossed the paper back down on the table. He'd have been convinced it was someone's idea of a joke, except that his experiences of the past half hour had convinced him that it was absolutely real.

Okay, he thought, *I'm playing your game, and I'm trying to play by your rules. But if this is going to last more than another few minutes, I think the least you can do is tell me what's going on and how to get back to the present.*

You are in *the present, Eddie,* whispered the unseen voice.

"I mean the real world's present," said Raven softly.

This is the real world.

"Then how do I get back to the phony world that I'm used to?" he asked.

Think hard, Eddie. You'll figure it out.

Somehow he knew the voice had suddenly abandoned him, at least for the time being. He wanted another drink, and didn't mind at all that people would see him paying for a drink at a rival bar (always assuming that the hotel *had* a bar), but he had the feeling that his reality was incomprehensible enough, and that booze would only make it more so.

He decided that maybe it was time to go home, get a night's sleep, and see if anything made more sense in the morning, but two things held him in place. First was the fact that he had no idea where he lived, and, second, he looked up and saw Ilsa approaching him.

He stood up to greet her, waited until she had seated herself on the couch, and then sat down next to her.

"I promised that I'd speak with you after Paul went to bed," she said. "Here I am."

"Thank you for coming," said Raven. "I appreciate it."

They were silent for a moment. Then she spoke up. "You're staring."

"You're worth staring at," he replied. *Damn,* he thought. *Bogart would have worded it better.*

"Surely I'm not here so that you could discuss my looks," she said with a smile.

"No, I'm content just to sit and stare while we talk," said Raven.

"About what?" she asked.

"Us."

"I told you," said Ilsa. "I've never seen you before."

"Then we'll talk about our separate lives," said Raven. "To begin with, what do you do?"

"I work with and for my husband," she replied. "He's a great man, Eddie, and he will do great things."

"I don't doubt it."

"And you?"

"I'm a saloon-keeper," he said with an expression that told her how little he thought of it.

"And before that?"

He shrugged. "I don't seem to remember anything important." He continued staring at her. "I know we've never met before," he said at last, "but do you get, I don't know, the *feeling* that we have?"

She looked puzzled. "I told you, we've never met before. This is my first trip to this country."

"Okay," he said. "One more question, and please don't be offended."

"I assume it's the same question all the men ask," replied Ilsa. "I'm not offended. I'm just tired of it."

He couldn't repress a smile. "No, it's not *that* question."

"All right, ask away."

"Have you ever been shot in the chest?"

She stared at him, frowning. "No, of course not."

"Or anywhere else?"

"No. Why?"

He shrugged. "Oh, no reason."

"Come on, Eddie," she said. "You had to have a reason."

"I knew a girl who looked exactly like you who *was* shot."

"That's terrible!" said Ilsa.

"I agree."

"She was killed?"

"Of course," said Raven.

"Then *I* have a question," said Ilsa.

"Shoot."

She frowned. "What?"

"Go ahead and ask your question."

"You say she was shot and killed?"

"Right," said Raven.

"Then why did you think I was her?" asked Ilsa.

"It's been a strange day."

"That's no answer," said Ilsa.

"I could invent more poetic and romantic ones," said Raven, "and certainly more logical ones, but that is as close to the truth as I can come."

She stared at him. "You don't seem drunk."

He shrugged. "You don't seem dead."

"I wish you'd stop speaking of this death fantasy," said Ilsa. "They've been trying to kill Paul and me just about everywhere we've been for the past six months."

"And you think you'll be safe on Europa?"

"Well, safer, anyway."

"I'll do what I can to help you."

"All we need are tickets," she said. "The ship leaves to-morrow."

"Just tickets?" he asked.

"Just tickets."

Then what the hell were these letters that the guy with three arms and three eyes was talking about?

"I think the woman you want to talk to runs a cut-rate rival to my place," said Raven. "Her name is Maserati. When you're both up tomorrow morning, I'll take you to her place and we'll get you the tickets, never fear."

"Are you sure she can do it?" asked Ilsa.

"There's nothing in this town you can't get," replied Raven. "For a price. I assume Paul has money?"

"We both do."

"Keep yours. I'll see that she charges Paul."

"It's both of ours," said the mirror image of the girl he had hoped to marry.

He tried not to wince as he nodded his head. "Both, right." He got to his feet. "Stop by my place when you get up and I'll take you to meet Maserati."

"I don't know quite what time that will be," said Ilsa. "If you're not there, where will we find you?"

He made a face. "Where else would I be but Eddie's Place?"

They said goodnight, he gave her a kiss on the cheek and restrained himself from hugging her, and then walked out the door.

It was a warm, muggy night, as he suspected most of the nights were, and he walked slowly back to the club, trying to memorize which stores and shops were where, admiring the ancient cars and noting the few that shouldn't have existed for another century or two. Mostly, though, he thought about Brff, Ilsa, and Maserati.

They're after tickets, he thought. *So what's with the letters of transit? What have the letters of transit got to do with anything?*

They're your *ticket out of here,* said the voice, which he now recognized as Rofocale's. *You're going to have only one chance at them, Eddie, so don't blow it or you'll be stuck here forever. And around here, forever is measured in days, or more likely, hours.*

5

"**G**et me a drink," said Raven to the bartender as he walked over and sat at his table. "On second thought, make it a whole bottle."

"With or without?" asked the lean bartender.

"With or without *what*?" said Raven irritably.

"With or without a glass?"

Raven merely glared at him. After a few seconds he sighed, put a bottle and a shot glass on a tray, carried it over to Raven, and set it down gently on the table.

"Don't drink too much tonight," said the bartender softly.

"Since when are you my keeper?" demanded Raven.

"We just got word," was the answer. "They're on their way from the airport."

"*Who* are on their way?"

"Why, the Anarchists, of course," replied the bartender. "And Colonel Massovitch is with them. He wouldn't be here if something major wasn't about to happen."

"Whatever it is, it doesn't concern us," said Raven. *How can it? I've only been in this world or illusion or whatever the hell it is for maybe four hours, tops.*

"He may still be upset from the last time," said the bar-tender.

Raven frowned. "The last time?" he repeated.

"Well, you did make him look like a fool in front of his men," said the bartender.

"Okay," said Raven. "Let me know when he comes in."

"I'm sure they'll all come in together. I'm told there are six of them, including Massovitch."

"Point him out to me as he comes through the door," said Raven.

"Point him out?" repeated the bartender. "Are you kidding?"

"Am I smiling?"

"But you know what he looks like!"

"Do it anyway," said Raven.

Suddenly Peugeot entered and approached Raven's table. "Invite me to sit down, Eddie," he said.

"Have a seat," replied Raven.

"Thanks," said Peugeot, seating himself. "Don't mind if I do."

"Pay me the posted rate and I'll pour you a drink," said Raven.

"Pour me a free drink and I won't arrest you for allowing gambling in here."

Raven shrugged. "Help yourself." Then: "To a small one."

"You're all heart, Eddie," said Peugeot. "And of course I'm all brain. Given the amount we drink, both of them beat the hell out of being all liver."

Raven chuckled at that. "So are you here to arrest Masso-vitch?"

"He outranks me," said Peugeot with a smile.

"Then maybe I'll make a citizen's arrest."

"I think maybe his being a bona fide trigger-happy maniac outranks both of us—especially when you remember that he's got five apprentice maniacs with him."

"So what's he here for?" asked Raven.

"Brff, of course," said Peugeot. "I *do* wish that man would put a vowel or two in his name."

"Could be worse," said Raven. "Could have a couple of s's in it. Then every time you discussed him with one of your lady friends you'd spit in her face."

"I suppose one must look at the bright side," agreed Peugeot.

"One could also answer my question. What's he here for?"

"Probably to threaten Brff. He can't arrest him, not here, but he can make things very uncomfortable for him." He paused. "And for *her*."

"What's she got to do with it?" asked Raven.

"Have you seen the lady?" asked Peugeot. "I guarantee Massovitch isn't the only man who'd kill for her."

"So you think he plans to kill two birds with one stone?"

"No," replied Peugeot. "But I can certainly envision him killing one and taking great enjoyment in violating the other."

"Not gonna happen," said Raven.

"Oh?"

"Not if I have anything to say or do about it."

"Ah . . . but *have* you?" asked Peugeot.

"I'm learning the ground rules."

"You sound like this is an American football game you're talking about," said Peugeot. "This is reality, Eddie."

"Yours," said Raven. "But it doesn't necessarily have to be mine or hers."

Peugeot picked up the bottle, read the label, and stared at

Raven. "This isn't *that* strong. You must have had an early start tonight, Eddie."

Sam, who had been playing one otherworldly love song after another, suddenly shifted to a military march. Raven looked at the door and saw that six uniformed men had entered. Well, five men and a scaly creature with huge fangs that poked through—not between—his lips, and claws on his hands that would have done a grizzly bear proud. Raven didn't need the bartender to indicate that this was Massovitch.

"Excuse me," said Peugeot, rising from the table. "Time for me to go be obsequious until you complete your master plan to destroy him and his toadies." He paused and stared at Raven. "You *are* working on a master plan, aren't you?"

Yeah, thought Raven, *but it only concerns two people, and you, pal, are not one of them.*

Peugeot reached the little group and invited them to "his" table, which was as far from Raven's as he could manage.

Thanks for that much, thought Raven, nodding toward Peugeot, who saw it and smiled back at him.

Sam walked over. "Mind if I join you?"

"Taking a break?" asked Raven.

"I played the only march I know. No sense playing sentimental stuff and getting 'em mad."

Raven shrugged. "Makes sense," he said. "Well, more than Massovitch and his clowns make, anyway."

Sam began staring over Raven's left shoulder and frowning. Finally Raven asked what he was looking at.

"Your pal," answered Sam. "The ugly little bastard with three eyes and three arms is staring at you, but he seems to be afraid to approach us. I think he doesn't want to be seen by

Massovitch and his men (and I use the word advisedly)." He shrugged. "Just as well. If they got their hands on him, we'd be days cleaning this place up."

"Well, I might as well see what he wants," said Raven, remembering Rofocale's words.

"I'll guard the booze," said Sam with a smile.

"Guard it in the bottle, not in the piano player," replied Raven, getting to his feet and walking to the small vestibule Sam had indicated. The little man with the two left eyes, the two right arms, and the painful limp was standing there, obviously waiting for him.

"You're still here!" he hissed.

"Where did you expect me to be?" asked Raven.

"Away! Elsewhere!"

"Give me my tickets to elsewhere and we'll talk about it."

"I don't have them with me!" snapped the little man. "I couldn't protect them! You know that!"

"Well, tell me where to find them, and when I get a chance—"

"When you get a chance?" repeated the man. "The letters of transit expire at noon tomorrow! Use them before then or they're just useless pieces of paper!"

"Okay, where are they?"

"They're very well hidden, so listen carefully."

"Let me pull out my pen so I can write this down," said Raven.

"We've no time!" the little man half shouted. "They're staring at us."

"Not to put too fine a point on it," said Raven, "but a man with three eyes and three hands is worth staring at."

"Be quiet and *listen*!" shrieked the man.

"Lower your voice or *everyone* will listen."

"You start at the roulette wheel. Then you—"

A shot rang out and the little man flew backward against a wall and collapsed in a heap.

"Poor shot," announced Massovitch, pocketing his pistol.

"What are you talking about?" said one of his men. "You got him right through the forehead."

"I was aiming at his far left eye," replied Massovitch in an annoyed tone.

"What now?" whispered Raven.

Now you start looking for the letters, said Rofocale's voice within his head. *You've got just under twelve hours to find them.*

And if I don't? thought Raven.

Then I hope you like your surroundings, because you will never be able to set foot outside again.

"Thanks for the encouragement," muttered Raven aloud.

6

"Was I encouraging you to do something?" asked Massovitch in an oily tone of voice. "I certainly hope not. I had hoped for a quiet, pleasant evening."

"I'll tell Sam to sing quiet, pleasant songs," replied Raven.

"Why don't we sit down and have a drink?" said Massovitch.

Raven shrugged. "As long as you're buying, why not?" He led Massovitch to an empty table and they seated themselves.

"What'll it be, Boss?" asked a waiter.

"Anything, as long as it's wildly expensive," answered Raven. "My companion is paying."

Massovitch grinned. "I like your style, Eddie Raven!" he said with a chuckle. "Under other circumstances I feel certain we could have been friends."

"You really think so?" asked Raven.

"Absolutely."

"Let's find out," said Raven. "Who was the greatest baseball player of all time?"

"Babe Ruth, of course," said Massovitch.

Raven shook his head. "It was Ty Cobb."

"You're wrong, of course," said Massovitch.

Raven shrugged. "You're welcome to think so."

"All right," said Massovitch. "The greatest football player?"

"Red Grange," said Raven.

"Slingin' Sammy Baugh."

"You're 0-for-two on the friendship test," said Raven. "You'd better quit while you're ahead."

"I thought you said I'm 0-for-two. How can that be ahead?"

"It's as close to being ahead as you're going to get," said Raven with a smile.

"Rubbish. I do not agree with either of your answers."

"I hope it makes you feel better."

"One more!" demanded Massovitch. "And this time I will demand proof."

"In a bar?" asked Raven, amused.

"We could walk out in the street if you prefer, but I still demand proof."

"Whatever makes you happy." The waiter appeared with the drinks, placing one in front of each of them. "The greatest racehorse?"

"Ah! An easy one!" exclaimed Massovitch.

"You think so?"

"Absolutely. It was Seabiscuit."

"Nice try," said Raven. "But it was Man o' War."

"Nonsense! Look at all the major stakes races Seabiscuit won! He was truly the People's Horse."

"Man o' War won twenty of twenty-one starts, and carried more weight than the handicappers ever put in Seabiscuit. Hell, even Citation was twenty-seven for twenty-nine before he was injured. You put Seabiscuit in a race with those two and Equipoise, you won't even be able to cash a show ticket."

"Damn your eyes, Raven!" bellowed Massovitch. "You will never leave this town alive!"

"That's a relief," said Raven.

Massovitch stared at him uncomprehendingly. "A relief?" he repeated.

"Yeah," said Raven. "I was afraid we were going to have to argue about the most beautiful woman next."

"You'd better hope she shows up here, because I meant what I said. You are going to die in Casablanca."

She's already shown up, thought Raven. *And she doesn't know who the hell I am.*

"There's worse places to die," said Raven aloud.

"Oh?" said Massovitch. "Where?"

"I'm sure you'll find one," answered Raven. "Of course, you won't be in any position to tell me about it, but . . ."

"Bah!" snarled Massovitch, getting to his feet. "I find your company boring!"

"Only boring?" asked Raven pleasantly.

"And infuriating!" Massovitch finished his drink with a single large swallow.

"I forgot to tell you," said Raven.

"Forgot to tell me *what*?" demanded Massovitch.

"The price for booze at Eddie's Place just tripled."

Massovitch uttered an obscenity, threw a bill on the table, and strode off to the far end of the room.

"You gonna let him get away with that?" asked Sam with an amused smile.

"You pay me twenty bucks for a shot of whiskey and you can be just as rude," answered Raven.

Sam looked at the bottle and chuckled. "Twenty bucks buys a dozen of these on the black market. Or probably even at the booze shop over on the next block."

"Well, since he didn't object, I suppose he feels he got his money's worth."

"He looks like he objects like all hell," said Sam. "He's glaring at you even as we speak."

"He objects to *me*, not the booze," replied Raven.

"Hey, Sam!" yelled a customer. "Play 'Heartbreak Hotel.'"

"Not classy enough," answered Sam. "How about 'Heartbreak Mansion'?"

"Never heard of it," said the customer.

"Neither did I," replied Sam. "But let's give it a whirl and see what happens."

He walked back to his piano and began playing, and the three-eyed three-armed little man approached Raven.

"I thought you were dead," said Raven.

"Oh, I was," replied the little man. "But for me, that is only a temporary condition." He paused. "May I sit down?"

"Be my guest."

"We are all your guests at Eddie's Place."

"As long as we seem to keep talking to each other, I suppose I ought to ask, have you got a name?"

"Of course I have a name," replied the little man irritably. "Everybody has a name. Around here, most people have three or four."

"I meant, would you care to share it with me?"

"Haven't I done so?" he asked. "I am Bogarti."

Raven stared at him, trying to remember the film. *Close enough*, he thought. *Peter Lorre was Ugarte. Of course, he only had two eyes and two arms, but what the hell.* At last he shrugged and took a drag on his cigarette. "Yeah, that sounds about right."

"So why are you still here, Eddie?" demanded Bogarti.

"If your letters of transit actually work . . ." began Raven.

"Of course they work!" snapped the little three-eyed man.

"If they do, then this is probably the only time I'll ever be in a position to drink as much as I want without having to pay for it," continued Raven. "Why not enjoy it for a few hours?"

"You are a fool, Eddie! Those letters expire at noon to-morrow!"

"East coast time?" asked Raven. "Daylight saving time?"

"Casablanca time, you fool!" exploded Bogarti.

Raven grinned. "You're almost as much fun to talk to as Massovitch."

"Why do you hate me so?"

"The alternative is unthinkable," answered Raven with an amused smile.

"I do not understand you at all," said Bogarti. Suddenly his eyes narrowed. "Unless you are waiting for the woman."

"What woman?"

"If you did not see her, then you are even a bigger fool than I thought." Suddenly Bogarti learned forward and lowered his voice. "Massovitch is glaring at you."

"He's got his men stationed all around the club," answered Raven. "He knows I'm not going anywhere right away." An amused smile crossed his face. "I think he's glaring at *you.*"

Bogarti turned and stared at Massovitch, who barely suppressed a snarl as he stared back.

"I think he knows I am the one who stole the letters," said

Bogarti nervously. He clasped two of his hands together on the table in front of him, trying to relax, but his third hand extended a forefinger and began drumming rapidly on the table.

"I've been wondering what you did with that third hand when the first two were otherwise occupied," remarked Raven. "Now I know."

"And?"

"And it would be difficult to be more boring."

"I didn't come here to be insulted by a doomed man!" growled Bogarti.

"Okay, I give up," said Raven. "Why *did* you come here?"

"To deliver the letters of transit, of course."

"No, you did that an hour or two ago. Why are you here *now*?"

"To negotiate, of course," said Bogarti.

Raven smiled. "To negotiate a price for letters you've already delivered?"

"To negotiate a price for telling you where I hid them when I brought them here this afternoon."

"I need them before noon tomorrow. How long were you going to wait before we haggled out a price?"

"Actually, I was going to wait until tomorrow morning, but . . ." Bogarti's voice trailed off into nothingness.

"But?" said Raven.

"But there's an excellent chance that Massovitch will kill you tonight." Bogarti lowered his voice confidentially. "The man is totally lacking in self-control."

"No wonder he doesn't look out of place here," replied Raven.

"So?" said Bogarti.

"So?" repeated Raven.

"So how much are you offering for the location of the letters?"

"Two free drinks," said Raven.

"Are you mad?" screamed Bogarti. "These letters are the only way to save your life."

"Make it one free drink," said Raven. "You're already too damned loud."

"I hope they kill you slowly and painfully," said Bogarti, getting up from the table. "I'll be in the vicinity if you come to your senses before noon."

"Is this man bothering you?" asked Peugeot, approaching the table.

"Yes," said Bogarti. "Absolutely."

"I was speaking to Eddie," said Peugeot.

"No more than most," replied Raven.

"I could lock him up for a few months," offered Peugeot. "I think we still have an empty cell." He frowned for a moment. "If not, I'll lock him in the same cell as Cemetery Grimes. He hasn't washed or changed prison outfits in all the years I've been here." He glanced at Bogarti. "Too bad one of those hands isn't holding a pen. It could write a fascinating memoir. After all, for who else would being shot in the forehead qualify as a minor flesh wound?"

"I think I'll just go over to that empty table and not bother anyone," said Bogarti, pointing to his destination with all three hands and walking off.

"I'm surprised you're still here, Eddie," said Peugeot. "You're operating under a deadline as I understand it, with an emphasis on the 'dead.'"

"The letters are in here somewhere," answered Raven. "How smart can Bogarti be? It took him maybe three minutes to decide on a hiding place and stash 'em. If I can't find 'em in twelve or thirteen hours, I deserve to be stuck here."

"I hate to be the bearer of unhappy tidings," said Peugeot, "but it's three thirty-five in the morning. You have less than eight and a half hours to find them."

"Then I'll have to put my thinking cap on," said Raven.

Peugeot shot him a knowing smile. "It probably wouldn't hurt to take your loving cap off."

"What are you talking about?"

"I *saw* Mrs. Brff," said Peugeot, still smiling. "And she's certainly worth risking all *this*"—he waved his hand around the room—"for. The trick, my friend Eddie, is to stay alive long enough to win her away from Brff and then have some time to enjoy yourself." He suddenly grimaced. "Damn!"

"What is it?" asked Raven, looking around for threats.

"I speak five languages fluently," answered Peugeot, "but I absolutely cannot pronounce that man's name!"

"We all have our problems, greater or lesser ones," said Raven. "Given the nature of mine, I hope you'll forgive me for not sympathizing overmuch with yours."

Peugeot smiled. "You know, Eddie, you're the only man in this town I feel any friendship or respect for—except myself, of course. Let me know where you're going with those letters and perhaps I'll come with you."

"They're good for only two people."

"I am staring across the table, and I only see one."

"You're a man of limited vision," said Raven.

"Of course!" exclaimed Peugeot with a sudden laugh. "They

ought to take away my French citizenship for not figuring that out instantly." He suddenly became serious again. "But if for any reason *she* is not inclined to lose a name that no one can pronounce . . . ?"

"I'll consider it," replied Raven.

"Good! I mean, look how well a totally corrupt officer like myself can live in a town like this. Think of what I could do in New York or London!"

"Forgive a personal question," said Raven, "but as long as you feel like that, why did you ever leave Paris?"

"That is not a personal question, Eddie," said Peugeot with a smile.

"Oh?"

The smile vanished. "It's an impertinent one."

"Forget I asked it."

"It is forgotten," said Peugeot, getting to his feet. "I'm sure you'll understand if I don't leave the premises until noon."

"You can keep Massovitch company," replied Raven. "Something tells me he's not leaving either."

Peugeot glanced at the front door. "Neither is Bogarti. Or her. How popular you've become!"

Raven looked in the direction Peugeot had indicated and saw the white-clad Ms. Maserati entering the club. She looked around, spotted Raven, and minced over to him, as only an overweight woman in a tight outfit and even tighter white shoes can do.

"Back so soon?" asked Raven.

"There are uneasy currents in the air," she said.

Raven resisted the urge to tell her to loosen her girdle. "And they've directed you back to Eddie's Place?"

"They tell me it may not be Eddie's Place much longer," said Ms. Maserati, "so I thought to make an offer for it again."

"I appreciate your persistence, but it's still not for sale."

"Everything's for sale if one can come up with the right price," she said with a knowing smile.

"Perhaps," said Raven. "But the right price is probably more than you can afford."

"Who said the right price had anything to do with money?" she asked.

I hope you're not peddling all three hundred pounds of your ass to me, thought Raven grimly. Aloud he said, "Okay, immediate free passage to Manhattan and a suite at the Waldorf."

An amused smile crossed her face. "Be reasonable, Eddie. It will be a much more pleasant negotiation than when you're desperate." She checked her elegant diamond-studded wristwatch. "Which, according to the grapevine, should be in another three or four hours."

"Come by my table then—if I'm still here—and we'll talk," said Raven.

"My offer will never be better than right now," said Ms. Maserati.

"That's hardly encouraging," he replied.

She gave him a humorless smile. "You'll never be less desperate than you are now." She looked around the room. "I see a nice empty table in the corner," she said. "I think I'll sit there until you're ready to talk business."

"You do that," said Raven. "And no pinching the waiters."

She uttered a sound that was halfway between a cough and a laugh, then began walking to the table in question.

"I've never seen the place this popular this late at night," remarked Peugeot, rejoining Raven.

"There have never been so many potential owners and killers knowing I only have until noon to get the hell out of here or face the consequences, whatever they may be."

"You know the consequences," said Peugeot. "You're here forever."

"Could be worse," replied Raven.

"Oh?"

"Could be in a grave forever. Or in a cell until they moved me to a grave."

"Or you could be one step beyond the city limits," said Peugeot. "I'm still interested in coming along if you choose the right location."

"First I have to figure out where Bogarti hid the letters of transit," said Raven.

"You *could* just buy them," suggested Peugeot.

"With what?" said Raven. He reached into his pocket and pulled out some bills and a handful of change. "I don't think he'll sell for . . . let me see . . . eighty-three dollars and sixteen cents."

"So sell to Ms. Maserati. If you don't, she'll just have that much more money to spend on white outfits that emphasize all her figure flaws."

"I may decide I like it here."

Peugeot smiled. "You like it here because Mrs. Brff is here. But will you like it when she leaves tomorrow?"

"Let's *hope* she leaves tomorrow," said Raven. "Colonel Massovitch swears she'll never leave."

"Colonel Massovitch doesn't give a damn about her, fool that he is," answered Peugeot. "He's only interested in detaining her husband."

Which makes us polar opposites, thought Eddie. *I don't give a damn about* him.

"Well, speak of the devil, or at least his wife, look who just showed up," said Peugeot.

7

Raven turned toward the entrance and saw Lisa standing there, looking uneasy. He immediately got to his feet. "Am-scray," he muttered softly.

"I beg your pardon?" said Peugeot, frowning.

"Beat it," said Raven. "I'm bringing the lady back to my table, and I want it empty when I get here."

He began walking over to where Lisa stood, and she relaxed noticeably as her eyes fell on him.

"Welcome back," said Raven.

"I couldn't sleep," she said.

"Come on over to my table and let me buy you something to get you wide awake."

"You're sure it's not an imposition?" she asked.

"Nothing about you is an imposition," he assured her.

"Thank you," she said, falling into step beside him.

"Here we are," he said as they reached the table. "What'll it be?"

"Whatever you suggest."

"Two weeks in the Caribbean," said Raven.

She smiled. "You're very sweet. I feel like I knew you in a different life."

He held up two fingers for the waiter, who nodded and walked over to the bar. "You did," said Raven.

She frowned. "I did what?"

"Know me in a different life."

"Don't be silly," said Ilsa.

"I'm being nostalgic," he replied. "There's a difference."

She glanced at the door. "I keep expecting my husband to come bursting through the door any minute."

"This time of night he'll figure out where you are," said Raven. "Almost every other spot in town is closed."

She smiled sadly. "Oh, he won't be looking for me. It'll be to meet some secret contact, or perhaps to confront Colonel Massovitch."

Raven stared at her. "How did you ever hook up with him? You don't seem to travel in the same circles."

"He was a world-famous patriot. I was . . . I *am* . . . nothing. I was flattered."

"Much as I hate to contradict a lovely lady like yourself, you're worth ten of him," said Raven. "Twelve when you smile."

A smile spread across her face. "I'm flattered, Eddie. But you're wrong."

"We'll have to agree to disagree."

The waiter arrived with their drinks. She took a sip, closed her eyes as she tasted it, and then smiled at him. "Just the thing for five o'clock in the morning in a strange land."

"Would you like something to eat with it?"

She shook her head. "No, thank you." Then, "Why is that little man staring at you? The one with three eyes."

"He has something I want, and he's waiting for me to make

him an offer." He stared at her. *Your husband has something I want, too.*

"What is it?"

"A ticket of sorts."

"To where?"

He smiled grimly. "Elsewhere."

She returned his smile, though without the grimness. "Elsewhere. It sounds enchanting."

"You never know," said Raven.

Eddie, said Rofocale's voice inside his head, *I can't believe it! You've got less than eight hours to save yourself, and you're sitting there flirting! Get those letters!*

They're here, thought Raven. *I just have to figure out where.*

By talking to the woman? demanded Rofocale.

"Are you all right?" asked Ilsa. "You seem . . . distracted."

"It's probably the hour."

"I can go back to the hotel lobby if—"

"No, I'm here for the duration."

She frowned. "The duration?"

Idiot! thought Raven. *Try to remember when and where you are.*

"Poor choice of words," he said aloud. "I mean that I'm here till noon." He frowned. "Well, *almost* till noon."

"It looks like a lonely life, at least from the outside," said Ilsa.

He smiled wryly. "You ought to see it from the inside."

"You need someone to share it with."

"That thought has occurred to me," he said. "So tell me, Lisa, how is *your* life?"

"Ilsa," she corrected him.

"My mistake," said Raven. "Ilsa."

"I am married to one of the most important men in the world. He is doing important things, and I am giving him moral and emotional support."

Raven forced a friendly smile to his lips. *Just as loveless as I thought. Maybe I* can *talk you into taking the other letter of transit.*

"He really is quite famous," she continued. "Is there anything you'd like to know about him? Anything at all?"

"Actually, there's something I'd like to know," said Raven.

"Just ask."

"How do you pronounce your married name?"

She smiled. "Mrs."

"Very good," he said with a chuckle. "I'll give you a ninety for that one."

"He took a vowel out to get a name on his passport that wouldn't set off alarms," she said, "and the new name stuck."

"That's as good a reason as any," said Raven, "and probably better than most." He paused. "By the way, can I order you another drink?"

"Just coffee, if you have it."

"It'll shock the kitchen, but yeah, we have it." He signaled the waiter and ordered two cups.

"If you'll excuse me," she said, getting to her feet, "I think I'll go freshen up while we're waiting for our coffee."

He stood up as well, watched her walk away, and then sat back down as Bogarti approached him.

"Are you ready to make an offer for them?" asked the little man.

"I don't know," replied Raven. "Are you ready to tell me where they are before I blow your brains out?"

Bogarti uttered a nasal laugh. "I told you, for me, death is merely a temporary condition. But kill me, and my silence about the letters' location will become a permanent condition."

Raven smiled. "We both know they're hidden somewhere in this room. How long do you think it'll take to tear the place apart, board by board?"

"You wouldn't do that, Eddie," said Bogarti.

"I'd have to," answered Raven. "After all, you'll be dead, and there will be nobody to tell me where they are."

"Surely we can come to an agreement," said Bogarti nervously.

"I'll up my offer," said Raven. "Fifteen dollars for one, twenty for the pair."

"They're worth thousands!" screamed Bogarti.

"To anyone but me?" responded Raven. "I doubt it."

"But we're talking about you!"

"We're talking about two letters of transit that I didn't even know existed twenty-four hours ago," said Raven.

"And they expire at noon!" yelled Bogarti. "So why won't you make an honest offer?"

"Okay," said Raven. "When you're right, you're right."

"How much?" asked Bogarti greedily.

"Fourteen dollars for one, eighteen for the pair."

"That's even less than you offered three minutes ago!"

Raven smiled. "As you just pointed out, they're that much closer to expiring with each passing minute."

"I hate you, Eddie Raven!" cried Bogarti, getting to his feet and stalking back to his own table.

"You've probably got a lot of company," muttered Raven as Lisa made her way across the room and reseated herself at the table.

"What an odd-looking little man," she remarked.

"He wouldn't look much better with only two eyes and two arms," answered Raven.

"He makes me very nervous," she said. "In fact, most of the people around here make me nervous. I can't wait to leave."

"Eddie's Place?"

She shook her head. "Casablanca."

He sighed deeply. "We have that in common."

She frowned. "What's keeping you? Have you somehow offended Colonel Massovitch?"

"I certainly hope so," answered Raven. "But he's not the reason I'm stuck here."

"So you need letters of transit too?"

"Doesn't everybody?" he asked wryly.

"Who sells them?"

"As far as I can tell, just one person," said Raven.

"Oh? Who?" she persisted.

"Our friend Three-Eyes," said Raven. "His slightly more formal name is Bogarti."

"What does he want for them?"

"We haven't got that far in the negotiations," answered Raven. "Hopefully we won't have to."

"I don't understand."

"They're hidden somewhere in here. If I can figure out where, they won't cost a cent. I'm no Muhammad Ali, but I don't think a little twerp like that can take them away from me once I've got my hands of them."

"Muhammad Ali?" she said, frowning.

"Sorry," he said. "Make that Joe Louis."

"Ah!" she said, smiling and nodding.

Try to remember when and where you are, Eddie, said Rofocale's voice inside his head, *or you may wind up staying here.*

Peugeot walked over to their table. "I couldn't help noticing the presence of the lovely Mrs. Brff," he said. "I hope you won't mind if I join you?"

"Would it do any good?" asked Raven.

"Not a bit," said Peugeot.

"Then please join us."

"Thank you," said Peugeot, pulling up a chair. "I think I will." He turned to Ilsa. "Has your husband left you behind?"

"Certainly not!" she said angrily.

"Too bad."

"I beg your pardon?" she said.

"It means he's still stuck here."

"We are *both* stuck in Casablanca," said Ilsa.

Peugeot shook his head. "Massovitch and the others have no interest in you. *He's* the one they want to keep here." He stared at her. "In fact, if our friend Eddie stops playing games and pays Bogarti what he wants, there are *two* letters of transit. He might be convinced to take you with him."

"Do I strike you as being that disloyal?" demanded Ilsa.

"No offense intended," answered Peugeot. "I simply assume your husband would rest easier knowing you were safely out of here, and in the company of a man who is almost as competent as myself."

"Enough," said Raven ominously.

"My lips are sealed," said Peugeot.

"Good."

"On *that* subject," added Peugeot. "I shall of course feel free, if not compelled, to share my wisdom on all other subjects."

"I can't tell you how grateful we are," said Raven sardonically.

"Oh, go ahead," said Peugeot. "Try."

"I just told you: I can't."

Peugeot checked his wristwatch. "I hate to mention it, Eddie, but you've got something less than seven hours left. I of course realize the game you're playing: As we get closer to noon, Bogarti will become more and more desperate, and will take much less than the letters are worth, since by noon they'll be totally worthless to anyone. And clearly this lovely lady's husband either doesn't know about them or doesn't give a damn, or he'd be here trying to outbid or out-search you."

"I assume there's a point that you're eventually going to get to?" said Raven.

Peugeot nodded. "Noble human being that I am, to say nothing of my intense dislike of Colonel Massovitch, if you have decided to search for the letters before paying Bogarti for them, I will volunteer my unsurpassed mental powers on your side of this battle of mental giants."

Do you know where they are? thought Eddie.

If I knew I would certainly have told you, answered Rofocale's mental voice.

You would? Why?

Don't be foolish, Eddie. You know very well why, or at least you should.

We'll argue that later, if I live past noon.

8

Raven looked across the table. "Okay," he said. "Go find 'em. Let me know if you need a hammer or a crowbar."

"I meant that I would supply help in the form of pure cerebration," replied Peugeot.

"Okay," said Raven with a shrug. "If you think you can look under the floor and behind the wallboards with just your mind . . ."

"I thought I'd put my massive brain to work, and then tell Sam where to look."

"Sam plays the piano. *You* look."

"Let's not be unreasonable, Eddie," said Peugeot. "I am a lieutenant in the police force. I haven't done an honest hour's work in years."

"I hate it when friends argue," said Ilsa, getting up. "I'll be sitting at that table"—she indicated an empty one halfway across the room—"until you're done."

She was walking away before Raven could tell her they weren't really arguing, and that he suspected they did this all the time, then realized that would have taken more explanation than he cared to give.

"Thanks," he said bitterly.

"Well, it does make your choice of what to do with the second letter of transit easier," answered Peugeot. "She's gone, and I'm still here."

"Being in your physical proximity is not the advantage you seem to think it is," said Raven, as the first rays of sunlight began shining in through the window. He looked across the room at Massovitch. "Doesn't he ever sleep?"

"He's probably wondering the same thing about you," said Peugeot in amused tones.

"If you really want to make yourself useful, find some way to distract him and get him the hell out of here before I unearth the letters," said Raven.

Peugeot smiled in amusement. "He has come to this place every night since he arrived, and I have never tried to order or entice him out of it. What do you think he'll conclude if I try on the one night that little three-eyed thief is here? I mean, surely he knows the letters of transit are missing by now."

"You're just a ton of help tonight," said Raven with a weary sigh.

"There's Ms. Maserati," said Peugeot, indicating the woman in white. "Along with owning a rival to this place, she sells and trades contraband all over the continent."

"So?"

"So she owns her own cargo plane, and I know she wants to buy Eddie's Place. You might effect a trade."

"And after we do I'll go to the airport and find a dozen of Massovitch's men waiting to arrest me," said Raven.

"You can be an incredibly bothersome man to speak with, do you know that?" said Peugeot irritably.

"It's been suggested a few times."

"Well," said Peugeot, "I'm going to the bar to have a drink with the one man I always get along with—myself."

And with that he got to his feet and began approaching the bar. Raven was going to signal Lisa to come back, or perhaps go over and join her, when he noticed Ms. Maserati approaching his table again.

"I'd ask if I may sit down," she said, "but you're just crude enough to say no, so I shall simply do so unbidden."

"Be my guest," said Raven. Then: "Strike that. Be my customer, and be sure to pay for your drinks when you leave."

"I admire you, Eddie," she said with an amused smile. "Such courage in the face of imminent disaster."

"Which of the many imminent disasters facing me are you referring to?" he asked.

"I *know*, Eddie," she said. "I think by now just about everyone in town knows."

"Everyone but me," answered Raven. "What do you think you know?"

"That if you're not gone from Casablanca by noon, you're here forever." She smiled again. "So I've come to make my final offer."

"Good!" said Raven.

"Ah!" she said. "You're ready to deal."

"No," he replied. "But I'm glad it's your final offer."

She stared at him for a long moment. "So you really intend to stay here."

"Absolutely not."

"Then listen to my offer."

"No."

She frowned. "But you just said . . ."

"Oh, I'm getting out this morning," answered Raven. "And I'm selling. But not to you."

"You haven't heard my offer."

"Let's get this over with," said Raven.

"Good. My offer is—"

"Don't understand me so fast," he said. He looked across the room. "Sam!"

"Yes, Eddie?" said the piano player.

"Come over here for a minute."

Sam got to his feet and walked over.

"How'd you like to own Eddie's Place?" asked Raven.

"I suppose I could live with the responsibility," said Sam.

"You got five bucks in your pocket?" asked Raven.

Sam dug into a pocket, pulled out a wad of bills he'd been tipped with, counted off five ones, and held them out to Raven.

"It's a deal, as of noon today," said Raven.

"Can I change the name to Sam's Place?"

Raven shrugged. "It's your club. Call it anything you want."

"Thanks, Eddie," said Sam, turning and walking back to the piano.

Raven looked across the table at Ms. Maserati. "Do we have anything further to discuss?" he asked.

"I hate you, Eddie Raven," she said coldly while getting to her feet.

"You're in good company," he said as she turned and walked to the door.

He got up and walked over to Lisa's table.

"How are you holding up?" he asked her.

"Truth to tell, I could use the coffee I ordered last night," she replied.

"Not a problem," he answered, signaling the waiter and making a sign with his hands that clearly meant 'coffee' to the man. "It'll be here in a minute."

"You're very thoughtful," she said.

He smiled. "You make it easy to be very thoughtful."

Eddie, said Rofocale's voice inside his head, *you're wasting time. You've got to get your hands on those letters.*

Not a problem, answered Raven.

Why not? You've only got a handful of hours, and you're no closer to getting them than when this started!

I'm hours closer. Trust me.

How can you be any closer when you refuse to negotiate?

I've got a deadline. But if he wants to sell to me, if they're earmarked for me, and obviously they are, then he *has a deadline too. The closer we get to noon, the more eager he'll be to unload them.*

"You seem distracted," remarked Ilsa.

"I'm sorry," replied Raven. "May I sit down?"

She smiled. "It's your club. You can sit anywhere you want."

"Next to you is where I want," answered Raven. He checked his wristwatch. "I should think your husband will be waking up any minute. I hope he doesn't panic when he finds you're gone."

"He'll know I'm here," she said.

"He will?"

"Where else would I be?" she asked. "In Casablanca everyone comes to Eddie's Place."

"Have either of you given any thought to where you're going next, in case you can't get to Europa?"

"I suppose that depends on Colonel Massovitch," she said. "Or perhaps you."

"Me?"

"Word has it that you plan to leave. Possibly you'll take us with you, or at least point out someone who can help us."

"The pudgy woman in white—Ms. Maserati—has done her share of smuggling, including people. Her club is two blocks to the south. You might talk to her."

"I'm told that the misshapen little man over there, I think his name is Bogarti, might be able to arrange passage out of here."

"Anything's possible," said Raven.

"Perhaps I should go talk to him."

"You might as well do it here, where I can keep an eye on you," said Raven. "I don't trust the little bastard."

She got to her feet. "Then if you'll excuse me for a few moments."

He stood up when she did, watched her approach the little three-armed man, and then returned to his own table, where Peugeot joined him.

"I had no idea she was blind," he said.

"What are you talking about?" demanded Raven.

"Why else would she spend time with Bogarti instead of with me, or even you?" said Peugeot.

"He has something she wants."

"The letters, of course," said Peugeot, nodding. "I can't imagine he has anything else anyone in the world could possibly want."

"True," agreed Raven. "Unless some undersize guy is looking for a beat-up suit with three arms."

Peugeot chuckled. "I *like* you, Eddie! I'm delighted that you're too obstinate to make a deal with Bogarti. The place just won't seem the same without you."

"I've already sold it."

"To Ms. Maserati?" asked Peugeot, making no attempt to hide his surprise and dismay.

"To Sam."

"Oh," said Peugeot. "You had me worried for a minute there. How many times have you sold it to him now?"

"A few," said Raven.

"Four? Five?"

"You never know," said Raven. "This time I might just put on a knapsack and take a stroll down to Cape Town."

"Somehow you don't strike me as a man who likes to take three-year strolls."

"Liking it's got nothing to do with it," replied Raven.

"Well, if you *must* walk south, try walking southeast," said Peugeot. "There's a charming girl I used to know who's living in Nairobi, and you can probably get there in under two years if you hurry."

"I'll keep it in mind."

"Or, as I thought we discussed last night, you can just meet Bogarti's price and take me with you."

"You don't even know where the letters of transit are good for," noted Raven.

"Elsewhere," said Peugeot. "What more do either of us need to know?"

"Not a damned thing, really," admitted Raven.

Peugeot looked across the room. "I see the young lady is returning to her table, and as far as I can tell, Bogarti hasn't gotten up to retrieve the letters from wherever he hid them, so I assume they didn't come to an agreement."

"I never thought they would," said Raven.

"Oh?"

"Like it or not, those letters seem to have my name on them."

"Then just lock the doors and don't give the little bastard anything to eat or drink until he turns them over."

"It's not that simple," said Raven.

"I don't know why not," replied Peugeot. "It certainly sounded simple when I said it."

"They expire at noon."

Peugeot checked his watch. "You've got a little more than three hours."

"I know."

"If I were you, I'd try dealing with him for the next hour, and if we hadn't come to an agreement by then, I'd beat the shit out of him until he told me where they were."

"It's not going to come to that," said Raven.

"You know something I don't know?" suggested Peugeot.

"I know a lot of things you don't know," answered Raven. "More to the point, I know something that Bogarti doesn't know, or hasn't figured out yet, but we'll make a deal before anyone beats the shit out of anyone else. Unless you annoy the hell out of me first."

"What a thing to say to your only remaining friend in all the world," said Peugeot in mock outrage.

"There's a friend right there," said Raven, pointing to Sam.

"Only until noon, at which time he'll start charging you for drinks."

"And there's another," added Raven, nodding toward Lisa.

"She may offer a consummation devoutly to be wished," replied Peugeot, "but she's hardly a friend. Why, you don't even know her first name. I heard you."

"True," answered Raven with a smile. "On the other hand, I don't know *your* first name either."

"François, of course!" snapped Peugeot. "All good Frenchmen are named François, except for a handful of Jacqueses and Pierres."

"I can't tell you how much better I feel, knowing who to sue in court," said Raven.

Peugeot uttered a hearty laugh. "Damn, but I've always liked you, Eddie!" he said. "Well, except when I haven't."

A well-dressed couple entered and walked directly to a table.

"Regulars?" asked Peugeot.

"They certainly act like it," said Raven.

"I know why people are still awake at this time of day," said Peugeot. "What I will never comprehend is why they wake up fresh and refreshed as these two seem to be."

"It's a strange world," agreed Raven. He saw Bogarti making frantic gestures toward him. "And about to get stranger."

"I think I shall leave you to your negotiations," said Peugeot, getting to his feet.

"We're not negotiating anything," replied Raven.

"You're not?" said Peugeot, surprised.

Raven checked his watch. "Too early."

Peugeot shook his head. "I simply do not understand you, Eddie," he muttered, walking off.

The moment he left, Bogarti walked over to the table and took his place.

"Why are you tormenting me?" demanded the three-eyed three-armed little man.

"Other than the fact that it's fun, you mean?" answered Raven.

"You have less than three hours to negotiate for the letters of transit," said Bogarti. "We both know you're not going to search for them, or else you'd have started looking last night. So why do you just sit there and ignore me? We both know those letters are your only ticket out of here."

"Oh, we'll negotiate," said Raven. "But it's too soon."

"Too soon?" screamed Bogarti, drawing stares from all around the room. "It's almost nine in the morning. Why won't you bid?"

"Because I know you're going to sell them to me," answered Raven. "They don't seem to be good for anyone else. Assuming that's true, *I* may be on a deadline, but so are you. I can't use them after the clock strikes noon, but then you can't sell them after that. So the closer we get to noon, the more reasonable your price figures to be. Hell, if I wait until eleven fifty-eight, you should be ready to take five dollars."

"Knowing that you are stuck here forever is worth more than five dollars to me," snapped Bogarti.

"More than a thousand?"

Bogarti paused, hand rubbing his chin, considering.

"See?" said Raven with a smile. "We're already negotiating."

"Why do you do this to me, Eddie!" demanded Bogarti. "I risked my life for those letters!"

"Really?"

"Well," admitted Bogarti, "the car *could* have run off the road."

"On a flat straightaway at twenty miles an hour?" asked Raven with a smile.

"Damn it, Eddie!" snapped Bogarti. "You'd better make an acceptable offer, and quick! I know something about the letters that you don't know!"

"You know at least two things," answered Raven. "Where they are, and what they look like. So what? When we hit on a price, and of course it's getting lower by the minute, you're going to fetch them and turn them over to me."

"It doesn't end there," said Bogarti with an evil grin.

"What are you talking about?"

"You have to activate the letters."

Raven frowned. "If there's some code word, I assume that's part of the deal. If I buy them and they don't work, I think you may safely assume that I would be *very* angry with you."

Bogarti shook his head. "No, nothing that simple."

"Okay, how complex?"

"You just have to answer a question or two."

"Okay, go ahead and ask."

"*I* don't ask," said Bogarti. "The letters of transit do."

"I get the answer right, I'm out of here, and if not, they don't work?" asked Raven.

"That's right."

"If I buy them and come up with the wrong answers, I'll want my money back."

"Certainly," said Bogarti.

Too fast, thought Raven. *That means you'll be out of here ten seconds after money changes hands, and probably beyond Casablanca's city limits by noon.* He frowned. *Still, what the hell choice have I got?*

"Okay," said Raven. "Three hundred dollars."

"We were talking about a thousand just a minute or two ago," replied Bogarti.

"That was talk," said Raven. "This is money."

"No."

"You didn't hear my whole offer."

"Oh?" said Bogarti, frowning.

"Right."

"Then make it."

"Here it is, and it's nonnegotiable," replied Raven. "Three hundred dollars until ten o'clock. Two hundred dollars until eleven. One hundred until eleven forty-five. One dollar thereafter."

Bogarti stared at him for a long moment.

"The clock's running," said Raven.

"I accept," said Bogarti.

Raven walked over to the cash register, pulled out three one-hundred-dollar bills, and brought them back to Bogarti, who grabbed them in one of his left hands.

"I hope you die!" growled Bogarti, pocketing the money.

"Someday I probably will," said Raven.

"Soon!"

"I hate to point this out, but if you don't give me the letters, and fast, I won't be the first one at this table to die."

Bogarti got to his feet, walked to the bar, reached his right hand behind a painting of a busty nude that hung on the wall above a row of bottles, and came away with an envelope, which he carried back to the table and handed to Raven.

"Here you are, little good may they do you."

"Thank you," said Raven. "Oh, one more thing."

"Oh?" said Bogarti suspiciously.

"Yeah," said Raven. "Your presence is no longer wanted in Eddie's Place."

"I'll be back when it's Sam's Place," promised Bogarti, turning to leave.

"If this quiz is as hard as you imply, I may flunk it, in which case it'll still be Eddie's Place tonight and you still won't be welcome here."

Bogarti muttered an obscenity and walked out of the building, while Raven looked at the envelope. He was about to ask Lisa once more if she'd like to escape with him, but just then Brff entered and walked over to her. She threw her arms around him and gave him a peck on the cheek, and he decided he'd be much happier—or less frustrated—thinking of her as Ilsa than Lisa, got to his feet, and walked through the kitchen and out the back door into an alley.

A moment later he found Peugeot standing beside him.

"I couldn't help noticing that you are in possession of the letters, and since letters imply plural, I was absolutely certain you wanted a traveling companion."

"Suit yourself," said Raven with a shrug. "First I have to dope these out."

"Just look for the word 'destination,'" said Peugeot.

"It's not that simple, according to Bogarti. Evidently these things are puzzles or questionnaires or something similar, and I have to answer them to activate them."

"If there are any questions about French women, I can be of inestimable service," said Peugeot.

"I suspect it's going to want more than measurements and phone numbers," said Raven.

"*Quel pitié!*" muttered Peugeot.

"Oh, well," said Raven, opening the envelope and pulling out a folded sheet of paper. "I might as well get this show on the road."

"You needn't read me," said the paper. "We can converse like normal beings."

Raven decided not to offer his own description of normal being. "Sounds good to me," he replied. "What do we do?"

"I ask you three questions."

"And I have to get them all right?"

"No," answered the paper. "Just get one right."

"And if I don't?" asked Raven.

"I go up in flames, as does your passage out of here."

"Okay," said Raven. "We might as well start."

"All right," said the paper. "Who is Howard Allen O'Brien?"

Raven frowned, trying to remember all the All-American football and basketball players he'd ever read or heard about.

"I'll give you a hint," said the paper.

"That'd be helpful," said Raven.

"I doubt it," responded the paper. "The hint is that Howard Allen O'Brien is not the name you know this person by."

"Beats me," admitted Raven. Another minute had passed. "Who is he?"

"*She* is bestselling author of vampire novels Anne Rice."

"She's a sex-change?" asked Raven.

"No, just a female whose parents gave her a male's name at

birth." There was a brief pause. "Are you ready for your second question?"

"Probably not, but let's have it anyway."

"What country's coins feature likenesses not of presidents, prime ministers, or kings, but rather images of Mickey Mouse and Star Wars?"

"And these coins are legal tender?" asked Raven.

"Absolutely."

"I don't suppose Disneyland qualifies as a country?"

"No."

"And I suppose all these questions and answers are verifiable somewhere?"

"Of course," said the paper. "You're stalling."

"I give up."

"I hardly blame you," said the paper sympathetically. "The answer is Niue, a small Pacific island, where the currency has images of Mickey Mouse and Star Wars."

"Really and truly?" asked Raven.

"Honest Indian," replied the paper. "Now, if you miss the third question, I will disappear in a sheet of flame, and you will be stuck in Casablanca for the rest of your life, however long or, more likely, brief it will be."

Peugeot backed away a few feet. "I'm rooting for you, of course," he said to Raven, "but there's no sense both of us getting badly burned, just in case."

"Thanks," said Raven dryly.

"Are you ready, Eddie Raven?"

"As ready as I'll ever be," answered Raven without much confidence. "Let her rip."

"I beg your pardon?" said the paper.

"Ask your question and let's get this humiliation over with."

"All right," said the paper, and suddenly there was a photo of a lovely lingerie-clad girl with long black hair, distinctive bangs, and a winning smile staring out at Raven. Above her was the caption "Betty Page, Queen of the Pin-Ups."

"Yeah, that's her, all right," said Raven. "I suspect every male over the age of twelve could identify her."

"The question," said the paper, "is, 'what is wrong with this?'"

"Other than the fact that she's not here in the flesh?" asked Raven.

"And that she's not French?" added Peugeot.

"Just answer the question," said the paper.

Raven stared at the image for a long minute. Everything was in perfect proportion, she had the right number of eyes, nostrils, arms, and legs; he couldn't spot a single thing wrong with it. He looked away, trying to clear his mind, then looked back—and saw it.

"Oh, shit!" he said. "Of course!"

"What is your answer?"

"You spelled her name wrong," said Raven. "It's B-e-t-t-i-e. Everyone knows that."

"Eddie Raven, you are right, and I shall now activate that portion of myself that will take you to your next location."

"I'm coming too!" said Peugeot—and vanished.

"What happened to him?" asked Raven.

"He is currently riding shotgun on a Wells Fargo stagecoach as it goes through Apache territory."

"Too bad," said Raven. "And no French girls waiting for him if he makes it to California." He paused. "Okay, what about me?"

"Where would you like to go?" asked the remaining letter of transit.

"I have a choice?"

"Not much of one, but yes."

"I've never seen Barcelona," mused Raven. "And I've always wondered if Bora Bora is as beautiful as James Michener made it sound. And Rio must be something to see during Carnival." He shrugged. "But I suppose when all is said and done, there's no place like—"

9

" ——Home," concluded Raven.

"Home *what*?" said an unfamiliar voice next to him.

He looked to his left and saw a rather tarnished robot walking alongside him. Next to the robot was a tall, slender creature that looked for all the world—*which world?* wondered Raven—like a scarecrow. And on his right was the strangest sight of all: a shaggy-maned feline creature wearing the torn remnants of what seemed to be a football uniform.

Walking just ahead of him was Lisa, who had an undersize Chihuahua on a leash.

It can't be, thought Raven. He looked down and saw that he was walking on a brick road. It may well have been yellow once, but it was so scuffed and covered with dirt that it was hard enough just to identify it as a road.

"Lisa!" he said. "What the hell is going on?"

She stopped and turned to him. "I'm Ilsa," she replied.

He shook his head. "You were Ilsa in Casablanca, but clearly you're Dorothy here."

"Don't call me that!" she said harshly.

"Don't call you Lisa?" he said, confused.

"Don't call me Dorothy!"

He stared at her. "I didn't mean to offend you."

She sighed deeply. "You couldn't know."

"You'd be surprised at how many things I couldn't know," said Raven. "Which one is this?"

"My mother named me Dorothy. In Greek it means God's gift. My dad came from elsewhere."

"Elsewhere?" he repeated.

"Well, North Elsewhere, anyway. Every time he got drunk he thought he *was* God, that I was his gift to give, and he kept trying to give me to his drunken friends—so my mother changed it, and until Dad can figure out what Ilsa's for, I'm safe."

"Interesting," said Raven, who actually thought it was minimally more horrific than interesting.

"And you are?"

"Eddie Raven."

"Eddie Raven," she repeated, frowning. "I feel like we've met before, but I can't remember where."

"Not in Oz, I can guarantee that," he said.

"But it's the only place I've ever been," she replied. "In fact, that's why I'm going to the Sapphire City—to see the Wiz and beg him to move me to a new venue."

"Any particular place in mind?" asked Raven.

"When I sleep, I dream about this strange, bustling city, with rooms beneath the ground that move on their own power, and buildings so tall that they almost blot out the sun, and people everywhere." She looked at him with a curious expression on her face. "In fact, I think *you* were in some of those dreams."

"I wouldn't be at all surprised," said Raven.

"Anyway, I want him to send me there."

"Sounds like an interesting place," said Raven. "Mind if I tag along?"

"I don't mind if *they* don't," she said, indicating her three companions.

Raven turned to them. "How about it, guys? Who knows? You might need another body on your side if things get rough."

"Couldn't hurt," said the lion. "I haven't seen a referee in miles."

"You got a name?" asked Raven.

"We just call him the Cowardly Lion," said the scarecrow.

"What's a big burly lion got to be afraid of?"

"My fans," said the lion.

"Your fans?"

The lion nodded. "We were playing the Leopards, down four points with three seconds to go on the clock. I went out for a pass, faked my defender out of his pants—that's literally, not figuratively; they're still laughing at him—got loose in the end zone, and then it happened."

"What happened?"

"I dropped the pass."

"And your fans were annoyed?"

"No," said the lion. "My fans were *homicidal*! So I ran off and hid. Then Ilsa found me and asked me to come along and protect her."

"Imagine that!" said the robot with a laugh. "The Cowardly Lion is Ilsa's protector!"

"I'll protect her against anything except a season ticket holder!" growled the lion.

"You got a name?" asked Raven.

"Yes and no," answered the lion.

"You want me to call you Yes and No?" asked Raven, frowning. "That's pretty strange even for here, wherever here is."

The lion shook his shaggy head. "No, I mean that I have a name, and I hate it."

"Oh?"

The lion nodded. "It's Leo." He frowned. "You ever meet a male lion that *wasn't* named Leo?"

"What if I call you Numa instead?" suggested Raven.

"Numa, Numa," mused the lion. "And there's not a single 'l' in it." He grinned. "Numa it is. I *like* it!"

Raven turned to the robot. "And you are . . . ?"

"I like Robby," he answered. "Almost all the robots I know are called Robby. But . . ."

"But?"

"But I walked away from my post, guarding the spam factory, to help Ilsa find the Wizard, and maybe protect her from him if push comes to shove—or, let's be honest, to *grab*—so I suppose I should be AL-76 since Isaac Asimov wrote a story called 'Robot AL-76 Goes Astray.'"

"Why don't we split the difference?" suggested Raven. "I'll just call you Al."

"Suits me," agreed the robot. "By Isaac, you're fitting in well already!"

Raven turned to the scarecrow. "And you?"

"Mostly I answer to 'Hey, you!'" said the scarecrow. "But if the Wiz can give me a brain boost, or at least a third-grade education, I'm going to call myself Einstein."

"Einstein it is," said Raven.

"Not yet," said the scarecrow.

"Why the hell not?" said Raven. "You've got to get used to hearing it, and I have a feeling that once we get to wherever it is we're going, I could yell 'Hey, you!' and get three hundred responses."

"That's true," admitted the scarecrow. "It always draws a crowd."

"Okay, we're in business," said Raven.

"Almost," said Numa.

"Almost?" repeated Raven.

"Ilsa's dog."

"If he's her dog, surely he's got a name."

"I agree that it's not much of a name," said Lisa. "One day I was walking along the road and suddenly there he was at the other end of the leash."

"Well, every dog my family had when I was a kid was called Shep," said Raven. "Most of them could eat this little fellow for breakfast, and it's a good, rugged, masculine name."

She nodded her agreement. "It beats Poochie," she said. "That's what I've been calling all four pounds of him."

They all commenced walking, and Raven turned to Lisa. "So how much does the Wizard charge for his services?"

"It depends on the services," she answered. "And he's the Wiz. The Wizard is his drunken brother who operates on the other side of the world."

"Give me a little time and I'll get the hang of it," replied Raven. "If I could dope out Casablanca, Oz ought to be a piece of cake."

Suddenly their way was blocked by a huge green tyrannosaur, standing on its hind legs. "Did someone say cake?" it bellowed.

"Dinosaurs can't talk," said Raven.

"Wanna bet?" said the tyrannosaur.

"Okay, they talk," said Raven. "Why don't you go kill a stegosaur or a triceratops and leave us alone?"

"Watch how you talk to the king of the world, chum!" growled the tyrannosaur. "I'm the absolute top of the food chain, in case it's slipped your notice."

"Don't annoy him, Eddie," said Einstein.

"Easy for you to say," said Numa. "Dinosaurs don't eat scarecrows."

"They probably don't eat robots, either," said Al. "If I knew how to fight, I'd be happy to take him on."

"Here, Shep! Here, Shep!" called Lisa, and they all turned to see the little Chihuahua, which had slipped out of his collar, racing toward the tyrannosaur. When he got there he growled once and bit the huge beast on the toe.

"Ow!" screamed the tyrannosaur. "What did he want to go and do that for?"

"Well, you *were* threatening us," said Raven.

"That's what carnivorous dinosaurs do!" whined the tyrannosaur, as a tear trickled down its cheek.

"Well, biting anyone who threatens its mistress is what guard dogs do," said Raven.

"It *hurts*!" whined the tyrannosaur.

"Oh, come on," said Raven. "Surely you get more than a nip on the toe when you kill your prey."

"Kill my prey?" it repeated, frowning.

"You know—your dinner."

"I buy my dinner at Hudson's meat market," said the tyrannosaur. "I just like terrifying people."

Lisa leaned over and whispered to Raven. "Maybe we should enlist it in our cause."

"Why not?" he replied. He turned to the tyrannosaur. "We're on our way to the Sapphire City. You want to come along?"

"Do they have good stuff to eat there?" asked the tyrannosaur. "Stuff that doesn't bite or fight back?"

"Beats me," admitted Raven.

"Then why are you going?"

"We're off to see the Wiz."

"The *Wiz*?" cried the tyrannosaur. "I'm outta here!"

And so saying, it turned and ran screaming into the distance.

"Appearances can be misleading," remarked Numa as Shep considered giving chase, evidently thought better of it, and trotted back to Lisa.

"Well, that was interesting," said Al. "Not totally unexpected, but interesting."

"Get a lot of chance encounters along the road, do you?" asked Raven.

"No more than two or three an hour," answered the robot.

"Well, let's see if adding a man to your party scares some of them off," said Raven.

"Who knows?" said Einstein. "Perhaps it would. If we had one."

"I haven't seen a man along this road in months," said Numa.

"What are you guys talking about?" said Raven. "*I'm* a man."

His four companions exchanged knowing looks.

"You really think so?" asked Einstein.

"Of course."

"I hate to be the one to tell you, Eddie," said Al. "But you're a Munchkin."

"The hell I am!" snapped Raven. "Look at me. I'm as tall as any of you!"

"How tall do you think we are, Eddie?" asked Numa.

Raven frowned. "Six feet?" he said.

"Try four feet," answered Einstein. "And a little less for Numa here."

"But Lisa—make that Ilsa—is no Munchkin, and I have her by five or six inches!" argued Raven.

"That was just to make you feel comfortable," said Lisa from behind him.

He turned to face her, and had to look up into her face. He considered the revelation for a minute, then shrugged. "Well, now I've got one more reason to see the Wiz."

"Which guild do you belong to?" asked Al.

"Guild?" repeated Raven, frowning.

"Every Munchkin belongs to a guild," replied Al. "The most popular is the Lollipop Guild."

"A bunch of insurrectionists," muttered Numa contemptuously.

"*Playkin* magazine gets all its centerspreads from the Lollapalooza Guild," added Einstein.

"Somehow, once you get a bit acclimated, Oz isn't all that different than the world I'm used to," said Raven.

Oh yes it is, and you'd better be prepared for it or you'll never see your own world again.

"Who said that?" demanded Raven, spinning around.

"Said what?" asked Numa, frowning.

I did, and it would behoove you to listen.

Rofocale? thought Raven. *Where the hell are you?*

Right where I've been all along.

The hospital?

Of course the hospital. I'm connected to half a dozen tubes that are keeping me alive. And the only way you're ever going to get back here is with the help of the Wiz.

There really is a Wiz?

Of course. Sometimes, Eddie, things are exactly what they seem. I thought you learned that in Casablanca.

Or wherever it was.

It was Casablanca. If you start doubting it, the odds against you surviving and escaping from Oz just tripled.

I'm here. I'm on what was once a yellow brick road. I'm accompanied by a scarecrow, a tin man, and a cowardly lion. I'm in the company of a girl I think I love, who was and maybe still is Dorothy. How the hell can I doubt it?

Just remember: This is not a book or a movie. You are in Oz, and powerful forces want you to remain there, alive or preferably dead. You must stay alert and adjust to whatever circumstance in which you find yourself. Because if you don't . . .

Raven waited patiently for Rofocale to finish the sentence. *If I don't?* he asked at last.

Then we're both dead.

10

"Let's take a break," said Einstein. "Scarecrows weren't made for hiking."

"Yeah, the Wiz'll keep for another hour or two," agreed Al, sitting down on the brick path.

"Besides, he's probably watching our every move," said Numa, also sitting down.

"You think so?" asked Einstein.

Numa shrugged. "He's the Wiz, isn't he?"

"Yeah," said Einstein. "What the hell, when you're right, you're right. Of course," he added, raising his voice to just short of a shout, "if he were a truly compassionate Wiz, he wouldn't make us fight our way through unknown dangers just to make our requests in person. He'd help us *NOW*!"

"He's brilliant and all-powerful," replied Al. "But I don't re-member anyone ever calling him compassionate."

"Besides, we're just tagging along to make sure nothing happens to Ilsa," added Numa. "If he helps us too, that's just so much gravy."

"Speaking of gravy, where does one grab a snack around here?" asked Raven.

"Beats me," answered Al. "Robots don't eat."

"Ever?" asked Numa.

"Well, not food," said Al. "Not that anyone else here would recognize it as food."

"You know," added Einstein, "I don't think scarecrows eat either. At least I don't remember ever having a meal."

"Do you ever feel hungry?" asked Numa.

"I don't know," said Einstein. "What does hunger feel like?"

"Well, *I* know what it feels like," said Numa. He turned to Raven. "Let's go kill and eat something small and defenseless."

"Let's do it the easy way," said Raven. "You got any fruit-bearing trees or bushes in this neck of the woods?"

"Lions don't eat fruit," growled Numa.

"Except when they're hungry," suggested Al.

"That goes without saying," replied Numa.

"So go find a grape tree or something similar," said Al to Raven. "If he's hungry enough, he'll join you."

"I *asked* you not to say it!" said Numa with a snarl.

Raven turned to Lisa. "You really enjoy their company?"

"They are my friends," she replied.

"I'd hate to see your enemies," said Raven.

"Too bad," she said. "We're going to pass by or through almost all of them."

"What the hell is a lovely girl like you doing with so many enemies?" asked Raven.

"In addition to offending the Wicked Witch of the Southeast?" she said with a bitter smile.

"Don't forget the Wicked Witch of the North Northwest," said Einstein.

"Or the Malign Witch of the West," added Al.

"That's *it*!" cried an unseen voice. "Find and defenestrate the Malign Witch of the West and your requests shall be granted!"

"Is that you, Wiz?" asked Einstein.

"You know anyone else who can contact you as a disembodied voice?" demanded the voice.

What the hell is this about, Rofocale? thought Raven.

I am not without my enemies, Eddie. That should be apparent to you by now. And one of them has placed the essence of the Malign Witch of the West into Murgatroid, my nurse. You've got to eliminate her before she eliminates me.

Then why not just ask me, instead of proposing it to these misfits?

Because you're going to need all the help you can get.

Even from them?

Especially from them, answered Rofocale.

You're the boss, thought Raven with a shrug.

You'd do well to remember that, Eddie.

Raven sensed that the connection was broken, and realized that all of his companions—well, all except Shep—were staring at him.

"Are you all right?" asked Einstein.

"Yeah, I'm fine," said Raven.

"You seemed to go into a kind of trance there for a minute."

"I'll do it from time to time," answered Raven, assuming that Rofocale would be contacting him again. "Pay no attention to it."

"He's just getting his thoughts all in a row," said Al. "You'll do the same thing someday, if the Wiz ever grants you the ability to have a thought or two."

"He'd damned well better!" said Einstein. "I'm risking my

straw for a reason. And it better be the right kind of mind. You can call me Einstein, and I'll answer to it, but I don't give a damn if E equals MC cubed or however it goes."

"So if you don't want to be another Einstein, what *do* you want?" asked Raven, curious.

"I want the brain of Throckmorton Billingsgate, of course," said the scarecrow.

"Throckmorton who?" asked Raven, frowning.

"You really don't know?" replied Einstein unbelievingly.

"No," said Raven. "Who was he?"

"The greatest handicapper in the history of hippo racing," answered Einstein.

"They have a lot of hippo racing in Oz, do they?" asked Raven.

"Not for the past thirty years," said Numa.

"But when it comes back, I have to be ready!" exclaimed Einstein.

"Well, if he can give you Billingsgate's brain *and* bring back hippo racing, he really is one hell of a wizard," replied Raven. He turned to Al. "How about you? What does a near-invulnerable robot want, besides something to fend off the rust?"

"I want to be governed by the Three Laws of Robotics," answered Al.

Raven frowned. "Aren't you?"

"No such luck," replied Al. "Last time I looked they were up to thirty-seven laws. Just keeping them all straight in my head takes up two-thirds of my waking hours."

"Waking hours?" repeated Raven. "Do robots sleep?"

"Damned if I know," answered Al. "So far all my hours have been waking."

Raven turned to Numa. "At least I can guess what your request is."

"You can?" said Numa.

"Sure," said Raven. "You want him to outlaw instant replay."

Numa nodded his shaggy head. "Got it in one."

"And you, Lisa?" asked Raven.

"Ilsa," she corrected him.

"Sorry. And you, Ilsa?"

"I told you before," she replied. "I want to go elsewhere."

"There are a lot of elsewheres on the map," noted Raven.

"When I get to the one I want, I'll know it," she said wistfully. "I feel like I've already been there in another life."

"There, there," said Numa, retracting his claws and patting her gently on the shoulder. "The Wiz'll get you there—wherever *there* is."

"You look a lot like her," said Einstein to Raven. "Except for the face, and the stubble, and the figure, and the gender, and—"

"Get to the point," said Raven.

"Perhaps you and she came from the same place."

"Don't be silly," said Al. "He's short, she's not. He's ugly, she's not. His voice is deep, hers isn't. He's flat-chested, she's—"

"We get the point," said Einstein. "But still, he looks a lot more like her than he looks like us."

"Let me assuage your doubts," said Raven. "Ilsa and I are both humans—or at least, we were, and if the Wiz is any good at his craft we will be again." He got to his feet. "Okay, rest period's over. Let's get moving."

The others got to their feet.

"About how far are we from the Sapphire City?" asked Raven.

"I don't know," said Numa. "None of us has ever been there."

"But we know it's at the end of the brick road," added Al.

"Could be a thousand miles," said Einstein. "Maybe we'd better rest a little longer."

"Could be a thousand miles," agreed Raven. "Maybe we'd better take fewer rests and walk faster."

Einstein glared at Raven sullenly. "I don't think I like you very much."

"I'm shattered," said Raven. "Now let's pick up the pace."

"I *knew* there was a reason I distrusted humans!" muttered Einstein. "Present *and* former."

They walked in silence, which Raven found himself appreciating more and more, for the next fifteen minutes, then stopped as the brick road reached the top of a ridge.

"What's down there?" asked Raven, pointing to a rather shabby fortress deep in a valley.

"You of all people ought to know," said Al.

"Just answer the question."

"It's a Munchkin fortress, of course," said Al. "And you being a Munchkin, whether temporarily or permanently, the job of enlisting them in our cause clearly falls to you. Well, you and Ilsa."

Raven considered it for a moment, then nodded his head. "What the hell," he said. "It can't hurt to ask."

"You don't feel pain, I take it?" said Numa.

"Spare me your wit," said Raven. "I'll do the talking, but we're *all* going down there."

"I'll face anyone but a cornerback or a safety," said Numa. "Count me in."

"I'll go too," said Al. "What's a few more dents to a negatronic robot who feels no pain?"

"I'll keep the home fires burning," added Einstein.

"You're a scarecrow," said Raven. "One spark and you'll go up in flames."

"Then I'll get ready to keep the home fires burning."

"That's mighty brave of you," said Raven.

"Brave?" repeated Einstein nervously.

"Staying up here all alone and unprotected," answered Raven.

"Alone?" said Einstein. "Who said anything about alone?"

"Everyone else is coming with me."

"Surely not Ilsa!" said Einstein.

"I can't protect her if she's stuck up here with nothing but a scarecrow," said Raven.

"But if she's up here, you won't *have* to protect her!" said Einstein desperately.

"Who knows what the hell might come wandering down the brick road?" said Raven.

"But . . . but she'll have Shep to protect her!"

"Shep probably weighs four pounds after overeating," said Raven. "How big was that tyrannosaur?"

Einstein turned to Lisa. "Ilsa, are you really going down there with these suicidal fools?"

"I'm on my way to see the Wiz," she replied, and then pointed down the road to the fortress. "He lies in *that* direction."

"Oh, well, it gets windy atop hills," said Einstein. "I wouldn't want to catch a chill. I guess I'll go with you." He paused as he realized they were all staring at him. "Well?" he demanded. "What are we waiting for?"

Raven turned and began walking toward the fortress as the rest of the little party fell into step behind him.

11

"Who goes there?" demanded a voice from atop the castle.

"*I* go here," said Raven irritably as he stood outside a barred gate. "It's been a long, unpleasant day. Now let me in."

"Who are you?"

"My name's Eddie Raven. I'm a Munchkin. That ought to be enough for you."

"But you are not traveling with Munchkins," said the voice.

"Not much gets by your eagle eye, does it?" said Raven.

"We're his manservants," said Numa. "Well, his Munchservants, anyway."

"All right," said the voice. "Advance and be recognized."

"We can't advance until you open the gate," said Raven.

"Oh," said the voice. Then, "Yeah." Then a sigh. And finally, "When you're right, you're right."

And with that, the gate slowly opened and Raven's party found itself surrounded by a dozen spear-carrying Munchkins.

"What is your purpose here?" demanded the one who seemed to be the leader.

"We're on our way the see the Wiz," replied Raven.

"The Wiz?" repeated the Munchkin, amid awestruck gasps.

"That way lies danger!" He frowned. "Or does it lie *that* way?" Finally he shrugged. "Either way, you're heading for a lot of trouble. You will have to pass terrible things and face unimaginable dangers."

"Good!" said Einstein.

"Good?" repeated the shocked spokesman.

"If I can't imagine them, I won't be afraid to pass by them," answered the scarecrow.

"I like the way you think, straw man," said another Munchkin. "Of course you won't survive your first day's march from here to the Sapphire City, but you'll die bravely, or at least mildly unafraid."

"How about inviting us in?" said Raven. "We could use some dinner, and a place to spend the night."

The leader turned and stared at Lisa for a long moment.

"Don't even think of it," said Numa. "That dog's a killer."

The leader jumped back, then turned to Raven. "All right," he said. "You will be our guests for the night. But the dog stays on a leash."

Lisa nodded her head. "Come on, Fang," she said. "No Munchkin meat tonight."

The Chihuahua walked up to her and sat down, leaning against her left ankle.

"Fang," repeated Raven with a smile. "I like it."

"Might as well use it," said Lisa. "He hasn't answered to Shep yet."

They walked into the castle, which was decorated with the heads of various animals and a few men as well.

"Our treasure," said the leader, nodding toward the trophies. "All got in glorious battle."

"Well," said another Munchkin, "actually, they were got in the aftermath of glorious battle."

"Some of which we didn't even participate in," said a third.

"How far are we from the Sapphire City?" asked Raven.

"Two, three, four days," said the leader with a shrug. "It all depends on earthquakes, landslides, typhoons . . ."

"Don't forget termites," said another. He turned to Raven. "A lot of the bridges are wood."

"Okay, I get the picture," replied Raven. "It probably wouldn't hurt to have a guide or two. Anyone here care to volunteer for the job?"

"What does it pay?" asked yet another Munchkin.

"Enormous emotional satisfaction," said Raven. He pulled his wallet out of his pocket and peeked into it. "And three dollars."

"I'm in!" cried three Munchkins at once.

"Me too!" yelled four more.

"I'm the leader," said the leader. "You can't leave me out."

When they were finally quiet again, Raven looked around the room, counting. "Twenty-three," he said. "Okay, you're all hired, and I'll leave it to you to figure out how to split three dollars twenty-three ways."

"That's easy enough," said the leader. "I'll take the three dollars, and my noble warriors will take the accrued glory of helping a Munchkin and five freaks of Nature reach the Sapphire City."

From the reactions, Raven thought he was going to witness the making of a new leader right then and there, but after a few minutes of howling in rage they fell silent again.

"Do we at least get to kill the baron?" asked one at last.

"The baron?" asked Raven.

"Baron Munchausen," was the answer.

"The *real* Baron Munchausen?" asked Raven.

"Of course."

"What's *he* got to do with anything?"

"He's suing us for perverting his name," answered the Munchkin. "We used to be the Little People, but then the leprechauns got mad at us, so we became the Munchkins. The case has been in court for a few decades now."

"But if you killed him, that might make up for paying us only three dollars," said another.

"We'll discuss it *after* we've seen the Wiz," said Raven. Then: "In fact, why don't you have the Wiz get the case thrown out of court?"

"Actually t-t-talk to the Wiz?" stuttered the leader, starting to shake. "Actually ask him for a favor?"

"Why not?" said Raven.

The leader probably had a valid answer, but he had already fainted dead away and was unable to offer it.

"Forget I mentioned it," said Raven. "By the way, just make sure the judge knows that on Earth half a billion kids know and love the Munchkins, and seven children, or maybe eight, tops, have heard of Baron Munchausen."

The leader opened his eyes, stared at Raven, and closed them again. "You're still here," he muttered.

"We're too weak to leave without a good meal and eight hours' sleep," said Einstein.

"For all of you?" asked the leader, reluctantly opening his eyes again and sitting up. "Or for each?"

"Each," said Einstein.

"Three days ago a dragon attacked the fortress," muttered the leader. "Yesterday the love of my life ran off with a traveling piccolo player. And now this." He sighed and shook his head sadly. "I'll say this for my luck: It's consistent."

"So what's for dinner?" asked Numa.

The leader turned to a Munchkin standing next to him. "What do you think?" he asked.

"Meat for the lion, oil for the robot, unicorn parmesan for the woman and the Munchkin, maybe a dead brontosaur for the thing she calls Fang." He scratched his head. "I don't know what scarecrows eat."

"Come to think of it," said Einstein, "neither do I."

"Surely you've eaten before," said the Munchkin. "Just tell us what it was."

"I can't remember on the spur of the moment," answered Einstein. "Nothing flaming, that much I know."

"Mock turtle soup, perhaps?"

Einstein shrugged. "Might as well give it a shot."

"Okay, follow me to the dining hall," said the leader, getting to his feet and walking into the interior of the fortress while Raven and his party fell into step behind him.

"Lot of skulls decorating the walls," remarked Al.

"Impressive, aren't they?" said the leader.

"You must be mighty warriors," said Al.

"Uh . . . those are Munchkin skulls," replied the leader.

"You honor your dead who fell in battle," said Numa. "Nothing wrong with that, except perhaps for its bizarre tastelessness."

"They didn't exactly fall in battle," said the leader. "They fell running *from* battle."

"But they weren't fast enough," added one of his advisors.

"And here we are," said the leader as they reached a large, round, stone chamber with a long wood table and a dozen chairs right in the middle of it.

A Munchkin came in from what appeared to be the kitchen and whispered something to the leader, who turned to Raven and Lisa. "No problem with the unicorn, but we don't seem to have anyone willing to get you the parmesan cheese for it."

"What's so difficult about that?" asked Lisa.

"You ever try to milk one of those parmesans?" demanded the kitchen Munchkin. "I don't mind slaughtering them, but a Munchkin could get killed trying to milk 'em."

"They don't want milk, they want cheese," said the leader.

The kitchen Munchkin frowned. "Cheesing 'em is even harder than milking 'em."

The leader turned to Raven and Lisa. "I'm afraid you'll have to have your unicorn plain." He paused, then looked up hopefully. "Of course, we *could* cover the damned thing with pterodactyl gizzards."

"Plain will be fine," said Lisa.

"Okay, give it five minutes, pay no attention to the screams, and we'll be ready to eat."

"The screams?" said Lisa. "They're not slaughtering our dinner right in the kitchen, are they?"

The leader chuckled. "No, of course not."

"Then why—?"

"That's because of Harry the Blade."

"Harry the Blade?" repeated Raven.

"Our chef," explained the leader. "He's half blind. I don't think anyone can remember a meal when he didn't accidentally slice a chunk out of his hand or arm."

"Not just his hand," offered another Munchkin. "There was that one time he put his knee on a piece of dragon that was still twitching long after it was dead," offered another Munchkin.

"Right," said the leader with a nostalgic smile. "Poor Harry! He was limping for a month."

"Okay," said Raven, "we'll do our best to ignore Harry."

"So what are you two doing in the company of four . . . four whatever they are?"

"I told you, we're off to see the Wiz."

"I was hoping you'd come to your senses."

"It's only been five minutes since I first told you," said Raven.

"Well, you know how it is with foolhardy self-destructive madness," said the leader with a shrug. "It comes, it goes."

"I'll keep that in mind during my few sane periods," said Raven sardonically.

"I suppose I should ask what you want from him?" continued the leader. "Maybe it's something we have right here." His assistant nudged him. "Of course, if we do, we'd have to charge you for it."

"The lady and I want to get back to midtown Manhattan," replied Raven.

The leader frowned. "Never heard of it. Do they have a lot of ogres there?"

"Not if you keep out of the bars," said Raven.

"Monsters? Cannibals? Creatures from the Underworld?"

Raven considered it for a moment, then shook his head. "No, they're mostly on Wall Street."

"And you are returning the lovely lady to her castle?"

"So to speak."

"Well, your story moves me, Eddie Raven," said the leader. "It moves me deeply. In fact, my army and I are coming along with you or my name is not Adlebert the Fourth."

His assistant leaned over and whispered hoarsely enough for Raven's party to hear: "It *isn't* Adlebert the Fourth."

The leader frowned. "Sixth? Seventh?"

The assistant shook his head.

The leader turned to Raven. "Evidently I have urgent business right here. I wish you every success, Eddie Sparrow."

"Raven," said Raven.

The leader shrugged. "Whatever."

Half a dozen waiters, each looking sillier than the last as they carried food, drink, and their oversize weapons with equal lack of dexterity, approached the table and began laying out the food.

"Well," said the leader, "what do you think?"

Numa took a bite and wrinkled his nose. "I think he should have cooked it."

"Hey, he sliced it," said the leader. "You can't have everything."

Raven found some fresh fruit buried beneath the still-twitching flank of whatever animal it had been, and placed it on Lisa's plate.

"You don't like fruit?" asked the leader, frowning.

"You don't see much chivalry around here, do you?" said Einstein.

"We ride horses," said the leader. "Or goats. Why would we drive chivalries?"

"And they're all still alive," muttered Al in amazement. "I guess the Wiz has never had a spare afternoon. That's all it'd take."

"Everyone's assuming the Wiz is our enemy," said Lisa. "That's wrong. We're going there as supplicants. Let's hope he has a good heart."

"And that he hasn't eaten it for lunch," added Numa.

"How many days did you say we were from the Sapphire City?" asked Raven.

"Two or three days, assuming," answered the leader.

"Assuming *what*?"

"Assuming nothing attacks or tries to hinder you," said the leader. "I put that at, oh, five hundred to one against."

"What in particular is likely to try to stop us?" continued Raven.

"Oh, it varies," answered the leader. "Legions of the undead, horse-size army ants, the Wicked Witch of the East, the Dirty Dozen . . ." He paused as one of his lieutenants nudged him.

"They're the Dirty Fifteen now," said the lieutenant.

"And then there's the usual," continued the leader. "Tyrannosaurs, stegosaurs, cankersaurs . . ." His assistant nudged him again. "Sorry," he said. "Those canker sores are so annoying I get them confused with all the four-legged saurs." He took a sip of his drink. "Then there's behemoths, gryphons, the occasional deranged minotaur." He paused. "Oh . . . and Betty Bedonia."

"Betty Bedonia?" repeated Raven, frowning.

"My ex-wife," explained the leader. "Most vicious creature walking the land. Of course, so far she's never attacked anyone but me, but still . . ."

"Okay, we'll keep her in mind." Raven looked around the table at his little team. "Are we all through eating?"

"God, yes!" bellowed Numa.

"Yes, please!" said Einstein with an emphasis on the "please."

"They even make oil taste like stale fish," added Al.

Fang merely growled.

"Thank our hosts, Eddie," said Lisa, "and let's get some sleep before we head off to the Sapphire City."

"I assume you have some empty beds somewhere in this fortress," said Raven, turning back to the leader.

"She can sleep in *my* bed!" cried one of the Munchkin warriors.

"No—mine!" hollered another.

"A private room for the lady and her guard dog," said Raven, "and another room for the other four of us."

"Yeah, we can arrange that," said the leader. He turned to Lisa. "Are you sure you wouldn't rather share *my* bed, Toots? It's got the softest mattress on the planet."

"No," said Raven. "She hates damp beds."

"It's not damp," said the leader, frowning.

"It will be after we slit your throat," said Raven.

The leader turned to Lisa. "On second thought, I've got just the room for you—and one next door to it for your ill-mannered friends."

"Don't kill him, Fang," said Raven. "He didn't mean to insult the rest of us. Probably."

"Absolutely not!" cried the leader, backing away from the table. "My flunkies . . . ah, my *fearless warriors* . . . will show you to your quarters. I'd do it myself, fearless host that I am, but I just remembered that I'm allergic to Munchkin-eating dogs."

"Really?" asked Einstein, arching an eyebrow.

The leader nodded. "I break out in hives, and frankly, we have more than enough bees around here already without giving them a new place to stay."

And with that he raced out of the dining hall, giving Fang an incredibly wide berth.

"Okay," said Raven, getting to his feet and gesturing for the rest of his crew to do the same. "Let's grab thirty or forty winks, and tomorrow we're off to see the Wiz."

12

They were up at sunrise, partially because the sun was shining into their eyes through the barred window, partially because they each had to make a run for the bathroom because of the previous evening's meal. Only Fang seemed hale and hearty, but only Fang had dined on a small horned chimera he'd killed upon entering its room with Lisa.

They were pretty much recovered, with all, including Lisa, vowing never again to eat at any palace, fortress, or roadside stand run by Munchkins, and then they set out on the brick road, which was a dirt-covered mauve for the first half mile, but turned red-brick-colored once they entered a forbidding forest.

"Beware!" screamed a banshee sitting atop a tall tree as they walked beneath it.

"*You* be a ware!" yelled Al. "I'd rather be a robot!"

"Death awaits you!" cried the banshee.

"I wonder . . ." mused Einstein.

"About what?" asked Raven.

"Does it mean that death awaits us at the end of a long and fruitful life, or that it's just beyond that next tree?"

"Or perhaps it's the name of a guide who can take us to Sapphire City," added Numa.

"It's not worth worrying about," said Raven.

"It isn't?" asked Numa.

"We'll find out soon enough," answered Raven. He suddenly came to a stop and frowned.

"What is it?" asked Lisa.

"I'm trying to remember the movie," he answered. "I don't recall what comes next."

"What's a movie?" asked Einstein.

Which is when he remembered that he wasn't in L. Frank Baum's Oz any more than he'd been in Humphrey Bogart's Casablanca.

"Forget it," muttered Raven, starting to walk again, and the rest of his party fell into step.

They came upon a quartet of very tall, very broad trees that were busy singing as a barbershop quartet, ignored the howls of outrage when Fang lifted his leg on one of them, and soon stumbled into a grass-covered clearing.

"It's very pretty," remarked Lisa.

"Nice rolling hills up ahead," added Einstein.

"And lovely flowers, always assuming they aren't poisonous," said Al.

"What do you care?" asked Numa. "Robots don't eat flowers. They don't even sniff them."

"How do you know what we sniff?" Al shot back. "Though I admit that there's never been a flower that smelled as good as motor oil."

"Uh, fellas . . ." said Numa.

"Don't interrupt," said Al. "You know zip about oil."

"No," admitted Numa. "But I know when we're in trouble."

"Is this an academic argument?" asked Einstein. "Or *are* we in trouble?"

"Unless one of you is on good terms with the Wicked Witch of the Southeast, I'd say we're in trouble," answered Numa. He turned to Raven. "Unless you summoned her here?"

"Never saw her before in my life," said Raven, peering into the sky, as a black-clad woman with a pointed hat circled lazily above them.

"Maybe she's just watching us, or reporting back like a traffic cop," suggested Al hopefully.

"I don't think so," said Raven. "After all, if you've identified her correctly, she's the Wicked Witch of the Southeast, not the High-Flying Traffic Observer of the Southeast."

"Well, when she lands, send her away!" said Einstein. "We're heading due east, so she has no reason to be here."

Raven simply stared at the scarecrow for a few seconds but made no reply.

"Should we move to cover, Eddie?" asked Lisa.

"She can reach us before we get to the trees," answered Raven. "Might as well just keep walking and hope she's looking for someone else." He turned and faced Einstein, Al, and Numa. "Have any of you guys done anything, now or in the past, to bring you to her attention?"

"Not me," said Al. "I mean, we didn't use any screws from her broom to fix my arthritis."

"Me either," said Numa. "Unless she was betting on the Lions the day I . . . well . . . you know."

"Nor me," said Einstein. "I mean, she's the Wicked Witch of the Southeast. She couldn't know about that sexy scarecrow's sister up north."

Yeah, thought Raven. *We're definitely not in Frank Baum's Oz.* He glanced at Lisa, who seemed more beautiful than ever. *Or Judy Garland's, either.*

"She's coming down," announced Lisa.

"Figures," muttered Raven. "I'll say this about our luck: It's consistent." He turned to Numa. "Be ready to growl hideously. It might convince her to go elsewhere."

"Growl?" whimpered Numa. "It's all I can do not to faint dead away."

Raven turned to Einstein and Al, but both were shaking so badly he expected them to collapse just about the time the witch touched down.

"You know anything about her?" he asked Lisa. "Or about witches at all?"

"Just that they're not very nice women," she answered.

Neither was my third-grade teacher back in grammar school, thought Raven, *but she didn't fly on a broomstick and threaten people. Exactly.*

"Okay," Raven told his companions, "she's circling around preparing to land, so be ready."

"For what?" asked Numa in a very unsteady voice.

"Whatever witches do," said Raven. "I'm a newcomer here myself. For all I know she's selling tickets to the witches' ball."

"You think so?" asked Al hopefully.

"You never know," replied Raven. *But I'd give five hundred-to-one against it.*

They looked up and watched as the witch continued her

descent. Lower and lower she circled, and they could hear her cackling as she approached them. Finally she touched down, held her broom in one hand, and approached them.

You're not half as ugly as I expected, thought Raven. *In fact, you remind me of someone, though I'll be damned if I know who.*

"So you picked up some defenders, did you?" growled the witch.

"Are you talking to me?" said Raven.

"You?" repeated the witch. "Who in blazes are you?"

"Just a traveler you don't want to mess with," replied Raven.

"So you have four of them," snapped the witch. "And you think they can help you?"

"If I need them," said Lisa, staring at the witch without showing any sign of fear. "And I probably won't."

"Let me handle this," said Raven, stepping ahead of her.

"He doesn't know, does he?" said the witch with a cackle.

"No, he doesn't," answered Lisa.

"Know *what*?" demanded Raven.

"Will you tell him, or shall I?" said the witch.

Lisa laid a restraining hand on Raven's shoulder. "Eddie, my name isn't Lisa or Ilsa or Dorothy—not since I graduated Sorcery School." She paused for just a few seconds. "It's Glinda."

"Oh my God!" exclaimed Numa. "What fools we were, protecting the Good Witch of the South—as if she *needed* our protection!"

Raven stared at her curiously. "You're a witch?"

She nodded. "I didn't mean to deceive you."

"I find this whole world more than a little bit deceptive," said Raven.

"You're not mad at me?"

"For being a symbol of good?" he said. "Of course not. Now, as long as you're a witch, vanish this wrinkled old crone—"

"I resent that!" said the Wicked Witch.

"—and let's be on our way," concluded Raven.

"It's not that easy," cackled the Wicked Witch.

"Why the hell not?" demanded Raven.

"You've been infiltrated!"

Raven looked at the scarecrow, the robot, and Numa. "Which one?" he asked.

Another cackle. "Look elsewhere!"

"Elsewhere?" asked Raven, frowning.

And as he was standing there, trying to interpret what she was saying, Fang walked over and bit him on the toe.

"Damn, that smarts!" he yelled.

Fang opened his tiny mouth to bite Raven again, but Raven was quicker, landing a mighty kick that should have sent the little Chihuahua flying fifty feet through the air.

"Goddammit!" bellowed Raven, dropping to one knee. "I think I broke my foot!"

"Here, Sweetie Pie," said the witch, and Fang bit his leash in half and walked over to her, where she picked him up and kissed him on his tiny nose.

"May I?" asked Glinda, pointing to Raven's foot.

"This one time," said the witch.

Glinda bent over, laid a hand on his foot, and chanted a brief little spell—and suddenly the pain was gone.

"You knew about the dog?" he asked, straightening up.

"Of course I did. Fang and I have been trying to convert each other ever since this pilgrimage began," answered Glinda.

"He's little, but he's the brains of the operation," said the witch. "Now, am I going to get some obedience, or am I going to start throwing some serious curses around?"

"Glinda will stop you!" said Einstein.

The witch emitted an evil chuckle. "She's my kid sister. I've had her number since she was five years old."

Raven turned questioningly to Glinda, who nodded her head sadly.

"Okay, you're here," he said to the witch, "you've got your little dog back, you've exposed your sister. What comes next?"

"I haven't thought that far ahead," admitted the witch. "My primary task was to find and hinder you, and expose *her*." She held the Chihuahua up to her face. "You're the mastermind. What do I do next?"

The witch and the dog were motionless for a full minute. Then she shrugged and said, "Are you quite sure?" The dog seemed to nod his head, and she put him back down on the ground, shrugged again, and said, "Well, you're the boss."

"And what did the boss say that seems to have distressed you so much?" asked Raven.

"He said we're to proceed unhindered," said Glinda.

Raven looked at the Wicked Witch. "Is that right?"

The witch nodded her head. "Regretfully."

"Then why the hell did you bother us in the first place?" demanded Raven.

"You had our leader," said the witch, indicating Fang. "We needed to get him back, especially if you had the skills to get to the Sapphire City and confront"—a nervous pause—"the Wiz."

Raven turned back Glinda.

"All right," said Raven. "We're still going to the Sapphire City to see the Wiz and find out what he wants to fulfill each of our requests. We're leaving Fang behind. Your sister's not going to bother us anymore. Since she was just here to get the damned dog, I assume no other supernatural blood relatives are going to hinder us from reaching the city. These three bozos"—he indicated Einstein, Al, and Numa—"are exactly what they purport to be, and not witches, wizards, or anything remotely similar in disguise. And you still want to get to the Sapphire City?"

"That's correct," said Glinda.

"Okay," said Raven. "Kick your sister good-bye and let's get across this damned field and back into the protection of the forest."

"I'm not going to kick her," said Glinda.

"But you'd like to, wouldn't you?"

"The last time she tried she was seven years old," said the witch, "and what happened to your foot was as nothing compared to hers. And I didn't lift the spell for a week."

"What can I say?" replied Raven. "You're a real sweetie."

The witch stared at him for a long moment. "I don't like you much, Eddie Raven."

"I see you like me enough to learn my name," he replied. "Nobody here gave it to you."

She gave him her best sneer, and then, with Fang tucked under her arm, she mounted her broom and flew off.

"What now?" asked Numa.

"Now we continue to the Sapphire City," answered Raven. "And stay alert."

"Why?" asked Al. "After all, the Wicked Witch and the

mastermind are both gone. There should be no more inter-ference."

"And what does that imply to you?"

The robot shrugged, which created a noisy clanking. "What *should* it imply?"

"That whatever's in the Sapphire City or on the way there has got even the Wicked Witch and her boss scared." He turned toward the city. "Let's get moving."

13

They entered the next forest, spent most of the day walking through it, annoyed but unimpeded by banshees flying overhead and occasionally swooping down toward them, and came to a large clearing just before sunset.

"Okay, we'll spend the night here," said Raven, sitting down with a tree trunk propping up his back.

"How do we want to divide guard duty?" asked Al.

"It all depends," said Raven.

"On what?" asked Einstein.

"On what kind of defenses a Good Witch can bring to bear." He turned to Glinda. "Any suggestions?"

She shook her head. "I'm a Good Witch. I can create lovely background music and transmute dry dead leaves into Macaroni Surprise, I can help heal wounds . . ."

"Heal wounds?" said Raven. "That's a start."

She shook her head sadly. "But I can't prevent them."

"Can you protect us from whatever the Wiz sends out?" asked Raven. "Always assuming he doesn't want us to get to the city."

"I don't know, Eddie," she said. "It depends what he sends against us. I can charm some of them, and logic some of them, but I can't physically defeat any of them." She uttered a most un-Good-Witch-like curse. "I wish I still had Fang. *He* could have protected us."

"He could also have killed us without drawing a deep breath," said Raven. He looked around his little group. "Okay, Al, you take the first watch."

"Why me?" asked the robot.

"Moonlight won't shine off your body a tenth as much as the morning sun. No sense advertising that we're here." He turned to Numa. "We'll do two-hour shifts. You're next."

"But I'm afraid of the dark."

"I thought you were just afraid of dropped balls and angry fans."

"Well, them too," admitted Numa.

"You're a lion, or so close to one as makes no difference. Use your nose. If you smell anyone coming toward us, let us know. Einstein, you're the third shift, and I'll do the last."

"But *I* should do the sunrise shift," complained the scarecrow. "Unlike Numa, I can't smell when anyone's approaching us. It makes more sense for me to stand guard when I can see the enemy."

"Problem is, they can see you too," said Raven.

"So what?"

"You *are* a scarecrow."

"Damn!" muttered Einstein. "I keep forgetting."

"Just keep alert on the morning shift, and maybe we can get the Wiz to add fifteen or twenty points to your IQ," said Raven.

"What about me?" asked the Good Witch, who Raven now had no trouble thinking of as Glinda rather than Lisa.

"You heal us if the Wiz or his hit squads beat the crap out of us."

"And give us some nice background music to sleep to," added Numa.

"And magic us up some porridge for breakfast," said Al.

"You've a puzzled expression on your face, Einstein," noted Raven.

"I'm just wondering . . ." said the scarecrow.

"About what?"

"You'll get mad," said Einstein.

"Try me," answered Raven.

"If she's a Good Witch, and she can cook breakfast out of twigs and dead leaves, and create beautiful music when we want to rest or sleep, and do other good witchly things, why are we risking our lives helping her get to the Wiz? You heard her: She wants to go to some huge alien city that's filled with traffic and people and strange noises. We want her *here*!"

"We want her to be happy," answered Raven, "and if that's what will make her happy, then that's what we want for her."

"But what about us?" persisted Einstein.

"If we actually get where we're going, there's every likelihood that you'll get a little brighter, Numa will get a little braver, and Al will have a few dozen fewer laws governing his behavior."

"And you," said Einstein. "What about you?"

"I've got to play it by ear," said Raven. "I don't know how I got here, and I don't know how to get back."

"I hate conversations like this," said Numa. "It keeps reminding me that this is a very strange world."

"No stranger than some others," said Raven, remembering his recent outing in Casablanca.

"I personally find that a terrifying thought," said Einstein.

"Really?" said Glinda. She stared off into the distance. "I find it a comforting one."

14

"Hey, you!" said the sharp voice. "Wake up."

The sharp voice was accompanied by a sharp point, which was the end of a spear and was jabbing Raven's shoulder.

Raven sat up and found that his little party was surrounded by an armored squad of spear-carrying Munchkins. He glared at Einstein, who was rubbing his eyes and yawning, then shrugged. After all, even if the scarecrow hadn't fallen asleep during his watch, what could the five of them do against some twenty armed warriors?

"What do you want?" Raven muttered, twisting his torso to avoid the continual prodding of the spear.

"Why have you invaded our territory?" demanded the Munchkin who had been jabbing him.

Interesting, thought Raven. *Now that I'm a Munchkin too, you guys don't look fat and harmless the way you did in the movie, or the illos from the book.*

"We're not invading it," said Raven. "We're passing through it on our way to the Sapphire City."

"You're sure?" said the Munchkin, arching a shaggy eyebrow.

"Yeah, I'm sure," said Raven, pushing the point of the spear aside again and getting to his feet.

"You're not a member of the guild?" persisted the Munchkin.

"What guild?"

"The Lollipop Guild, of course."

"No," said Raven. "We're just passing through."

A couple of armed Munchkins were staring at Glinda. "*She* could be a member," said one enthusiastically.

"Of the Lollipop Guild?" asked Raven.

"Of the Lollapalooza Guild," answered the Munchkin.

"They may all look like her," said another, "but they're the toughest fighters on the planet."

"Then perhaps they'd like to lend us their services," said Glinda.

"It all depends who you're at war with."

"No one," she answered.

"Then what are you doing here?" said the Munchkin. "Or did we ask that already?"

"We're on our way to see the Wiz," said Glinda.

"Ohmygod ohmygod ohmygod!" cried the Munchkin. "Funny—you don't *look* crazy!"

"So will you, or your Lollapalooza Guild, help us get there?" asked Raven.

"Certainly not!" said the first Munchkin, the one who'd awakened Raven. "We're a one-day march from the Sapphire City. Once there, you walk another hour to reach the Wiz's palace." He frowned, as if doing the mental math. "That means you've got a life expectancy of twenty-five hours and thirty seconds."

Another Munchkin shook his head. "Have you forgotten? He's moved his office to the second floor."

"Ah! Right!" said the first Munchkin. "Make that twenty-five hours and one minute."

"I assume that means none of you or your lady friends are going to accompany or help us?" said Raven.

"You assume none of us is willing to risk instant, painful, hideous death for absolutely no profit or reward whatsoever," said the first Munchkin. "You must have been the brightest one in your class."

"All right," said Raven. "If you're not going to help, at least step aside and let us pass."

"Through our territory?" said the Munchkin. "I hardly think so."

"What'll it take to change your mind?" said Raven.

Suddenly the still morning air was pierced by the loudest, most hideous roar Raven had ever heard, and the ground started shaking as if some huge creature was approaching them, measured step by measured step.

"It's changed!" cried the Munchkin as the others all fled. He handed his spear to Raven. "Here, you're going to need this."

"It sounds a little too large to kill with a spear," said Raven, taking the spear and studying it.

"It's not for him!" cried the Munchkin as he began racing after his companions. "It's to put your friends and yourself out of your misery before Megasaur does it for you!"

"I've never heard of a species called Megasaur," said Raven, frowning.

"It's not a species, it's a name!" yelled the Munchkin just before he was out of earshot. "*His* name!"

Then he was gone, and Raven's little company gathered together, looking nervously at the forest ahead of them.

"Anybody got anything resembling a weapon with him?" asked Raven.

There was no answer.

He turned to Glinda. "You got any spells for keeping Megasaurs at bay?"

"I don't even know what a Megasaur *is*!" she replied.

"Okay," said Raven. "We play it by ear."

And as the words left his mouth, there was a rustling of trees and bushes directly ahead of them and suddenly a metallic gray being stepped forward, a spear in its hand. Its ears were pointed upward, its chin pointed down, its mouth filled with impressive-looking fangs, and a tail ending in a sharp point trailed behind it.

"Could be worse," muttered Raven.

"How?" asked Numa in a tremulous whisper.

"There's only one of him," said Raven. "And he's no more than a foot taller than Shaquille O'Neal." The Megasaur unleased a mighty bellow. "Got gum problems, too."

"I admire your optimism," said Numa.

"Do you just roar and bellow, or do you talk, too?" said Raven, stepping forward.

"I roar, I bellow, I talk—and I kill," said the Megasaur ominously.

"So do we," replied Raven, "except for the roar and bellow part. And there are five of us. So wouldn't you rather talk?"

"But you're five little ones!" said the Megasaur with a growl.

If you know a spell—any *spell*—*that might help us, now would be a good time to use it,* thought Raven.

And it was as if Glinda had read his mind, for suddenly she—or her image—began to grow. Soon it towered some twenty feet above the others. She turned her face toward the Megasaur and scowled.

"Talking's good," said the Megasaur, and the growl was totally gone from its voice. "Nothing like a nice chat."

"Then lower your weapon . . ." began Raven.

"Now!" bellowed Glinda.

"And let's talk."

The Megasaur lowered the point of its spear to the ground, took a quick look at Glinda, and released the other end of it. Al moved over and picked it up.

"Nice day, isn't it?" said the Megasaur.

"Well, it just got a little nicer in the past few seconds," interjected Einstein.

"Think the Assassins will take it all this year?"

"The Assassins?" repeated Numa, frowning.

"Murderball," said the Megasaur.

"I didn't know it was a sport," answered Numa.

"You'll have to forgive me," said the Megasaur. "I like genial conversations, but I'm a little out of practice."

"You can make up for it by telling us why you were threatening us," said Raven.

The creature looked confused. "That's what Megasaurs do," he said at last. "It's our nature."

"You just threaten anything that isn't a Megasaur?"

"As long as it's smaller than us," confirmed the Megasaur.

"For no reason at all?" said Einstein.

The Megasaur shrugged. "What can I say? It's a biological imperative."

Raven stared at it for a long moment.

"You're making me very uneasy," said the Megasaur.

"Sorry," said Raven. "But you've just given me an idea."

"Oh?"

Raven nodded his head. "Yeah. How big is the Wiz?"

"Smaller than you," said the Megasaur. "About the size of a deformed lady Munchkin, but not as pretty."

"Then I think you have an opportunity to behave according to your nature," said Raven. "We're on our way to see the Wiz. Come along and protect us."

"I'm in the *threatening* biz, not the *protecting* biz," said the Megasaur.

"You'll actually pick up a new trade," said Raven.

"I will?"

Raven nodded. "By threatening him, you'll be protecting us."

"Hey, I could charge double for that—if I ever start charging." A morose look crossed his face. "You'd be surprised how few people offer to pay for being threatened."

"So do we have a deal?" asked Raven.

The Megasaur nodded its massive head. "Why not?"

Glinda suddenly appeared as her true size again.

"You know," said Raven, "despite your appearance, you're easier to deal with than Bogarti or Massovitch."

"Who are they?"

"A couple of people I wish you'd met," answered Raven. He looked at his companions. "Are we ready to continue?"

"Welcome to your doom!" cried a hollow unseen voice. "I eagerly await your arrival."

"Who was that?" asked Raven.

Numa and Einstein tried to answer, but were trembling too much.

"I assume it must be the Wiz," said Glinda, frowning.

"Are we sure we want to go through with this?" asked Al, who was shaking so badly and so squeakily that the trembling of his metal body all but drowned out his words.

"You know anyone else who can get us out of this world?" said Raven.

There were no answers.

"Besides, we've got a Megasaur to protect us." He turned to the creature. "I never did catch your name. I'm Eddie, she's Glinda, and they're Einstein, Al, and Numa."

"I'm . . ." The Megasaur paused uncomfortably.

"Surely you have a name," said Al.

"Yes," said the Megasaur. "But all the guys make fun of it."

"We're in no position to make fun of anything," Raven assured it.

"Okay," said the Megasaur reluctantly. "But promise you won't laugh."

"We promise," said Einstein.

"All right," said the Megasaur, summoning up its courage. "It's Daffodil."

"Daffodil?" repeated Numa, fighting back a chuckle.

"My mother thought they were the prettiest flowers in the world, and when the egg hatched, she thought I was the prettiest baby."

"Could be worse," said Einstein. "Could be Petunia."

"You think so?" asked Daffodil hopefully.

"Absolutely," assured the scarecrow.

"Or Marigold," added Al. "You wouldn't have wanted to spend

your childhood—assuming Megasaurs *have* childhoods—being called Mary by all your playmates."

"Answering to Daffy wasn't a lot better," answered the Megasaur as a tear rolled down its cheek.

"We'll call you anything you want," said Raven. "Just come along and protect our little party."

"Anything?"

"That's what I said."

"When I was a kid I used to read pulp magazines, and the toughest dude in any of them was always a guy named Dillinger." It paused, then asked hesitantly, "Could I be Dillinger?"

"Well, it's easier to say than Bonnie and Clyde," replied Raven. "What the hell—Dillinger it is."

"Okay, let's go!" said Dillinger. "And woe betide anyone who stands in our way, including that self-centered little bastard who rules the universe."

"The whole universe?" asked Numa nervously.

"Well, the known parts of it, anyway," said Dillinger.

The Megasaur turned and began walking toward the Sapphire City, and the little group fell into step behind it.

15

They walked for three hours, and then Numa and Einstein demanded a break.

"I thought you were in a hurry," growled Dillinger.

"The Wiz will still be there tomorrow," said Numa. "My feet may not be, unless I can give them a rest."

"Some hunter!" said Dillinger.

"You want a long hunt, get a cheetah," said Numa.

"Or something with bones in its feet," added Einstein.

"Okay," said Dillinger. "Fifteen minutes, no more."

The entire group sat down, and Raven turned to the Megasaur. "Since you've had experience with the Wiz, tell us a little about him." *Like, please, does he look as harmless as Frank Morgan?*

"Well, he's self-centered, and sadistic, and close to being all-powerful, and of course he's got a terrible temper and is capable of awesome feats of magic," answered Dillinger. "But of course you know that."

"People come to him for favors, right?" asked Numa.

"In a manner of speaking," agreed Dillinger.

Numa frowned. "Explain, please."

"Well, the usual favor is 'please stop torturing my husband,' or 'may I have my vision and hearing back if you're through playing with them?'"

"Sounds like they're begging for mercy, not for favors," commented Raven.

"Oh, now and then he gets a request that doesn't involve a cessation of pain," answered Dillinger. "Usually something on the order of fixing it for a three-hundred-to-one shot to win the Sapphire City Derby."

Glinda turned to her original three companions. "Are you sure you want to continue? I *have* to go, but—"

"We're with you to the end!" said Al.

"Probably," confirmed Numa.

"Please tell me his castle's lit by electric bulbs and not torches," said Einstein.

"You three do what you want," said Raven. "The lady and I are going."

"Just what favors are you seeking?" asked Dillinger.

"I don't think it would make much sense to you," said Raven.

"Try me."

Raven shrugged. "Okay. Midtown Manhattan."

"You're absolutely right," answered Dillinger. "It makes no sense at all." It turned to Glinda. "And you?"

"I'm still working on it," she said. "I thought I knew, until yesterday."

"Is it getting darker?" asked Numa, frowning.

"It's only late morning," said Al.

"And there is no rain on the horizon."

Raven looked up. "Those aren't rain clouds."

"What *are* they?" asked Al.

"Spear-carrying flying apes," answered Dillinger. "They're part of the Wiz's private guard."

"Must be twenty, maybe thirty, of them," said Raven, looking up.

"We'll know soon enough," added Einstein. "They're headed directly at us."

"Why?" asked Numa.

"The Wiz likes his privacy," said Dillinger.

"Surely we can *discuss* it!" said Numa desperately.

"I don't think so," said Raven as the apes swooped down toward them. He turned to Glinda. "You got any useful magic up your sleeve?"

She shook her head as she watched the apes approach. "Not for a situation like this. Becoming twenty feet tall just gives them a bigger target."

Raven turned to Dillinger. "Give me your sword."

"But I might need it if I lose my spear."

"They're going to go after the ones with the weapons first," said Raven. "You want to be their only target, be my guest."

"Here, have a sword," said Dillinger, drawing its sword and handing it to Raven.

He took it, walked a few steps to his right until he was standing next to Glinda, and asked softly, "Do you know what he looks like?"

"The Wiz?" she said.

"Yeah."

"No," she answered. "I've never seen him." Suddenly she smiled. "But I know what he sounds like."

"Good!"

"You want me to call them off right now?"

"No, they'll never buy it. But if we survive the first assault, tell them you were just testing us and they should go back to base or wherever the hell they came from."

"All right."

Then they could hear hideous war cries as the apes went into their final dive.

"This is going to be *fun!*" cried Dillinger, holding its spear at the ready.

"I admire your idea of fun," muttered Raven.

The nearest ape headed straight for Dillinger, and was impaled on its spear a second later. They next two attacked Raven, who found that chopping off parts of a charging enemy was minimally less difficult than he had imagined.

Einstein stood where he was, made no attempt to escape, absorbed three spear thrusts, and sent two of the apes plummeting to the ground.

"Idiots!" he chuckled. "You think spears can stop someone with no nervous system and no skeleton?"

Al grabbed an ape's spear, thrust the handle into the ape's belly, waited for the ape to fall to the ground, knelt down beside him, and began choking him. Four more spears were thrust at him. Each bent or broke with a loud clang.

"Fools!" he said. "You fight scarecrows with fire and robots with rust-inducing water!"

Son of a bitch! thought Raven, as he hacked away at two more apes. *We're actually gonna come through this intact!*

But even as he said so, there was a hideous scream off to

his left. He turned to see a large lance protruding from both sides of Numa's torso. Blood spurted up like a fountain, and then the lion lay still except for some spasmodic twitching.

"You have done well, my children!" boomed a voice, and Raven knew it was Glinda following his suggestion. "I could not be more proud of you. But it is time to return to your quarters now."

"Aw, let us stay and kill the others!" complained one of the apes.

"We have lost half your number in this exercise," answered Glinda in the Wiz's voice. "That is enough. Return immediately!"

"You're sure?" said the ape.

"Yes."

"Absolutely sure?" the ape persisted.

"If I have to ask you again, you will not live to see your quarters, or even another minute."

"Let's go, apes!" cried the ape, flapping its wings. "Last one back is a monkey's uncle!"

In seconds they were gone, and Raven and the others went over to examine Numa.

"Is he really dead?" asked Einstein.

"No pulse, no breathing, no nothing," said Al, a tear running down his cheek. He wiped it away. "Damn! If I cry, I'm gonna rust."

"Dead as a doornail," said Dillinger. "Always assuming doornails were alive once. Well, let's be going."

"No," said Glinda. "We have to bury him first."

"He'll never know the difference," said Dillinger.

"Perhaps not," she replied. "But we will."

Dillinger looked at Raven. "You seem to be the leader. What do you say?"

"We'll bury him."

"Anyone got a shovel?" asked Dillinger.

Raven looked around at the dead apes. "We'll use their spears," he said, and a moment later he, Al, and Einstein were digging a shallow grave.

He's really dead, thought Raven. *We're definitely not in Frank Baum's Oz—not the book, not the movie, not anything where happily-ever-after is automatic.*

16

They walked for a few more hours, put together a dinner of fruits and berries they gathered from their surroundings, and were prepared to take turns sleeping and standing guard when Dillinger announced that Megasaurs didn't sleep—at least, it was pretty sure they didn't—and it would stand guard all night.

Raven opened his eyes at dawn, and was about to say something when Glinda, who'd been sleeping next to him, prodded him gently on the shoulder, held her finger to her lips for a moment, and then pointed to Dillinger, who was standing with its back propped against a tree, spear in hand, snoring peacefully.

"I guess they *do* sleep," whispered Raven.

"At least for an hour or two," she agreed.

Einstein and Al were both up within another half hour, and finally Dillinger started growling and twitching, finally yelled "Take that!" and stabbed the air with its spear, then stood there blinking its eyes furiously.

"Are you okay?" asked Einstein.

Dillinger frowned. "Except for the humiliation."

"What's a little humiliation among friends?" said Al.

"*Are* we friends?" asked Dillinger.

"Of course," said Einstein.

The Megasaur smiled. "Really? I've never had a friend before."

"We should always be open to new experiences," said Raven. "And speaking of new experiences, let's get on with our quest for the Sapphire City."

"We'll get there by lunchtime," said Dillinger, "depending of course on how late or early we get hungry."

"Maybe we should have breakfast first," suggested Al.

"Carry what's left of dinner and eat it as we walk," said Raven.

"Right," said Dillinger. "Do what my pal says."

A minute later they were proceeding along the trail through the trees. About an hour later they could see the Sapphire City shining atop a hill perhaps a mile ahead of them.

"It's beautiful!" enthused Glinda.

"Look at those buildings!" said Raven. "It's like someone took the most impressive and exotic buildings from Earth, covered them with sapphires, and arranged them all into this city."

"We could pretend to be tourists and examine it for a couple of days before making our nonnegotiable demands on the Wiz," suggested Einstein.

"You do what you want," said Glinda. "I'm here on business."

"We all are," agreed Raven.

"Not all of us," Dillinger corrected him. "I'm here for my friends."

"Okay, friend," said Raven. "Can we see the Wiz's palace from here?"

"See the tall building with the truly impressive dome, surrounded by the four turrets?" asked Dillinger.

"That's his palace?"

"Right."

"Okay, let's go there," said Raven.

Dillinger laid a huge hand gently on Raven's shoulder. "You don't want to, good buddy."

"Oh?"

"He doesn't live in his palace," explained Dillinger. "That's just to attract and divert the enemy."

"Where *does* he live?" asked Raven.

"See that ugly little split-level about half a mile to the left of the palace?"

"The thing with the rough walls?"

"Greenstone," said Glinda. "Like brownstone, only uglier."

"And he lives there?" asked Raven.

"Lives there, works there, sleeps there," answered Dillinger.

"Then that's where we're going," said Raven. He paused for a moment. "How well guarded is it?"

"Hardly at all."

Raven frowned. "Are you sure?"

"Guards would just attract the enemy. That's why they're all at his palace, though of course he can summon them whenever he wants."

"Seems impractical as all hell," said Raven.

"He *is* the Wiz," replied Dillinger. "He's more powerful than the whole damned army put together."

Raven sighed deeply. "Yeah, I suppose he is."

"I wonder he if knows we're here?" said Glinda.

"Of course I know!" cried a voice inside their heads. "I'm the Wiz!"

Raven and Dillinger held their weapons at the ready, looking around them, but there was no one to be seen.

Rofocale, thought Raven, *are* you *the Wiz?*

There was no response.

"All right," said Raven. "Let's go through that one forested patch and we're there."

They walked down a long grassy slope for perhaps a quarter of a mile, then followed the brick road as it led them through what had seemed like a few thousand trees.

"Uh . . . Raven," said Einstein after a moment.

"What?"

"These tree trunks . . ."

"Thick, aren't they?" interjected Al.

"I just leaned against one for a minute," continued Einstein nervously.

"And?" said Raven.

"The damned thing's alive!"

"You never saw live trees before?" said Raven.

"Damn it, Eddie—this one *moved,* and then it *purred*!"

Frowning, Raven studied the tree closest to him.

"Son of a bitch!" he muttered.

"What is it, Eddie?" asked Glinda.

"He's right. The damned thing's *breathing*!" He turned to Dillinger. "What do you know about this?"

"They won't bother us," said Dillinger. "If the Wiz didn't want us to make it to the city, they'd have swallowed us already."

Raven stared long and hard at the nearest "tree," trying to spot its mouth. "Damned good camouflage," he said after a minute.

"Did anyone save anything from breakfast?" asked Raven.

"I have an apple," answered Al. "Well, *kind* of an apple."

"Toss it on the ground near one of the trees," said Raven.

Al produced the half-eaten apple and rolled it in the direction of a tree trunk. Suddenly the bottom ten feet unwrapped itself from the tall, dead, branchless tree trunk that it had coiled itself around, opened a huge mouth glistening with yellow fangs, grabbed the apple, swallowed it with an audible gulp, and then the huge snake resumed its former position and was once again almost indistinguishable from the forty-foot-tall tree that housed it.

"And it didn't even thank me," said Raven sardonically.

"Thanks, pal!" croaked the snake.

"Let's get out of here!" said Glinda, starting to walk forward as the others all fell into step behind her.

It took another twenty minutes to put the last snake/tree behind them, and now they were within two hundred yards of the city wall.

Let us in, thought Raven.

Silence.

You had to have heard me, he continued. *Let me in.*

Who do you think you're talking to?

You, the Wiz, Rofocale—you're all one and the same.

I hate to disappoint you, Eddie, but I'm Rofocale, and I'm still sedated on my hospital bed.

You're not the Wiz?

Certainly not.

Shit! You got any suggestions on how to get him to send us back?

Us?

Me and Lisa. Pay attention!

I told you—I'm heavily sedated. But not so much that I

don't know you're referring to Glinda the Good Witch, and not Lisa, the girl who was with you in Mako's shop.

We'll argue about that if I survive the next couple of hours. How do I beat him?

You don't want to beat him, Eddie. He's more fragile than you think. One good blow could kill him, and then you're stuck there forever—and in that venue, your forever can probably be measured in hours, perhaps only in minutes.

Has he got any weakness?

We've all got some weaknesses, Eddie. You should know that.

What are they?

Silence.

Damn it, Rofocale! What are they?

Sorry . . . Eddie . . . meds are kicking in againnn . . .

Raven could tell he was no longer in communication with Rofocale. He stood still for a moment, blinking his eyes.

"Are you okay?" asked Glinda.

"Yeah," he replied. "Just a little dizzy spell."

"If you want to put off facing the Wiz for another day or week or month, that's okay by me," said Einstein.

"Yeah, the closer we get, the less important my request seems," added Al.

"Nobody's holding a gun to your head," said Raven. "Glinda and I are going. If you want to stay behind, or go back home, wherever home is, you're free to do so."

"What about me?" said Dillinger.

"I thought you wanted to confront him," said Raven.

"I thought so too," said Dillinger. "But you all have things to ask him for. Me, I don't need anything."

"Don't be so sure of that," said Raven.

"Oh?"

"Once you prove that you got us through every layer of protection he's got, why shouldn't the Wiz put you in charge of all the forces protecting him and the Sapphire City?"

"Yeah, why shouldn't he?" agreed Dillinger. "You got a point, Eddie Raven. And to show you how grateful I am, I'll kill you as swiftly and painlessly as I can once he orders me to."

"You're all heart," said Raven.

"If we're all through talking, shall we continue?" suggested Glinda.

"Right," said Raven, starting to walk forward again.

He concentrated, and thought he could sense a groggy, distant Rofocale.

Are you awake again?

Briefly. Good luck, Eddie.

Got any hints to share about the Wiz? Any at all?

He's just like every other tyrant, only more so.

Thanks a heap.

I'm sorry, Eddie. It's these drugs. They're keeping me alive, but they make it hard to think or concentrate.

Let's try one single question: Has he got the power to send Lisa and me back home?

He's got the power to send you to this or any other universe at any point on this or any other calendar.

And beyond that he's powerless?

I think that's a joke, or a wry comment, or at least insincere, but I'm so groggy I can't . . . I can't . . .

And again Raven sensed that the connection was broken.

"Are you all right, Eddie?" said Glinda. "It looked like you had another dizzy spell."

"Probably just nerves," said Dillinger. "It's not every day that one makes nonnegotiable demands of the most powerful creature in the universe."

"I'm fine," said Raven. He turned to the Megasaur. "Besides, you're going to talk to him first, so he'll be used to hearing demands by the time I speak."

"Me?" demanded Dillinger, turning a bright shade of red-orange. *"First?"*

"Right."

"But . . . but *you're* the one who wants to speak to him the most!" said Dillinger. "You're the reason we've come all this way."

"We *all* have essential requests to make of the Wiz," said Glinda. "Only you needed to have one suggested to you."

"So if he gets annoyed by requests . . ." began Al.

"Best to start with a nonessential one so he can get all the hostility out of his system," concluded Einstein.

"Oh my goodness!" said Dillinger, staring at its left wrist. "I'm late for a meeting of Megasaurs for Satan!"

"You're not wearing a watch," said Al.

"I traded it for a roasted piglet last year," said Dillinger. "But I remember exactly where the hands formerly were." It began walking back the way they'd come.

"Was it regular time or daylight saving time?" asked Einstein.

"Yes!" it yelled back, and then it vanished into the reptilian forest.

"Was that wise, I wonder?" said Glinda. "We might have needed it."

"He got us this far," answered Raven. "We ought to be able to make the last hundred yards or so without him."

"Besides, my uncle used to tell stories about how Megasaurs ate scarecrows," added Einstein.

"Nothing eats scarecrows except cows and horses," said Al. "Well, and goats and sheep and deer and pigs and elephants and—"

"Enough!" cried Einstein. "You're giving me such a headache!"

"Take it easy, guys," said Raven. "Your first duty, and mine, is to get Glinda to the Wiz, unscathed. Everything else comes after that."

"Right," said Einstein. He turned to Glinda. "Forgive me. I just get so nervous when I think of herbivores."

She reached out and held his prickly hand. "It's all right." She paused and stared at his hand. "I'd pat it with my other hand, but . . ."

"I quite understand," said Einstein. "You don't want to draw blood, especially your own, this close to the Wiz."

She nodded her agreement, held on to his hand for a few more seconds, and then gently released it.

"You see any guards on the nearest wall?" asked Raven, staring at the city.

"Not a one," answered Al. "I see a batch off to the right, guarding the palace."

"So based on what we were told, they're no threat to us," said Raven.

"We hope," agreed Al.

"All right," said Raven, taking Glinda by the hand and starting forward. "We're no closer to the Wiz or to home than we were five minutes ago, and none of us is getting any younger. Let's go."

And with that, he began approaching the wall of the Sapphire City.

17

They reached the barred gates and paused.

"I keep expecting someone to say 'Who goes there?'" admitted Raven.

"I don't see anyone any closer than the palace," said Glinda.

"All right," said Raven, opening the gates. "What's the worst that can happen?"

"Don't ask," said Einstein, looking around nervously.

They approached a narrow gate which opened wide for them, entered the city, and found themselves on a series of sparkling blue streets that kept turning in upon themselves. Finally they found one street that went off to the left in a relatively straight line and followed it to the unimpressive little house they had seen from beyond the city walls.

"If Dillinger was telling the truth, and at the time it had no reason to lie, this little ramshackle building is the Wiz's residence or office or both," said Raven. He raised his voice a bit. "You know we're here, don't you?"

"Not so loud!" said an unseen voice. "I've got a horrible hangover."

"Open the door for us," said Raven.

"Wait a minute. I've got to get where the sun won't blind

me." There was a pause, and then a crash. "Damn!" And then, "I never liked that lamp anyway." Another pause, and a loud click. "Okay, Eddie Whoever-you-think-you-are, and the Good Witch from wherever, and the straw thing, and the metal monster. Enter."

"At least he didn't add 'at your own risk,'" said Raven, opening the door.

"I figured it didn't need saying," croaked a voice from within the building.

"I'd better go first," said Al, stepping ahead of Raven. "What's a couple more dents to a robot?"

Raven nodded and let Al walk ahead of him and Glinda, while Einstein brought up the rear.

The foyer was a small, circular room, filled with a strange display. There were weapons galore, none of them functional: sword handles without blades, pistols and rifles without triggers, poison bottles marked so boldly that no one could mistake them for anything else (and which Raven noticed were all empty), and even a suit of armor minus metal plates to cover the heart.

"What do you make of that?" mused Raven aloud.

"If I was a little smarter I could tell you," answered Einstein.

"You gonna stand out there gawking all day?" said a high nasal voice.

"Where are you?" asked Raven.

"There's only one doorway leading from the foyer," said the voice. "I'll give you three guesses."

"Even I don't need more than two," said Einstein. "Probably."

"Come on, come on," said the voice. "I haven't got all day."

"Haven't you?" said Al.

"Actually, I have aeons," said the voice. "But *you* don't."

Raven took Glinda's hand and stepped through the doorway at the back of the foyer, followed by Al and Einstein. They found themselves in what seemed to have once been a vast library, with hundreds of feet of bookshelves and bookcases running to the ceiling in most places. Perched atop a stool behind an antique wood desk was a skinny little man with a large nose, an angular chin, and dark piercing eyes. He wore a robe covered with exotic symbols, and a pointed hat.

"You're the Wiz?" said Raven.

"Is that a question or a statement?" replied the little man.

"Take your choice."

"Damn! I like you already!" cried the little man. "Right! I'm the Wiz."

"Good," said Raven. "We've come to—"

"Don't say it!" snapped the Wiz. "Let me guess!"

Raven shrugged. "Whatever makes you happy."

"Guessing makes me happy," said the Wiz. "Just between you and me, I haven't been wrong since November of 1735."

"Must be nice to be the Wiz," commented Raven.

"It has its compensations."

"So why are we here?"

"To ask for favors," answered the Wiz. "That's the only reason anyone ever comes to visit." He brushed a tear from his cheek.

"If you wouldn't make it so difficult to see you," said Glinda, "maybe people would visit you more often."

"You're right," agreed the Wiz. Suddenly he growled deep in his chest. "I hate it when people are right."

"Then let's get our business over with, and you can go back to hating people from afar."

"I like the way you think—or did I say that before?" replied the Wiz.

"Something similar, anyway," answered Raven.

"Good!" said the Wiz. "I haven't read three million books so I can repeat myself."

"Where are they?" asked Einstein.

"Where are *what*?" demanded the Wiz.

"Your three million books. This library's totally empty." He rubbed a forefinger along a shelf, raising a cloud of dust. "And it looks like it's been empty for ages."

"Well, of course," said the Wiz. "Who needs a book once you've transferred it?"

"You mean read it?" asked Einstein.

"Almost the same thing," replied the Wiz. "I pick a book up, concentrate as hard as I can, and presto!, the whole damned thing is transferred to my memory." Suddenly he smiled. "And the way I know is because none of the words remain on the pages; they're all fighting for space between my ears."

"That's a fascinating talent," said Einstein enviously.

"It can be annoying at times," said the Wiz. "When I'm looking at a triple hot fudge sundae, the last thing I want to remember is the health book that warns what an extra gazillion calories can do to your heart." Suddenly he smiled. "Not that I have one, of course, but still . . ."

"So shall we begin our negotiations?" said Raven.

"Might as well," said the Wiz. "As long as you've braved untold hardships." He paused. "I don't suppose you'd like to tell me about them?"

"Some other time."

"Just as well," replied the Wiz. "Sometimes hearing about them gets me so excited I can't function."

"Then let's begin," said Raven firmly.

"You sound like you're giving me orders," said the Wiz. He inhaled deeply, and seemed to grow until he'd tripled his size. "I don't like it when people give me orders." He doubled in size again, until he was a muscular giant who had to kneel down and bend over to fit into the high-ceilinged room. "Understand?" he bellowed.

"You look goddamned uncomfortable," remarked Raven.

"Well, now that you mention it . . ." said the Wiz, blinking his eyes three times in succession and shrinking down to what they assumed was his normal appearance.

"You scare a lot of people with that parlor trick?" asked Raven.

"It works better when I'm outside and standing up straight," admitted the Wiz.

"Okay, *now* are you ready to deal?"

"Sure," said the Wiz. "You do a service for me, I do one for each of you. But me first. After all, I'm the Wiz."

"Okay," said Raven. "What do you want?"

"I need a queen," said the Wiz. He looked long and hard at Glinda, then nodded his head as if he'd made a decision. "This one will do as well as any, if she'll agree to wear low-cut blouses and short, tight miniskirts."

Glinda was about to protest, but Raven spoke up first.

"That's our most valuable treasure," he said. "Are you open to the only counteroffer we're prepared to make?"

"Of course," said the Wiz.

"Okay," said Raven. "You want her, she's yours."

Glinda looked shocked. "Eddie!"

He held his hand up. "In exchange, we want your life and your city."

The Wiz frowned. "I can always replace my life, but it's too much work to build another Sapphire City. I reject your offer."

"And we reject yours," said Raven. *Rofocale,* he thought, *if you're awake and paying attention, I could use some help, some suggestion, something.*

And suddenly Rofocale's voice came through loud and clear inside his head. *Make the best deal you can and get here quick. I'm in deep trouble!*

Your wounds?

I've got doctors for that. Just get here!

The Wiz looked at the assemblage, then pointed a bony forefinger at Einstein. "You first," he said.

"Me?" said Einstein nervously.

"You're a ready-made broom and dust mop. I need someone to keep the place clean."

"How many rooms is it?" asked Einstein, looking around. "Five, six?"

"Three hundred and fifty-two," answered the Wiz. "What do you want in exchange for being my housekeeper?"

"A brain," came the prompt reply.

"You already have one, though I agree it's difficult to find."

"A better one," said Einstein.

"Okay," said the Wiz, pulling a deck of cards out of his pocket, briefly shuffling them, and placing them on his desk.

"Tarot?" asked Einstein, frowning.

"IQ," was the answer.

"I don't understand," said Einstein.

"That's because your IQ is functioning at about a seventy-five. Cut the cards."

Einstein reached a hand out. "Just cut them?"

"Right," confirmed the Wiz.

"And this will determine my new IQ?"

"Not if I have to miss lunch waiting for you to cut the god-damned cards," growled the Wiz.

"Okay, okay," said Einstein with a sigh. He reached out, let his hand hover above the deck for a few seconds, and finally cut to a card.

"What does it say?" asked Raven.

"One hundred forty-three."

"That's your new IQ," said the Wiz.

"Is that good?" asked Einstein nervously.

"It's about twice as good as you were," said the Wiz.

"O happy day!" cried Einstein.

"Tell me that after you've cleaned a couple hundred rooms and the first ones are already dirty again," said the Wiz. "Sometimes it's better not to have a brain at all."

"I'll make up poems and stories as I clean," said Einstein, "and recite them to myself."

The Wiz shrugged. "I suppose it'll work. Half the writers and poets I know haven't got your IQ or anything close to it, and it's never stopped them." He turned to Al. "Okay, metal man. You're next."

"Good," said Al. "I want—"

"Me first," interrupted the Wiz. "I thought I explained the ground rules."

"I apologize," said Al. "What favor or service do you want?"

"My magnificent brain never stops working," began the Wiz, "but I tire easily, especially in this wimpy little body that I use to fit into some of the rooms in this house, and over at the castle."

"I can't give you more energy," said Al.

"No," agreed the Wiz. "But we can rig up a harness so I can sit on your shoulders while you carry me from place to place."

"Yeah, you look light enough," said Al.

"I shall not be an inconsiderate jockey or passenger," continued the Wiz. "I promise never to eat more than five double cheeseburgers at a sitting, accompanied by maybe an extra-thick malt or two." He paused. "And now what can I do for you?"

"I've got too many laws running through my negatronic brain," said Al. "Half the time when people think I'm sleeping or resting, I'm just frozen, sorting through which of the thirty-seven laws I must obey takes precedence."

"So how many do you want?" asked the Wiz.

"Well, Isaac Asimov always gave his robots three laws—but then, they always got into trouble."

"How about an even dozen?" suggested the Wiz. "Not too many, not too few."

"Deal!" said Al excitedly.

The Wiz mumbled a spell, then looked up. "How do you feel?"

Al frowned. "Lighter."

"You *should*," chuckled the Wiz. "You're carrying twenty-five fewer laws now." He turned to Raven. "And you and the lady?"

"We want to go home," said Raven, and Glinda nodded.

"Is that nearby?"

Raven shook his head. "It's not even in this world."

"Hmm," mused the Wiz. "That'll take a *big* favor." He stared at Glinda. "You're sure you won't trade her?"

"Not a chance."

"Okay," said the Wiz. "Make a suggestion. You've been more bother than you're worth."

And in that reply Raven saw his perfect offer: "I've really been bothering you?"

"Absolutely."

"Okay," said Raven. "Return us home and we promise that neither of us will ever tell any of our countrymen how to get here."

"Anyone of your race and species," said the Wiz, frowning as he considered the offer. "What do I care what country they come from?"

"Deal!" said Raven.

He reached out his hand to shake on it—

18

And found himself back in the hospital room, reaching out his hand toward Rofocale, who was still connected to half a dozen tubes.

"What the hell is going on?" muttered Raven.

We're both in immediate danger, answered Rofocale's voice within his head. *They're coming to get us, even as I communicate with you.*

"*Who* is coming to get us?" demanded Raven.

No time! came the answer. *They've already entered the hospital. We've got to get out of here!*

Raven looked around the room, saw a wheelchair in the corner, and rolled it over to the bed, then paused.

What is it?

"You're connected to oxygen and half a dozen tubes."

Rip them all out—and HURRY!

Raven did as he was told, lifted Rofocale, and transferred him to the wheelchair.

There's a service elevator off to the right. Use it. They're coming up the main elevator, and we don't want to run into them.

Raven wheeled Rofocale out into the hall, saw that there were no doctors or nurses walking back or forth, and began pushing the wheelchair at a trot. He rounded a corner and entered a service elevator, then waited for the doors to close.

"Okay, you're safe for the moment," said Raven. "Always assuming people were really coming after you when and how you said." Then: "Shit!"

What is it, Eddie?

"Lisa!" answered Raven. "If these guys really mean business, I've got to go back for her! Hell, you seemed in such trouble I didn't even pay attention to her!"

It's all right, Eddie.

"What do you mean, it's all right?" snapped Raven. "If these guys are half as dangerous as you seem to think . . ."

She's not here, Eddie.

Raven frowned. "What the hell are you talking about?"

You each opted to go back to your home world.

"Right," said Raven. "And this *is* our world."

This is your *world, Eddie—not hers.*

"What are you saying?" demanded Raven.

I'll explain later. But right now they're reached my room and realized that we've left. There are—let me count—four of them, plus one they left covering the exit in the lobby.

"What the hell did you do to make them so mad at you?"

They're not after me, *Eddie. It's* you *they want.*

"Me?" said Raven. "I don't even know who they are!"

But they know who you *are.*

The elevator stopped at ground level.

"This place got a basement?" asked Raven.

Let me examine it. A brief pause. *Yes, we can descend one more level.*

"Okay, let's give it a shot. Maybe there's some other exit

from down there. And once we've got a little breathing room, I want some answers."

You deserve them, agreed Rofocale, as the elevator reached the basement level and Raven emerged behind the wheelchair.

"And first and foremost is this nonsense about Lisa."

Movement to your left, Eddie.

Raven turned and stared into the darkness. "Probably a mouse," he said.

Probabilities are meaningless where the Master of Dreams is concerned.

"Who?" demanded Raven.

Lower your voice, Eddie. We, well actually you, *are being hunted by the Master of Dreams.*

"Sounds like something from a bad comic book."

He is much more than that.

"Has he captured Lisa?"

No, Eddie, he has not.

"Then maybe that was her off to the left."

It wasn't.

"Okay, where is she?"

Not in this world.

"Are you saying that she really was killed back in Mako's store?" said Raven unbelievingly. "Then who was Ilsa back in Casablanca, or the witch in Oz?"

No, she's alive, Eddie—and she's been trying to help you. She has that much control over her fate.

"Then why isn't she here?"

She chose *where to go. Eventually her reasons will become clear—if we live that long.*

There was a sudden crash.

Raven looked into the shadows and saw a grotesque, mildly human shape emerging from behind a pile of empty crates.

"I've got nothing to fight it with!" said Raven. "Hang on, if you're capable of grabbing the chair's arms!"

He began pushing the wheelchair at a dead run, and saw a flickering exit sign in the distance. The creature took up the pursuit, but evidently it couldn't see any better in the dark than Raven could, because it kept colliding with crates and boxes.

Raven and the chair made it to the exit half a dozen paces ahead of the creature, which shied back from the sudden brilliance of a nearby streetlamp, and Raven promptly slammed the door and was gratified to hear the lock slide into place.

"Well, that's that!" he muttered.

It's not over.

"What are you talking about?" said Raven. "We're out. It's in. And the bad guys are still in your room or on the main floor."

This is no mere mortal you're up against, Eddie. This is the Master of Dreams, with almost-unlimited resources. Don't let your guard down for an instant.

"I don't know if I believe any of this," muttered Raven.

Did you believe Casablanca and Oz?

"Okay," said Raven. "I'm listening."

We've got to get to my room, which is just about the only spot that's impregnable to his powers.

"Where is it?"

About four blocks from here.

"That's a relief. I was afraid you were going to tell me to take you there on the subway."

Just get me to the end of this alley, and I'll direct you.

Raven began pushing the chair, and shortly came to a cross street.

"Okay," he said. "Right or left, sidewalk or alley?"

Left to the cross street, then right. And stay near the lights where possible.

Raven turned left, came to a corner, and began pushing the wheelchair across the street when he heard a hideous roar and saw something that dwarfed a huge grizzly, at least ten feet tall and covered with armor plating, bearing down on them. It roared again, then charged.

Raven couldn't see any place where he could move the chair out of the line of attack. Then he saw headlights out of the corner of his eye, waited until the creature was within a dozen feet of them, and then, pushing the wheelchair ahead of him, raced across the street.

There was a loud honking, and an even louder crash as a delivery truck rammed into the creature. The driver stuck his head out the window and began cursing a blue streak, as the creature got slowly and painfully to its feet and offered a weak bleat in return.

Raven watched from the far curb, then began pushing the wheelchair up the street once he was sure the creature was in no condition to pursue him.

"Where to now?" he asked softly when they came to the next corner.

Straight ahead for another block.

"Any hint as to what might be waiting up ahead?"

He's got an entire menagerie, Eddie. After all, he is *the Master of Dreams.*

"We're going to have to talk about that if we survive the next couple of blocks," said Raven grimly.

He began walking up the block, and had gone about fifty feet when he heard a shriek from directly overhead. He looked up and saw a winged creature with a long beak filled with gleaming teeth gliding down toward him.

"Suggestions?" he hissed as he maneuvered the chair around a lamppost, the only cover for thirty feet in any direction.

The creature slowed its flight and began circling the lamppost, a few feet lower with each circle. Finally it reached its neck out to its full length and tried to clamp its jaws shut on Raven's left arm. Raven pulled back just in time, and as he heard the jaws clamp shut he reached out with his right hand, grabbed the creature by its beak, closed his left arm about its throat, and swinging it like a living, misshapen baseball bat crashed it against the lamppost.

The creature tried to shriek, but it came out as a weak gurgle. Raven kicked it into the street and began pushing the chair again as screeching tires told him that a car was trying to avoid hitting the creature, and a loud crunch confirmed that it hadn't been able to.

"How much farther?" he asked as he began pushing Rofocale's chair again.

Get to the corner, turn right, second building you come to.

"Every apartment building around here locks its front door at dusk, if not around the clock. You're in a hospital gown. How do we get in?"

The door will recognize me.

"You'd better be right," muttered Raven.

He continued pushing, made it to the last corner, and was about to turn to the right as Rofocale had directed when he found an enormous serpent blocking his way.

"Just a typical evening stroll in Manhattan!" he muttered, looking around for anything he could use as a weapon, and finding nothing.

The serpent slithered forward, staring unblinkingly at Raven. Suddenly he heard a honking down the street and saw a convertible holding a quartet of drunken young men happily screaming obscenities as they careened down the street.

"Damn it!" said Raven. "If they're as drunk as they sound, we may come through this in one piece!"

He picked up a garbage can from the corner, yelled to attract the driver's attention, and threw the can into the street.

"Idiot!" yelled the driver.

Raven's response was an obscene gesture.

The car veered and made a beeline toward Raven just as the serpent was beginning its final charge. Raven stepped back, pulling the chair with him, and watched as the car crashed into the serpent.

The serpent wheezed, blood gushing out of its mouth. The car's motor died, and all four young men were unconscious.

"Okay," said Raven, pushing the chair into the street to get around the senseless combatants. "Which one?"

The next building.

Raven rushed the chair up to the door of the building, which irised to let them through.

"Please tell me your apartment is on the ground floor," said Raven.

Go through the door on the left. It will open for us.

And indeed it did, revealing a very small elevator.

Second floor.

"There are no controls," noted Raven.

It knows.

A moment later the door slid shut behind them, and in a few seconds they emerged onto the second floor. There were three doors, and one of them instantly opened. Raven pushed the chair inside, and found himself in a sparsely furnished living room.

He lifted Rofocale out of the wheelchair, carried him over to a small, beat-up sofa, and set him down.

"You okay?" he asked.

A little the worse for wear, but otherwise okay.

"Then perhaps you'll tell me what the hell is going on? My girl was shot dead right in front of me, then turned up as an Ingrid Bergman clone in Casablanca and a witch in Oz. And I never saw you before in my life, but suddenly we're conversing by . . . I don't know . . . telepathy, I guess."

And you remember nothing else, Eddie?

"No, of course not," said Raven. "I mean, hell, isn't that enough?"

And you want answers, of course.

"Damned right I do."

Then you'll be pleased to know that your answer is *obtainable. You've but to go and retrieve it.*

"Okay," said Raven. "Is it nearby? In Manhattan?"

Nothing is ever that simple, Eddie. The answer lies in Camelot.

Raven frowned. "John Kennedy's Camelot? Lerner and Loewe's Camelot?"

No, Eddie—the real *Camelot.*

"Camelot, if it existed at all, was centuries ago."

It existed.

"Okay, say it did, for the sake of argument. How do I travel through time?"

The same way you traveled to a Casablanca café that never existed, and an Oz that exists only in the mind of L. Frank Baum and the hearts of children. Time and space are not arbitrary constants, Eddie; once you realize that all times and places coexist, you need never leave this city or even this room to travel wherever and whenever you wish.

"And Lisa will be there?"

I wouldn't be at all surprised.

"You know," admitted Raven, "after the last few days, neither—"

19

"—Would I."

He wasn't aware of any feeling of motion, or any lapse of time, but he knew he was somewhere else—with an emphasis on the *else.* He looked down and found he was wearing a rather nondescript robe.

"Okay," he muttered. He placed a hand to his head. "No crown," he muttered. He suddenly realized he was wearing a sword. He drew it from its scabbard and studied it. "A bit rusty, nothing special about it in any way, no writing on it. Definitely not Excalibur." He looked around at his surroundings. "Okay, so I'm clearly not Arthur. And while Merlin doesn't necessarily have to have what I think of as a magician's hat, or even a wand, there doesn't seem to be anything magical at all about me or my trappings."

Lancelot? "Not very likely. I've never held a sword in my hand, not even a toy sword when I was a kid. Besides, isn't *he* a part of the Round Table? I mean he couldn't run off with Guinevere if he didn't have access to her. And even if he hasn't done so yet, he's still part of the Round Table."

He frowned. "Okay, I'm clearly not one of the principals . . .

so what the hell am I doing in Camelot anyway? I'm not the king, the wizard, any of the knights, so I've got no clout."

He closed his eyes and hurled a thought to Rofocale. *You might have chosen a better persona for me. How the hell am I going to access anything I need?*

There was no response. He wasn't sure whether or not he'd really expected one. He sent another thought, demanding to know more about his mission, also with no answer.

He looked around the landscape. There was a rather nice castle about half a mile behind him, and some raggedly dressed peasants herding some equally ragged hogs and sheep in the distance. Nothing that looked the way a thousand years of British poets and historians would dedicate themselves to describing it.

"Well," he muttered, "I'm not going to get answers out here in the middle of nowhere. Maybe someone at the nearby castle can enlighten me."

He turned and began approaching the closest, and minimally most impressive—or, to be more accurate, least *un*impressive—castle. A couple of medium-size dogs of very indeterminate parentage ran up to greet and accompany him.

"Well, *you* seem to know me, anyway," said Raven, petting each in turn. "And since you do, and I can't see a goddamned door, lead the way."

The dogs frisked and barked, and he fell into step behind them. As he got closer he saw that the castle was surrounded by a moat, and as he drew closer still he saw that the moat was empty. Nevertheless, a drawbridge lowered as he approached, and he walked across it, accompanied by the dogs.

"Lunch will be another hour, my lord," said a man in what Raven considered to be a shabby uniform of the Arthurian era. He bowed low, and since Raven didn't know how to salute him or indicate that he could straighten up, he simply nodded his head and continued walking forward.

A woman carrying folds of cloth in a basket emerged from a room, almost bumped into him, blushed, curtsied, and disappeared back into the room.

Good God, are you all afraid to talk to me? thought Raven. *Who the hell am I—and how am I going to find out if no one will meet my gaze or speak to me?*

He walked a few steps, then stopped and stared at an image on a painting that hung on a wall. It showed two young men in armor, each with a friendly arm around the other, each smiling, each sporting youthful beards.

He stopped, hands on hips, turned to study the painting, and tried to spot anything identifiable in the background. He must have been staring for a few minutes when a feminine voice spoke in low tones right next to him.

"Is it not straight, my lord?" asked the voice. "I cleaned some cobwebs off it yesterday. I may not have been as careful and precise as I should have been."

He turned and looked at the speaker, who was either in her late teens or early twenties, a pretty face topped by flaming red hair.

"No, it's quite straight," said Raven. Then: "What do *you* think of it?"

"A very fair representation, my lord."

"You really think so?"

She nodded. "Of course, you were younger. You are more mature and handsome now."

"Thank you," said Raven. "And the other?"

She frowned. "The other?"

He pointed to the taller, somewhat older, man in the painting.

"As you say, sir, he looks every inch the king that he is."

So that's *Arthur!*

He turned to the young woman. "Thank you."

She frowned again. "For what?"

"For your opinion."

"But I am just a servant girl."

"Just as there can be inferior kings, there can be superior servants," said Raven.

"The only king I know of is Arthur," she said, "and of course he is flawless."

"How often have you seen him?" asked Raven.

"I have seen him ride past with his army three . . . no, four . . . times since I came to work here eight years ago."

"I mean, close up, not from a distance."

She lowered her eyes and looked uncomfortable. "Oh, sir, you know the answer to that."

"Enlighten me."

"Just once, when you and he had your falling-out during the banquet and he left with his men before the final course was served. Surely you remember, sir."

"Yes, I do," answered Raven.

"Is there anything else, sir?" she asked uncomfortably.

What the hell can I ask, without out-and-out demanding my name?

"No, I guess not," he said. "And your name is?"

She stared at him as if he might be expected to start baying at the moon even though the sun was still out. "Arabella, sir."

"Arabella," he said with a smile. "Of course."

She turned and vanished into one of the many rooms that lined the corridor in which he found himself.

He remained where he was, still facing the painting, still trying to figure out who he was, besides a friend—or at least a one-time friend—of Arthur's.

He felt a hand on his shoulder, and a friendly voice spoke up. "I wouldn't worry, my lord. He'll get over it before much longer."

Raven turned to face what appeared to be a battle-hardened knight. "You really think so?"

The knight smiled and nodded his head. "Everyone knows that Arthur and Mordred are like brothers."

Great! thought Raven bitterly. *Thanks a heap, Rofocale. You not only got me sent here, but made me the least popular villain in the whole goddamned kingdom!*

20

Raven sat in a room by himself, perched on a stool, his elbow on his knee and his chin on his hand, considering his possibilities.

Since Lisa had been in Casablanca and Oz, it made sense that she was in Camelot too, and that almost certainly meant she was Guinevere.

Now who the hell else was there? he wondered, trying to remember *The Once and Future King*, or even the musical *Camelot*.

Well, there was Lancelot, of course. And Sir Ector and Sir Pellinore. Oh, and Merlin.

The more he thought about it, the more it seemed to him that Merlin was the man to seek out for answers. After all, who knew more about things mystical than the greatest sorcerer of his era, perhaps of *any* era?

That led to more questions. First, where could he find Merlin, and second, could he travel in the open? If he and Arthur had become enemies, was it safe to travel very far from his castle, especially by daylight?

Damn it, Rofocale—this one makes Oz look like a piece of cake! Why the hell couldn't you have chosen—I don't know—ancient

Athens, where Hecate figures to have been easier to deal with than Arthur's good buddy Merlin. Or wherever the hell Circe reigned.

Suddenly he frowned.

Or do I need a magician at all? I didn't have one to get out of Casablanca.

No, said Rofocale's voice somewhere inside his head, *but the letters of transit did not obey the laws of the physical universe.*

"You're alive!" muttered Raven out loud. "I thought I'd lost you."

I am harder to kill than you think, Eddie Raven.

"So what the hell am I doing in Camelot?" asked Raven. "Or Casablanca or Oz, for that matter."

Don't you know?

"If I did, I wouldn't be asking."

Your archenemy transported you to Casablanca and has been hindering your return to your world ever since.

"You mean to *our* world," said Raven.

I meant what I said.

"Great," muttered Raven. "Now I've got half a dozen more questions to ask. Let me start by asking who is my archenemy?"

Why, the Master of Dreams, of course. That's why he keeps transferring you to venues that never existed.

"Why is he my archenemy?"

They gave me powerful medications at the hospital which I must continue to take. The thoughts came slowly, hesitantly. *I cannot stay awake. We will speak again when this batch wears off. Good luck, Eddie! Be alert—even in Camelot there are those who want you dead.*

And suddenly Raven knew that they were no longer in contact.

"Okay," he muttered to himself, "who's the easiest to reach, and who's the likeliest to know how I get home?"

He thought about it for a few moments and decided that Merlin was the likeliest to know how to help him. Then he tried to remember Mallory and all the other chroniclers of Camelot to find out what his relationship to Merlin was—friend, enemy, son, brother? There were enough chronicles, no two told quite the same story, and while Mallory was the most popular there was no reason to believe that it was any more accurate than any of the others—Geoffrey of Monmouth, Chrétien de Troyes, Robert de Boron, John Leland, half a dozen more, no two of whom saw it alike. Arthur married Guinevere; Arthur killed Guinevere; Guinevere ran off with Lancelot; Guinevere died young; Guinevere killed Arthur.

It would be nice if he could pick and choose, but of course all but one version—in fact, a minimum of all but one version—were false. No one even agreed on where Camelot was, except that it didn't evolve into London.

I'm running blind, thought Raven. *But the one thing they all agree on is that Merlin was a magician. In some he's Arthur's mentor, in some his enemy, but in every one he's a magician, so that's the place to start.*

And then, for the first time, he thought of Lisa.

She must be Guinevere, he mused. *Living in the castle—assuming there is a castle, in Camelot, married to someone who evidently hates my guts. I want to see her, but maybe this isn't the world to go out of my way to do it in. She was unattached as Dorothy, and predisposed to care for me in*

Casablanca, but if she's the queen, she runs off with Lancelot, not with Mordred.

Or does she? Camelot has half a dozen conflicting versions. Maybe the one in which I find myself also strays from any accepted text. After all, Mallory and the others were poets and mythmakers, not historians.

He sighed heavily and considered his options. *But maybe I'll hunt up Merlin first. There's every possibility that Mallory and some of the others were telling the truth, Arabella confirms that he's angry with me, and besides, I don't know where the hell his castle is.*

Of course, he didn't know where Merlin's castle was either, but he decided he was less likely to be killed while looking for it.

21

Raven had the cook pack him some food, asked a couple of servants where Merlin's castle was, got contradictory answers, and kept on asking until three in a row gave him the same answer. Then he put the food in a primitive backpack, walked out the front door of his castle, and headed in a southeasterly direction.

He'd gone perhaps three miles when he decided to take a break, and sat down on a large rock. He rested about ten minutes and was just about to start off again when an elderly—the description that came to mind was ancient—man in armor rode up on a horse that looked every bit as old.

"Avast, there!" said the man.

"Hello," replied Raven.

"Have you seen it?"

"Have I seen *what*?" asked Raven.

"Why, the Questin' Beast, of course."

Raven was torn between saying no and asking what the Questin' Beast looked like. He settled for the former.

"Damn!" said the old man. "That is the most elusive creature on God's Earth." He paused. "Do you mind if I sit down and join you?"

"There's room enough for two on the rock," said Raven. "Be my guest."

"Thanks," said the old man, dismounting. "I must say, Mordred, that you don't seem to be the cad that most people make you out to be."

"Thank you, I think," said Raven. "And you are?"

"Sir Pellinore, of course!" said the man. "Don't you recognize me?"

"You've aged," said Raven.

"True, true," admitted Sir Pellinore. "Comes from spending the last twenty-five years chasing the damned Beast."

"At least it's given you a purpose in your pending old age," said Raven.

"That it has," admitted Sir Pellinore. "And what, may I ask, is *your* purpose, Mordred? Surely it goes beyond sitting on a rock with the sun beating down upon you?"

"I need to speak to Merlin."

Sir Pellinore frowned. "I don't believe he likes you." He paused. "Of course, hardly anybody does."

"I still need to speak to him," said Raven. "Can you tell me where to find him?"

"Certainly," said Sir Pellinore. "The only thing I can't find is the damned Questin' Beast."

"Well?" said Raven after a brief pause.

"Oh!" said Sir Pellinore. "You want me to tell you! I thought you just wanted to know if *I* knew."

"Yes, I'd be most appreciative if you'd tell me."

"In his castle, of course."

"And where is his castle?" asked Raven.

"Off that way," replied Sir Pellinore, pointing to the south and east.

"Is it far?"

"Not if you're an elephant," was the answer. "Too damned far if you're one of those little insects that gets born, breeds, and dies all in the same day."

"Thanks, I think," said Raven.

"Tell you what, Mordred," said Sir Pellinore. "I'll accompany you."

"I'd greatly appreciate it," said Raven. "You're sure you don't mind?"

"The Questin' Beast is as likely to be in that direction as any other." He frowned. "I'd offer to let you ride behind me, but I've put on a little weight, and of course this armor weighs a lot, and . . ."

"Not a problem," said Raven. "I'll be happy to walk alongside you and the horse."

"Then it's settled. As soon as I get the energy to stand up and climb back onto the damned horse, we'll begin."

"Has the horse got a name?" asked Raven.

Sir Pellinore frowned. "He had one once. Damned if I can remember what it is." He shrugged, sending his armor clanking. "Probably he wouldn't recognize it even if I used it." Suddenly he smiled. "Tell you what," he said. "*You* name him!"

"I've never named a horse before," said Raven. "I wouldn't know where to begin."

"At the beginning, of course."

"Well, I *do* know some horse's names," said Raven. "Not a lot, but some."

"That's a start," said Sir Pellinore. "What are they?"

"Silver. Trigger. Champion. Topper. Man o' War. Secretariat. Seattle Slew. Oh—and Black Beauty." He paused, trying to come up with more names.

Sir Pellinore stared at his mount. "Well, he's not silver and he's not black, and I don't know what a trigger is. I guess Champion will do nicely."

"I'm sure the Autry estate will be proud," said Raven.

"The Autry estate?"

"Never mind," said Raven. He reached out a hand. "Let me help you up."

The process was noisier and more awkward than anticipated, but finally Sir Pellinore was on his feet.

"Thank you, Mordred," he said. "You're a very nice, thoughtful, helpful man." He frowned. "I wonder why everyone hates you so?"

Raven wanted to say "Innate prejudice against New Yorkers," but didn't feel like explaining what and where New York was, so he simply shrugged his shoulders. "Beats the hell out of me," he said at last.

"I didn't know you were a religious man," said Sir Pellinore.

"I'm not."

"But isn't that what you ask your priest to do in some of the more esoteric ceremonies—beat the hell out of you?"

"Just an expression."

"Be careful when and how you use it," said Sir Pellinore. "Or you may find someone taking you up on it."

Raven smiled. "I can tell you're going to be a useful guide in many ways. Shall we begin?"

"I need a log, or a rock, or a chair," said Sir Pellinore.

"This armor weighs more than I do, and I'm not the man I once was."

"Try this," said Raven, standing next to the horse and cupping his hands. He had to lower them more than a foot before Sir Pellinore could reach them, and then realized that the old knight wasn't kidding about the weight of his armor, but finally he sat astride his horse.

"Have you ever considered going into battle *without* armor?" asked Raven.

"Against the Questin' Beast?" said Sir Pellinore. "Are you quite mad?"

"Not quite," said Raven. "I've never seen the Questin' Beast. What kind of weaponry does he bring to a battle?"

"He's huge, and powerful, and hideous, and of course unforgiving," answered Sir Pellinore.

"Teeth?"

Sir Pellinore held his hands ten inches apart. "This long."

"Really? What does he eat?"

"I've no idea," answered Sir Pellinore. "Anything smaller than himself, I should think."

"Does he breathe fire?"

"He breathes air, just like everything else on Earth."

"Let me rephrase that," said Raven. "Does he exhale fire?"

"I've never gotten close enough to tell."

"Let me get this straight," said Raven. "You've been hunting the Questin' Beast for thirty years . . ."

"Longer," interjected Sir Pellinore.

"And you've never gotten close enough to tell what he eats, or if fire is part of his arsenal?"

"That's right."

"Well, I'm sure glad you haven't wasted your time," said Raven.

"You don't seem to understand, Mordred," said Sir Pellinore. "The honors that will befall the man who slays the beast will be greater than any man other than Arthur himself can achieve or expect."

"Well, it's a little late in the game to change goals now," agreed Raven. "But may I make one suggestion?"

"Certainly."

"I assume you've yet to get within one hundred feet of the Beast?"

"Well, eighty feet, anyway," said Sir Pellinore.

"Then why not lose the armor? You've never seen a flame, he certainly doesn't throw them eighty feet or more if he throws them at all, and think of how much more comfortable you'll be with at least fifty fewer pounds of armor—to say nothing about how much cooler you'll feel."

"By God, Mordred, you're *far* better than people say, even those few people who actually like you!" Sir Pellinore unhooked the armor covering his torso and arms and let it fall noisily to the ground. "I'll take care of the legs when next we stop."

"Feel better?" asked Raven as Sir Pellinore took half a dozen deep breaths and exhaled them with a beatific smile on his face.

"I almost feel like I'm ninety again!" enthused the knight. "Now let's go see the wizard who hates the sight of you and see if I can return the favor!"

22

They'd traveled for a day and a morning, and were thinking of stopping by a grove of apple trees and having some lunch when Raven saw a magnificent white horse approaching them, with a tall knight in shining armor sitting atop it.

"We've got company," he said.

"Yes, I see him," answered Sir Pellinore.

"Anything to worry about?"

The knight shook his head. "No, it's just Lancelot."

"*Sir* Lancelot?" asked Raven.

"I don't suppose he's been demoted since last I saw him," confirmed Sir Pellinore.

"What kind of quest can he be on that's brought him all the way out here?" mused Raven.

"I don't know," said Sir Pellinore. "But it damned well better not be the Questin' Beast. He belongs to *me*, and I'll kill the man who disagrees with that."

"I think we're about to find out," said Raven. "He's heading this way."

Indeed, the white stallion began approaching them at a

slow but steady trot, and Raven had to shield his eyes from the glare the sun made on the knight's shining armor.

"Bright," he muttered.

"Show-off," replied Sir Pellinore. "I could polish *my* armor to within an inch of its life too, but why let the enemy know you're coming until you're upon him?"

"I hope he knows we're not the enemy."

"There's every possibility," said Sir Pellinore. "He's not the brightest knight in the kingdom, but he pretty much knows friend from foe."

"But he's never seen me before," muttered Raven.

"You're with me," said Sir Pellinore. "That makes you my friend or my prisoner. Either way, it should stop him from running you through until we chat a bit."

"*Should*, not *will*?" said Raven nervously.

"He's known for his bravery, not his brainpower," answered Sir Pellinore. "Don't worry too much. If need be, I'll protect you."

"I can't tell you how comforting that is," said Raven grimly.

"I'll explain to him that you've become my apprentice Questin' Beast hunter," said Sir Pellinore.

"I'm Mordred," said Raven. "He'll never buy it."

"He's *physically* awesome," came the reply. "It doesn't necessarily extend above his neck and especially between his ears."

"I hope you're right," said Raven. "He's too damned close for us to run anyway, even if Champion can hold both of us on his back, which I doubt."

"Surely you weigh less than my armor," said Sir Pellinore.

"I wouldn't bet on it," answered Raven.

"Ahoy, there!" called Sir Lancelot in a deep, strong voice.

"Ahoy?" repeated Raven, frowning. "We're nowhere near the water."

"We're in a sea of grass," replied Sir Lancelot, "and besides, I couldn't think of another greeting on the spur of the moment." His horse cantered up to them and came to a halt some twenty feet away. "Hello, Pellinore. May I assume you're apprenticing to learn dark, evil, deceitful ways from Mordred?"

"Certainly," answered Pellinore as Raven glared at him. Then he smiled. "You'd be wrong, but assume any damned thing you want. What brings you out this way, Lancelot?"

"Guinevere," said Sir Lancelot.

"She's around?" asked Raven, scanning the grassy plain.

"God, I hope not!" said Sir Lancelot. "That woman simply will not stop throwing herself at me. Any day now Arthur is going to have the rest of the Round Table cut me into fish bait!"

"I was told that Guinevere was beautiful and stately and brilliant and charming and everything one could want in a woman," said Raven.

"She is all of that, and more," agreed Sir Lancelot.

"Well, then?" asked Raven.

"You have said it yourself," replied Sir Lancelot. "She is everything one could want in a woman."

"Then I don't understand," said Raven, frowning.

Sir Lancelot's expression softened and became almost beatific. "Sir Gawain is everything one could want in a man."

"Suddenly everything is making sense," said Sir Pellinore.

"*She's* married," continued Sir Lancelot. "*He's* not. It would be immoral to pursue her, let alone distasteful."

"So *she* pursues *you*," said Sir Pellinore.

"'Am I not beautiful?' she asks, and of course I say that she is. 'And well-mannered, and sweet, and thoughtful, and considerate, and a fabulous cook on those rare occasions I visit the kitchen?' and I confirm all of that. 'Then what is it that I am not?' she whispers as she sneaks up and embraces me. And my answer always sends her into paroxysms of rage."

"What is your answer?" asked Sir Pellinore, though Raven would have been happy to offer even money that he knew Lancelot's reply.

"'What you are not,' I tell her regretfully," replied Sir Lancelot, "'is Sir Gawain.'"

"I'm surprised she didn't convince Arthur to have you assassinated," remarked Sir Pellinore.

"I am the greatest warrior in the kingdom," answered Sir Lancelot. He frowned. "She convinced Arthur to have Sir Gawain assassinated." A tear rolled down his cheek. "He barely escaped, and I have been searching for him ever since."

"If we see him, we'll tell him you're looking for him," said Sir Pellinore.

"I have a suggestion," said Raven, who still wasn't sure what kind of reception he could expect from Merlin. "We're on our way to Merlin's castle to seek his wisdom. Surely the greatest wizard in the kingdom can help you locate Sir Gawain." *Or tell you that he's dead,* he added silently.

"That's a splendid suggestion," said Sir Lancelot, "and I'll be happy to join you."

"Good!" said Raven with a sense of relief.

"And the likelihood that the dozens of knights Arthur has sent after me will deduce that I'm on my way to Merlin's castle is no better than fifty-fifty."

Raven suddenly decided that having the greatest warrior in the kingdom accompanying them wasn't necessarily the best of all possible ideas.

23

"One . . . two . . . three . . . four!"

Raven opened his eyes. The sun had barely risen above the horizon. Even the crows were still asleep.

"Oh, my God!" he muttered, shutting his eyes tightly. "It's barely morning."

"One . . . two . . . three . . . four!"

Raven sat up on the grass. "What the hell is going on?" he demanded.

"Ah! Good morning!" said a totally nude Sir Lancelot.

"You're the greatest knight of the Round Table," said Raven. "How the hell did you let someone steal your armor?"

"No one stole anything, Mordred," answered Sir Lancelot with an amused smile.

"Then I repeat: What the hell is going on?"

"I'm doing my morning exercises," answered Sir Lancelot. "I can only do fifty push-ups and run a mile with my armor on, but without it I'm good for five hundred push-ups and three miles without taking a deep breath!" He smiled at Raven. "You should try it some time."

"I don't *want* to be the greatest knight in the kingdom," muttered Raven. He yawned. "I just wish I wasn't the most sleep-deprived." He looked around. "What happened to Sir Pellinore?"

Sir Lancelot pointed off to his left. "He's sleeping behind that log."

"Yeah, I suppose it'll take more than a manly voice scream-ing out numbers to wake you when you're in your nineties," said Raven.

"It's been my observation that people that old cherish every moment of wakefulness they can experience, and sleep only with the greatest reluctance," noted Sir Lancelot. "Of course, very few of them need their energy to go after the Questin' Beast."

"Does it really exist?"

"Certainly. Why should you doubt it?"

"Near as I can figure it, he hasn't even seen the damned thing in thirty or forty years," answered Raven. "That's a lot of beast to take on faith."

"The second he stops believing in it and searching for it, *it* will find *him*," said Sir Lancelot. "You know the way things work around here, Mordred."

"Sometimes I forget," said Raven.

"That's probably why you make so many enemies and near-fatal mistakes," said Sir Lancelot knowingly.

Suddenly there was a flurry of action behind what Raven now thought of as Sir Pellinore's log.

"Take *that*, you foul creature!" cried the old man's voice. "And *that*! And don't you dare beg for mercy, for you've long since used up my supply of it."

Raven and Sir Lancelot exchanged glances, and both began walking over to the log, where they found Sir Pellinore, still sound asleep, with a small limb in his hand, wielding it like a longsword.

"Don't beg!" yelled Sir Pellinore. "I hate it when you beg!"

"Sir Pellinore!" said Raven. "Wake up!"

"Reinforcements won't save you!" cried Sir Pellinore, swinging the branch in a wide arc.

"Is he often like this in the morning?" asked Raven.

"I really couldn't say," answered Sir Lancelot. "I've never gone hunting with him."

Raven put his foot down on Sir Pellinore's hand, preventing him from rolling over and swinging the branch again.

"Get off my arm!" yelled Sir Pellinore. "Questin' Beasts don't have enough brainpower to stand on a man's sword arm."

"Good morning, Sir Pellinore," said Raven.

The old man opened his eyes and looked above him. "Mordred, you've changed," he said with a frown. "Suddenly you look exactly like Sir Lancelot."

"I *am* Lancelot," was the answer. "Mordred is the one standing on your arm."

Raven took a couple of steps back. "Are you awake now?"

Sir Pellinore surveyed his surroundings from right to left. "No Questin' Beast," he said unhappily. "Yes, I guess I'm awake."

"Then let's grab some breakfast and be on our way," said Raven.

"You two eat," said Sir Lancelot. "I've still got to do the rest of my exercises and my three-mile run."

"You sure you can't skip it until we reach Merlin's castle?" asked Raven.

Sir Lancelot shook his head. "Gawain would never forgive me."

"Stern taskmaster, is he?" said Raven.

"He's not any kind of a taskmaster," answered Sir Lancelot.

"Then why—?"

"Because it sounds better than saying Gawain would never touch me," said Sir Lancelot.

"Sorry I asked," said Raven.

"So am I," agreed Sir Lancelot.

They helped the elderly knight to his feet, went searching for his horse when he couldn't remember where he'd tethered it, found it attached to a tree about a quarter mile distant, and brought it back.

"Well, I'm famished!" announced Sir Pellinore. "What's for breakfast?"

"Didn't you bring any?" asked Raven.

"A knight lives off the land," replied Sir Pellinore with dignity.

"The land looks pretty barren," remarked Raven.

"Well, in truth, usually a few leaves and some tree bark will suffice," admitted Sir Pellinore. Suddenly he smiled. "Or sometimes sunflowers, depending on the time of year."

"That's hardly enough for a knight in training," said Sir Lancelot with a frown.

Or even a New Yorker just trying to get home, added Raven mentally.

"Stop staring at me!" snapped Sir Pellinore. "I'm a knight, not a chef, damn it!"

Raven looked around. "Which tastes less awful, the grass or the leaves?"

"Knights of the Round Table don't eat green things," stated Sir Lancelot firmly.

"Certainly they do," said Sir Pellinore. "It hasn't been *that* long since I've dined at Arthur's castle, and I fondly remember the wonderful cabbage and those exquisite brussels sprouts, and—"

"We don't eat *unprepared* green things," amended Sir Lancelot. He gazed off in the distance, and suddenly tensed. "Wait here!"

"What is it?" asked Sir Pellinore.

"A wild boar, half a mile off to the right. Now *that's* a proper breakfast for a knight!"

He took a couple of steps in the boar's direction.

"Don't you want your horse?" asked Raven. "Or your armor?" Pause. "Or even your clothes?"

"I haven't done my morning roadwork yet," replied Sir Lancelot, breaking into a run.

"Of course he hasn't done any roadwork," said Sir Pellinore as he and Raven watched the knight race off. "There isn't a road within miles of here."

"That's a lot of running," mused Raven. "I can't help but feel sorry for him."

"Feel sorry for the boar," said Sir Pellinore. "Lancelot is probably going to be in a grouchy mood by the time he catches him."

Good mood or poor, Sir Lancelot caught the boar within eight minutes, considered strangling him, decided his companions were too hungry to wait, ran him through with his sword, hefted the three-hundred-pound corpse onto his shoulders, and jogged back, laying it at Sir Pellinore's feet.

"I caught him," he said. "You cook him."

"Why bother?" said Sir Pellinore, opening the hide and cutting off a slice of the boar's flank. "It's a warm, pleasant day and he was a warm-blooded animal. Why burn a perfectly good meal?"

Sir Lancelot shrugged. "Man's got a point." He buried his fingers in the boar, brought them together, and pulled out a chunk.

Raven was torn between eating the raw boar or trying a handful of grass, but decided on the boar since the grass wasn't cooked either.

"Not bad at all," remarked Sir Lancelot after swallowing a couple of mouthfuls. "I may start eating all my meat like this."

"I've tasted Guinevere's cooking," replied Sir Pellinore. "In truth, there's not much difference."

"Certainly there is," said Sir Lancelot. He patted the boar's corpse. "This meat isn't burned to a crisp and smothered with foul-smelling spices."

The mention of Guinevere reminded Raven that he still hadn't encountered Lisa, or whatever character Lisa had become in Camelot. He was sure he'd find her in this world, and he was dead certain that she was a major character—after all, Ilsa and Dorothy were clearly the most important females in Casablanca and Oz—so it made sense that she must be Guinevere.

Raven frowned. If she was Guinevere, then perhaps he *wouldn't* encounter her in Camelot, at least not if Merlin could give him the key to returning home. But he couldn't leave her behind, not even as the queen of all she surveyed, which wasn't all that much for a twenty-first-century Manhattan woman.

So should he go to Arthur's castle first? And if he did, and survived, was he supposed to wait there until Merlin showed up, if indeed he ever did? Or could Merlin transfer Lisa back to Manhattan even from as far away as Arthur's castle, which was just a brief stretch of the legs compared to transferring them both to New York.

"Well?" said Sir Pellinore, interrupting Raven's train of thought.

"Well what?" he replied irritably.

"We've been waiting for twenty minutes while you went into some kind of trance," said the old knight. "I'd warn you that your food was getting cold, but that seems somehow counterproductive given the current circumstances. So instead let me simply ask if you're ready to proceed?"

"Yes," said Raven, tossing what was left of his handful of meat onto the ground. "Let's go."

Sir Lancelot donned his clothes and armor, the three men began walking, and Raven took the opportunity to ask some questions about Camelot.

"Tell me about the Round Table," he began.

"It's more oblong," admitted Sir Lancelot. "But Knights of the Oblong Table just doesn't roll off the tongue, if you see what I mean."

He paused. "It may be some time before I see it again."

"Why?"

"Arthur is insanely jealous," replied Sir Lancelot.

"But you left Guinevere and the castle behind," said Raven, frowning.

"It's enough that Guinevere keeps throwing herself at me," answered Sir Lancelot. "The fact that I repulse her advances doesn't seem to count for as much as the fact that I advance her pulses."

"But that's ridiculous!" said Raven.

"Go tell Arthur and that yenta he married."

"Yenta?" repeated Raven. "Where did you ever learn a word like that in Camelot?"

"Merlin studies the ancient grimoires from distant lands, and of all the magical words in the world, that was the one he felt best describes Guinevere. Truth to tell, I don't even know what it means."

Raven tried to remember what little he'd read about Sir Lancelot and Camelot in the past. Finally one incident came to mind.

"Have you fought against the Black Knight yet?"

"No," replied Sir Lancelot.

"But he keeps challenging you," said Sir Pellinore.

"That's because everyone knows I'm the greatest of the knights," answered Sir Lancelot. "But I truly hope it doesn't come to that."

"Why not?" asked Raven curiously.

"I don't mind that he's black, and I don't mind that he wants to prove himself," said Sir Lancelot. "I just don't know why he has to do it in mortal combat against me."

"He's black?" said Raven, surprised. "I thought it was just the color of his armor."

"Maybe it is," answered Sir Lancelot. "I've never seen him without the armor, so I don't know. But why should I let him kill me just to prove he's good enough to be a Knight of the Round Table or whatever he wants to be, and why should I kill someone I don't know just because he has delusions of grandeur?"

"You know," said Raven, "you're almost too reasonable to be a knight."

"There's always a chance that Gawain and I will cast our armor aside and go live barefoot and bare-everything-else in the mountains."

"There are mountains?" said Sir Pellinore, surprised.

"Somewhere," answered Sir Lancelot. "With a little luck we'll find them before a war or a tournament or a sex-crazed queen finds me." He turned to Raven. "But first, we must accompany Mordred to Merlin's castle so that he can solve his own problem." He smiled at Sir Pellinore. "His problems are more immediate, while I can guarantee that your Questin' Beast and my romantic entanglements aren't going anywhere anytime soon."

And so saying, the three men and their steeds began walking toward Merlin's castle.

24

It was midafternoon when Sir Lancelot came to a halt and peered off to his left.

"What ho?" he murmured.

"Ho?" said Sir Pellinore, frowning. "It's a kind of laugh, I think."

"Except in certain parts of Manhattan," added Raven, trying to see what Sir Lancelot was looking at.

"Try not to understand me so fast," said Sir Lancelot. He frowned, and then smiled. "Yes, by God, I do believe it is!"

"Is what?" asked Sir Pellinore.

"Gawain," answered Sir Lancelot. "The dear boy has come looking for me." He turned to his companions. "I have to desert you in the middle of your quest, but in truth we're only an hour or two away from Merlin's castle. Just keep walking in this direction until you come to a small river, then turn left and follow it and it will take you right to the castle."

"Have you any message for him?" asked Sir Pellinore.

"I was never on my way to see him," said Sir Lancelot. "Give him my regards and regrets, but I must be on my way."

And so saying, he mounted his horse and began galloping off in Gawain's direction.

"I hope it *is* Gawain," remarked Sir Pellinore. "Anyone else could die of heart failure just at the sight of our greatest knight bearing down on him."

"Well, let's continue on our way," said Raven. "The sooner we get there, the sooner we can relax and hopefully count on Merlin's hospitality for dinner and perhaps a little something to drink."

"True," agreed Sir Pellinore. "And if he withholds it, at least we'll have an hour of daylight to hunt up a meal somewhere."

They continued on, and after a few minutes Raven turned to Sir Pellinore. "As long as I'm the one who wants to see him, maybe you could tell me a little something about what he's like."

"Wizardly," was the answer.

"Anything a little more specific?" said Raven.

"Very absorbed in his work," replied Sir Pellinore. "Oh . . . and a bit cranky."

"Cranky?"

Sir Pellinore nodded. "And forgetful."

"Of what?"

"Mostly of things."

"Thanks a lot," said Raven.

"Oh—and try not to pay much attention to his pets."

"Very demanding, are they?" asked Raven.

"They're very a lot of things," confirmed Sir Pellinore. "And whatever you do, don't pet one."

"He's that jealous?"

Sir Pellinore shook his head. "He'd love to have you pet them."

"Then I don't understand," said Raven.

"Believe me, you don't want one of them following you home. Or anywhere else, for that matter."

"You make his castle sound as formidable as he himself is," remarked Raven.

"Well, he did build it himself," answered Sir Pellinore.

Raven frowned. "Brick by brick?"

"Spell by spell."

"Is he a young man, or middle-aged, or—?"

"No, he's quite old," answered Pellinore. "He probably wasn't here when God was creating the Earth, but it's said that he played cards with Moses and Ramses, neither of whom ever spoke to him again."

Raven frowned. "I think I was happier when I didn't know anything at all about him."

Sir Pellinore nodded his agreement. "Most people are." He grimaced. "Especially those who have met him."

Raven decided that the less he knew about Merlin, the less uncomfortable he would be about meeting the mage, so he stopped asking questions and just walked in silence. The terrain became a bit more rolling after another forty-five minutes, and then they came to the river and turned left—and after thirty more minutes they could see the castle in the distance.

"Well, there it is," said Sir Pellinore. "What do you think of it?"

"Reminds me of covers for *Weird Tales* and some of the other horror magazines I've seen reproductions of," answered Raven. "And he actually lives there?"

"Absolutely."

"Well, let's go knock on the front door."

"Uh . . . it's not quite that easy," said Sir Pellinore. "When we get a little closer you'll see the moat."

"Filled with moat monsters?" asked Raven uneasily.

"Filled with *something*," answered Sir Pellinore. "It varies from day to day." He paused thoughtfully. "Sometimes from hour to hour."

"Why does anyone ever visit him?"

"For the same reason you're here," said Sir Pellinore. "You have a problem. Only the Master Mage has the solution."

"You know," said Raven, "I've been so intent on getting here I never thought to ask: Does he want payment for his services?"

"Do you have any money with you?"

"No," replied Raven.

Sir Pellinore smiled. "Then it doesn't really matter, does it?"

Raven shrugged. "I don't know. He might want an arm or a leg, or a decade of servitude, or—"

"Hush!" said Sir Pellinore. "He might be listening. No sense giving him any ideas."

Raven nodded his head, fell silent, and continued walking. Suddenly Sir Pellinore came to a stop.

"What is it?" asked Raven.

"Champion—my horse," answered Sir Pellinore. "Suddenly he remembers this place. He doesn't want to go another step."

"So tie him to a tree, and give him enough slack to graze," said Raven. "I have a feeling if you just turn him loose he may go all the way back to Arthur's castle."

"A telling point," agreed Sir Pellinore. "Will fifty yards be enough, do you think?"

"Plenty," said Raven.

Sir Pellinore reached into a saddlebag, withdrew a long rope, tied one end to a tree and the other to the horse's bridle.

"If we stay overnight, I'll have to come back in the morning and lead him to the river to drink."

"I find that encouraging," said Raven.

Sir Pellinore frowned. "Encouraging?"

"That we expect to be alive in the morning."

"I said I expect to live through the night," said Sir Pellinore. "I don't believe I mentioned you."

"Thanks a heap," said Raven. "Let's start walking."

When they were still fifty yards from the river, an owl took off from a nearby tree and flew low over their heads.

"Beware all who would enter the castle of Merlin!" it cried. "Things unimaginable await you!"

"Nonsense!" said Sir Pellinore. "They may be hideous, but I can imagine all of them."

"Fool!" cried the owl. "Poor doomed fool!"

"Not quite a welcome mat," muttered Raven.

"It's just to frighten salesmen away," said Sir Pellinore.

"I'll bet it works," said Raven.

"On humans," agreed Sir Pellinore. "But you haven't seen some of our salesmen. Or should I say, sales*things*?"

They reached the water in another minute.

"I don't see a drawbridge," said Raven. "Or a boat, for that matter."

"Those are for *normal* moats," explained Sir Pellinore.

"What does *this* castle use?"

"It varies," answered the ancient knight. "I'm sure all will be made clear once Merlin has had his fun."

"His fun?" asked Raven nervously.

Before Sir Pellinore could answer, a huge green creature broke through the surface of the moat and stared at them.

"Who goes there?" it demanded.

"Mordred and Sir Pellinore," answered the knight.

"And for what foul purpose?"

"We come as friends, of course," said Sir Pellinore. "And *he*," he added, indicating Raven, "is a supplicant."

"Why should I believe you, rather than kill and eat you right now?" said the creature, baring its enormous fangs.

"Give me that," said Raven softly, taking Sir Pellinore's sword from him. "Now you listen to me, Plug Ugly," he said, raising his voice and facing the creature. "It's obvious that Merlin is watching every second of this meeting, and if he's half the wizard he's supposed to be, he knows we're telling the truth, and he's just using you to amuse himself. I'm not impressed with either of you, and if you make one more threat or insinuation, I'm going to wade right into the moat, cut your ugly head off, and practice kicking field goals with it."

"No! Don't hurt me!" screamed the creature, tears streaming out of its eyes as it backed away. "No more threats, I promise!"

"What's a field goal?" asked another voice.

"Invite us in and I'll explain," replied Raven.

"Why are you here, Mordred?" demanded a highly cultured voice, which he assumed was Merlin's. "We don't even like each other."

"I'm here to pick your brain."

"Sounds painful," said Merlin.

"Just an expression," said Raven. "I am here as a supplicant, seeking knowledge that only you can supply."

"That's more like it," said Merlin's voice approvingly. "And what about the old geezer?"

"Sir Pellinore has been my guide and companion."

"You trust *him* to guide you?" said Merlin with a chuckle.

"He got me here, didn't he?" said Raven.

"Damn, you're right," admitted Merlin. A pause. "I just hate it when other people are right."

"So are you going to let us in now?"

"You and Pellinore, yes," said Merlin. "The horse, no. It takes forever to clean the carpets. Leave him where he's tethered."

"Deal," said Raven. "Now what?"

"Follow the silver."

Raven looked around. "The silver *what*?"

Sir Pellinore tapped him on the shoulder and then pointed to the moat, where a five-foot-wide strip of the water had turned a very bright silver.

"We walk across that?" asked Raven.

"It's wide enough, and it's a straight line," said Sir Pellinore.

"But it's still water," complained Raven.

"Am I not Merlin?" demanded Merlin's voice.

"Okay," said Raven. "But bring the green creature over."

"Why?" asked Merlin.

"Because if I drown, I'm not dying alone."

"Age has improved you, Mordred," said Merlin. "I almost like you."

"Remember that when I get to the castle and start asking questions," said Raven.

"We'll see," said Merlin. "Getting across the moat is one thing. Actually entering the castle is quite another." Pause. "Would it distress you if I were to give vent to a sinister cackle?"

"I don't know," said Raven. "Would it distress you if I killed all your moat monsters and then turned around and went home?"

"Do you remember that I said I almost liked you?" asked Merlin.

"It wasn't that long ago," answered Raven.

"Well, forget it."

"I'll do my best. Now can we start walking across the moat?"

"You always could," replied Merlin. "But now you can do it safely." The green creature surfaced a few feet away. "And here's my favorite moat monster, as per your request."

Raven turned to Sir Pellinore. "You ready?"

Sir Pellinore tentatively reached a foot out to the silver strip of water, found that it was solid despite its shimmering appearance, and began walking. Raven fell into step behind him. The creature opened its mouth wide, but Raven couldn't tell whether it was a smile or a yawn.

"Once you reach the other side of the moat," said Merlin, "walk straight to the iron gate, pay no attention to the dragon, and don't pet the snakes atop the gorgon's head."

"I'll try to control myself," answered Raven.

"Just as well we left the horse behind," said Sir Pellinore. "I remember that dragon. He could eat a bigger steed than mine in one gulp."

"By the way," said Merlin, "do you have any books with you?"

"No," replied Raven.

"I don't mean grimoires or the like," said Merlin. "I read anything." There was a pause. "I still haven't read one Jane Austen novel—*Mansfield Park*."

"She won't be born for another thousand years," said Raven, frowning. "Maybe longer."

"What is that to the greatest mage in history?" Merlin shot back.

"I wish I'd had you with me the last couple of times I went to Belmont Park," said Raven.

Then they were at the castle, and after resisting the nonexistent urge to pet the dragon or fondle the snakes, he and Sir Pellinore passed through the doorway and began walking into the mysterious interior of the magical castle of Merlin the Magnificent.

25

"Looks much bigger from the inside," said Raven, trying to make out the ceiling a couple hundred feet above them.

"The size varies, according to my mood," replied Merlin's voice.

"And what is your mood right now?"

"Expansive," answered Merlin.

"Okay, which way do we go?" asked Raven.

"Makes no difference," said Merlin. "All roads lead to me."

"Do any of them pass by the kitchen?" asked Sir Pellinore. "My appetite is returning, now that I realize we're going to live."

"Have I said that?" growled Merlin.

"Now that I realize we're probably going to live," amended Sir Pellinore.

They walked ahead for another hundred feet, then found their way blocked by a wall of ancient books.

"What now?" said Raven.

"Are you not thrilled and mystified and fascinated?" said Merlin.

"By a bunch of books?"

"You say that as if they're common objects."

"Where I come from, they are," said Raven.

"You come from Camelot, Mordred," said Merlin sternly.

"Where I've been, then."

"Really? And you can read?"

"Of course I can read."

"That makes two of us in the entire kingdom," said Merlin. "No, make that three. I forgot that Arthur can read some of the printing on that damned sword of his."

"I hope I'm not required to read my way past this damned wall," said Raven.

Suddenly he was confronted by a tall, slender man with a long white beard, a beautifully embroidered robe, a tall conical hat with the figures of the zodiac on it, and a wand in his left hand. He brought the wand up to his mouth, the top of it morphed into a lollipop, he licked it, and it became a wand again.

"You're Merlin, of course," said Raven.

"Who else would I be?" replied the bearded mage.

"It's Merlin, all right," said Sir Pellinore. "I can tell by the wart at the tip of his nose."

"The castle, the dragon, the magic spells, they don't convince you, but you know I'm Merlin because of a facial blemish," said the magician severely. "I'm starting to remember why I don't like you very much."

"No offense meant," said Sir Pellinore hastily.

"I hate to think of how obnoxious you can be when you *do* mean to offend," said Merlin. He turned to Raven. "But back to you and literature, Mordred. Do you think he was crazy?"

"Do I think *who* was crazy?" asked Raven, puzzled.

"Captain Queeg, of course."

"I can only offer an opinion based on the movie."

Merlin shook his head. "I'd ask what a movie is, but I'm afraid you might tell me. Maybe we should discuss the bird instead?"

"The bird?"

Merlin nodded. "Right. I've still got a chapter or two to go. Do you think it will wind up with the fat man or the broad? Or does Sam Spade dope it out and get it back?"

"Telling you would spoil it for you," replied Raven.

"Hah!" said Merlin. "I *knew* you didn't know."

"I most certainly do," replied Raven.

"Rubbish!"

"None of them wind up with it," said Raven. "It's a phony—and Sam Spade sends the girl over for killing his partner."

"Arrrgh!" screamed Merlin.

"Is something wrong?" asked Raven. "You sound like you're in agony."

"You ruined it for me!" whined Merlin. "Now there's no sense finishing the damned book."

"You *did* ask."

"Only because I was sure you'd never read it!" growled Merlin. "I was just showing off."

"Look," said Raven, "we don't have to discuss books at all. We could address my problem instead."

"We'll get to it," said Merlin. "But you're the first person I've been able to discuss literature with in centuries."

"But my answer seems to have distressed you."

"From this point on I'll only discuss books I've finished," said Merlin.

"But *then* we discuss my problem?"

"Absolutely, probably," answered Merlin.

"What the hell does that mean?" asked Raven.

"It means if neither of us dies of old age before the book discussion is over."

"Forget it," said Raven. "We talk books for one hour. Then we discuss my reason for coming here."

"I suppose so; it's better than nothing," said Merlin. "I agree."

"Okay, go ahead."

"Where to start, where to start?" muttered Merlin. "Sometimes it's difficult, having 37,409,574 facts in my head." He grimaced. "For example, I can tell you with absolute certainty who's going to win the 2134 Super Bowl."

"Really?"

Merlin nodded. "Definitely." Suddenly he frowned. "But for the life of me, I can't tell you what a Super Bowl *is*."

"Must be awkward at times," said Raven, against his will feeling some sympathy for the old wizard.

"You've no idea," muttered Merlin. He was silent for a moment. "You're sure you don't have a copy of *Mansfield Park* with you?"

"Afraid not."

"I suppose it wouldn't answer the question I've been puzzling over all day."

"What is that?" asked Raven.

"Romeo and Juliet are a pair of well-spoken but shallow teenagers who know each other for less than a week before they die. Why is *that* his most popular play?"

"Beats me," admitted Raven, whose notion of high theatrical art leaned more toward musical comedies with lots of dancing girls.

"Ah, well, let's get on to *real* literature."

More real than Shakespeare? thought Raven, but kept his mouth shut.

"Poetry," explained Merlin. "The highest literary art form. And there is one particular poem I've been wanting to analyze for years. In fact, it was when I got a little tipsy and tried discussing it at a banquet that Arthur banned me from his castle and made me live out here amid the birds and the flowers and all of Nature's other disgusting creations."

"And what poem was that?"

"How thoughtful of you to ask," said Merlin. "It is Mallory's *Le Morte d'Arthur*."

"*The Death of Arthur,*" said Sir Pellinore. "I can see why he might not have been too thrilled with it."

"An understatement," said Merlin, and promptly began a scholarly analysis of the poem.

It was quite some time later that he paused for breath.

"I think your hour's up," said Raven.

"It feels more like five minutes," complained Merlin.

"It's been an hour, maybe more."

"But I was just getting to the good parts," whined Merlin. "The parts about *me*."

"Next time."

The ancient mage shrugged. "All right—fair is fair. What did you want, Mordred? A spell to entice that gorgeous cook in Arthur's kitchen? A sure tip on the pending battle between Sir Lancelot and the Black Knight? Just name it."

"I was cast here from my own land by a magic spell," said Raven. "I need a spell or at least some mechanism to get back."

"And that is your request?"

"Partially."

Merlin frowned. "Partially?"

"There is every chance that the woman I love is here too, but under a different guise." He paused. "You see, I appear to you as Mordred, but in my own world I am Eddie Raven. If she's here, and I suspect that she is, she will appear as someone you're all used to, just as I do—but *I* will recognize and know her as Lisa, and of course I want to take her back with me."

"That's quite a request," said Merlin.

"You're said to be quite a wizard," replied Raven.

"There are only two master magicians in all of Camelot, and you're talking to the best of them," said Merlin.

"That's why I'm here," said Raven. "So . . . how do I get back? Is there some incantation, some particular spot I have to go to, or what?"

"I'll need some time to work on it," said Merlin. "After all, I need to determine not only *where* to send you, but *when*."

"And with whom," added Sir Pellinore. They both turned to him. "I know, I had my eyes closed, but I was listening, not sleeping." He paused. "Well, not entirely. Not during the good parts of the poem, or when Mordred was explaining his problem."

"I shall retire to my quarters to think about it," announced Merlin, "and will surely have an answer for you in the morning, Buzzard."

"Raven."

Merlin shrugged. "Whichever." He turned and began walking into the darkened interior of the castle. "I strongly recommend you two stay here. Wander too far into the dark, and you may never find your way out, always assuming you make it through the night uneaten."

His voice became weaker, and soon he was out of both sight and earshot.

"I hope he can help me," remarked Raven, sitting down on a large, not very comfortable, wood chair.

"So do I," said Sir Pellinore. "Because if he can't . . ."

"I'm stuck here forever?"

"Probably not," said Sir Pellinore. "But the only other master of magic with the skills to return you to your time and place is Morgan le Fay, and you don't want to deal with her."

"Morgan le Fay," repeated Raven. "Yeah, I think I remember reading about her. Is she any good at her craft?"

"Her skills are unquestioned," replied Sir Pellinore. "But while Merlin might charge you an arm and a leg for his services, she'll charge you that same arm and leg, and see to it that they toil in her service for the next half century."

"Then let's hope that Merlin can dope out the proper spell," said Raven.

"He's pretty good," agreed Sir Pellinore. "And when all is said and done, Atlantis probably wasn't his fault." He paused thoughtfully. "Well, at least, not entirely."

26

They were up with the sun, and as they were wandering around, trying to find the kitchen, Merlin suddenly materialized out of empty air.

"Good morning," said the mage. "Well, as good as it can be when the sun is still in the eastern half of the sky."

"Have you solved my problem?" asked Raven eagerly.

"Not entirely," replied Merlin. "I came up with three spells that will transfer you to other worlds, but I suspect none of them is the right one."

"You're sure?"

Merlin frowned. "Do you live in a chartreuse and mauve world peopled by talking dinosaurs?"

"No."

"Or one with seventeen human sexes, none of which are women?"

"No," said Raven.

"I'll bet Sir Lancelot would like it," added Sir Pellinore.

"I thought not," said Merlin. "Well, I shall keep trying."

"What about the third world?" asked Raven.

"Don't ask."

"I've got to," said Raven.

Merlin sighed deeply. "It was populated by a few million versions of myself," he said, frowning. "Every one of them better looking and more powerful."

"So what do I do now?"

"I'm still working on it," answered Merlin. "You mentioned that the two of you wanted to go to Arthur's castle. I happen to have some business there, so why don't I just transport us?"

"And Champion," said Sir Pellinore.

"Champion?" asked Merlin, frowning in puzzlement.

"My noble steed."

"You mean your rickety used-up old horse?" said Merlin.

"He who insults my horse dies!" yelled Sir Pellinore, his hand moving to the handle of his sword. He jerked it a couple of times, but nothing happened. "Damned thing's stuck!" he muttered.

"How fortunate for me," said Merlin. "I'd have gone crazy trying to decide which of the best three thousand spells to use on you had you actually pulled the damned thing out of the scabbard."

"Well, I can't present myself at court with a sword that won't come out," said Sir Pellinore. "If I promise not to use it on you—this time, at least—will you magic it out for me?"

"Certainly," said Merlin. He pointed a bony forefinger at the sword and muttered a chant in ancient Aramaic.

"Thank you," said Sir Pellinore, sliding the sword out of its scabbard. Suddenly he looked down at it and frowned, as it began writhing and hissing. "Uh . . . Merlin?"

"Boy, some people are never happy," muttered Merlin. He uttered a brief spell in Swahili, and the snake became a sword again. "You could have done your enemies much more damage if I hadn't changed it back."

"To say nothing of my friends," said Sir Pellinore.

"Well, yes, there *is* that," admitted Merlin. "Shall we go?"

"How about some breakfast first?" said Sir Pellinore.

"That's not a bad idea," said Merlin. He reached into the air, snapped his fingers, and suddenly was holding a small crystal globe on his hand. "Here—catch!" he said, tossing it toward Sir Pellinore. It had become a ripe cantaloupe before it reached him.

The magician turned to Raven. "How about you?"

"I'll have some eggs Benedict," said Raven, wondering how the magician would first conjure and then deliver it.

Merlin made a mystic sign, suddenly had a pair of chimera eggs in his left hand, and tossed them to Raven. "Here you go—and my name's Merlin, not Benedict."

The eggshells broke as Raven caught them. "I guess I'm not that hungry after all," he said, looking for something to wipe his hands with.

The magician uttered a brief chant, and suddenly Raven had a damp towel in his hands.

"We might as well go," he said after cleaning his hands off.

"Fine," said Merlin. "Follow me." He headed off in the direction of a thick wall.

"But the door's *that* way," said Raven.

"Only when I will it to be," answered Merlin. He uttered another brief chant, and suddenly the wall vanished just long enough for the three men to pass through to the outside. Merlin then led them to a raft that was tied to a small dock on the castle side of the moat, all three walked aboard it, and then it began hovering some ten feet above the water. Merlin directed it to Champion in still another language, it landed, Sir Pellinore spent a few minutes leading the suspicious horse onto the raft, and then they were aloft again, this time rising to a height of more than a hundred feet.

"I could get used to traveling like this," said Sir Pellinore after they'd been cruising above the ground for an hour. He looked over the edge of the raft and waved to a surprised peasant below him.

"What's that?" asked Raven, pointing to a large, beautifully kept castle in the distance.

"Oh, *that*," said Merlin with a contemptuous sniff. "It's Morgan's, of course. She is *such* a show-off. Every window sparkling clean, every flower in bloom, no shrub out of place."

"Morgan le Fay?" asked Raven.

"She's as fey as they come," growled Merlin. "Now let's talk about something enjoyable, like war or torture."

"Um . . . I hate to interrupt," said Sir Pellinore, "especially when you're about to discuss such delightful topics, but . . ."

"But?" said Merlin.

"I know it's a beautiful day, and the sun is shining down upon us," he said uneasily. "But . . ."

"But *what*?" demanded Merlin.

"But I'm freezing!"

Merlin chuckled. "Of course you're freezing! You're traveling into the wind wearing nothing but your underwear."

"Damn!" said Sir Pellinore. "I never thought of that. I took my armor off to make it easier for Champion, and I never donned it again. I don't even remember where I left it."

"I'll magic up a new set for you before we land," said Merlin.

"How soon will we get there?"

"Maybe another hour."

"Uh . . . not to complain or nag," said Sir Pellinore, "but I could use it right now. I'm afraid to look, but I have a feeling my extremities are turning blue."

"Not a problem," said Merlin. He snapped his fingers. "Presto!"

"I'm still freezing," complained Sir Pellinore. He tried to say something more, but was drowned out by the enormous oof from the surprised Champion.

"Uh . . . Merlin," began Raven, blinking his eyes rapidly to make sure that he wasn't imagining a shining set of silver armor covering every inch of the horse from head to tail.

"Oops!" muttered Merlin. Two quick spells denuded the horse and dressed Sir Pellinore in a truly impressive suit of armor. "Better?" asked the mage.

"Much," said Sir Pellinore, and Champion seemed to nod his head in agreement. "Thank you, Merlin."

"The day will come when you'll render me a service in return," said the magician.

"Me?" said Sir Pellinore, surprised. "What service could I possibly render to the greatest mage in the world?"

"I've always wondered what Questin' Beast flank tastes like," came the answer.

"Then it shall be yours, just as soon as I catch it!" promised Sir Pellinore.

"Good. I wasn't in a hurry anyway."

Raven looked down as more cultivated land began appearing, and after a few minutes he saw a magnificent castle in the distance.

"Arthur's?" he asked.

Merlin nodded. "Arthur and those endless knights of his. Ten or twelve I could understand, but he's up past forty now. Noisiest banquet table you've ever encountered."

"Well, he'll be minus Lancelot and Gawain, and of course Sir Pellinore won't rejoin him permanently until he catches the Questin' Beast," said Raven.

"Or it dies of old age," added Merlin. "And it's *still* a confusing place to eat and live." He shook his head sadly. "There are so many plots against the throne."

"Jealous, ambitious knights, I presume," said Raven.

Merlin shook his head. "A jealous and ambitious queen."

Raven shook his head. "There must be some other explanation. Lisa's simply not like that."

"There is no other explanation," replied Merlin. "And her name is Guinevere."

"I want to talk to her."

"That shouldn't be a problem," said Merlin.

"Oh?"

"You're a man. I'm not aware of any other prerequisite."

"What's Arthur like?"

"Like a king."

"Okay," said Raven. "What's a king like?"

"Like Arthur, of course."

"I've seen everyone from Sean Connery to Richard Burton portray him, plus a bunch of actors who were no longer hanging around by the time I was born, and no two seem to have the same interpretation."

"I know none of these names."

Raven grimaced, then sighed deeply. "At least he doesn't start singing 'Camelot' at the drop of a hat."

"Kings wear crowns, not hats," said Merlin, frowning. "And there's nothing he likes better than to sing, especially after he's had a flagon or two of wine."

"You're not being very helpful," said Raven.

"I am flying you to meet the king and demanding no tribute," replied Merlin. "*I* call that helpful."

Raven nodded his head. "Yes, you're quite right. I apologize."

"Good!" said Merlin. "Still, it would have been amusing."

"What are you talking about?"

"Throwing you over the side of the raft and seeing if you could develop wings before you hit the ground."

"Has anyone?"

"Not during my lifetime," answered Merlin. "Or theirs."

Raven decided it was time for a change of subject. "What's the protocol once we land?"

"We'll enter the castle and I'll introduce you to Arthur," replied Merlin. "I hope the king isn't too distracted. I understand there's all kinds of fuss over some new knight named Galahad, but in the end he probably won't prove to be any more special than the rest of them." He paused. "We'll also get you assigned to some quarters. I think it would be a good idea for you to share them with Sir Pellinore."

"Oh?" said Raven. "Why?"

"He should be just about immune to Guinevere's charms by now," said Merlin.

"Well, I like that!" snapped Sir Pellinore.

"The point is that you *don't* like that," explained Merlin. "At least, not for the last fifty or sixty years."

"Well, when you put it that way . . ." said Sir Pellinore.

"All right," said Merlin. "Any further questions?"

"Just the same one," said Raven. "How soon will you be able to magic me home? Me, and possibly Guinevere?"

"Certainly no more than a day or two," answered Merlin. "Perhaps a week." He paused. "A month at the outside."

So much for dealing with the greatest mage in history, thought Raven bitterly.

"They see us," said Sir Pellinore.

"They're so far away," said Raven. "How can you tell?"

"One of them just fired a flaming arrow at the raft," answered Sir Pellinore. "Barely got halfway high enough, and we're still a few miles distant, but they know we're here."

"And that's the way they greet strangers?" asked Raven, frowning.

"Oh, we're no strangers," said Sir Pellinore. "They have to know that Merlin's aboard and steering this thing."

"Then why shoot a flaming arrow?" persisted Raven.

"Maybe they meant to miss, just as a form of greeting or acknowledging our presence," suggested Sir Pellinore.

"Or maybe it was because of certain romantic promises that were taken somewhat more seriously than they were given," added Merlin with a frown.

"We'll know soon enough," said Sir Pellinore.

"We will?" asked Raven.

The old knight nodded. "If they shoot another as we get closer . . ."

The raft started dropping lower in the sky. "Another five minutes and we'll be on the ground," announced Merlin.

Sir Pellinore stuck his head over the side of the raft. "No more arrows," he announced.

Half a dozen knights on horseback rode out of the castle and formed a circle around where they expected the raft to land.

"Recognize any of them?" asked Raven.

"That's Sir Ector, and over to the left is Sir Gareth, and next to him is Sir Kay, and . . ." The old knight rattled them all off, surprising Raven with his eyesight.

Merlin manipulated the raft with great precision, and it finally touched down in the center of the knights' circle, in the shadow of King Arthur's castle.

"Tell me, Mordred," said Merlin, clearly proud of his piloting, "did you ever think you would come down gently from the sky to land in the very heart of Camelot?"

Raven thought back to his experiences in Casablanca and Oz, as well as walking to Merlin's castle in the company of Sir Lancelot and Sir Pellinore, and replied, "Even the world's greatest magician couldn't picture some of the places I've been and things I've done." He took a deep breath. "Time to do one more."

27

A team of knights in shining armor approached.

"May I request the purpose of your visit, Merlin?" asked the leader.

"I just thought I'd grab an exquisite meal or two, say hello to Arthur, and see if he needs anything magicked," answered the mage.

"And you, Mordred?"

"I wish to speak to the king," replied Raven. "And to the queen as well."

The questioner arched an eyebrow. "The queen?"

"Briefly," said Mordred.

That response brought a number of smiles, and Raven turned to Merlin with a questioning expression.

"Briefly is her specialty," whispered the magician.

"And what about you, Sir Pellinore?" asked the leader.

"I'm just giving the Questin' Beast time to recover from his wounds, compassionate soul that I am." He paused. "Then the hunt is on again."

"Still haven't caught him, have you?" said the leader with a chuckle.

"I notice *you* haven't tried your hand at hunting him down," said Sir Pellinore irritably.

"I hunt down Arthur's *real* enemies," answered the leader. "Who has the Questin' Beast ever harmed?"

"You mean besides the last five kings?" Sir Pellinore shot back.

"Bah!" said the leader. "We have this conversation every time."

"Not so," said Sir Pellinore. "Three times ago we discussed the cute little redheaded cook who had just arrived." He paused. "Well, *you* discussed her. *I* listened, due to my knightly manners."

"Enough!" growled the leader, turning and heading into the palace. "Come with me or not, as you choose."

"All three of us?" asked Raven.

"Unless there are more of you that I'm blissfully unaware of," was the answer.

They proceeded down an impressive hallway, lined on both sides with tapestries portraying prior royalty, and stopped at a doorless empty room.

"Sir Pellinore, you look like you're going to collapse under all that armor," said the leader. "You can change into something rusty and falling apart but more comfortable in here."

"Then what?" asked Sir Pellinore.

"I'll send one of the cooks to escort you to the knights' quarters," said the leader.

"Let me guess," said Sir Pellinore. "The redhead."

"No, this one is gray-haired, wrinkled, stooped over, and toothless," answered the leader. "I remembered how uninterested you were in the redhead."

"Thanks a heap," muttered Sir Pellinore, entering the room.

"Merlin, you know your way around almost as well as Arthur himself does," said the leader. "Why don't you do whatever it is you came to do, as long as it's not nefarious, and I'll take the ugly, traitorous little wart to see Arthur."

"May I assume the library's still in the same location?" asked Merlin.

The leader nodded. "No new grimoires, but a lot of wildly romantic poetry accumulated by the queen, some of it even in book form."

"*Some* of it?" said Merlin, frowning. "What about the rest of it?"

"Missives, letters, notes, all to the queen."

"Ah!" said Merlin, nodding his head. "Figures."

The leader turned to Raven. "All right," he said. "Come with me. And I apologize for the way I described you a moment ago. It just slipped out. Actually, you are physically perfect in every way, and the embodiment of all the noble virtues."

Raven stared at the leader for a long moment. "Are you quite well?" he asked at last.

"If you're not mad," replied the leader.

"Then perhaps you'll explain the praise," said Raven. "Even I know what I look like."

"It's your antecedents," said the leader.

"I don't quite follow you."

"As you know, there have been a number of histories written about Camelot and you are prominently featured in almost all of them."

"I still don't understand," said Raven.

"In some you're just the ugly immoral little traitor you appear to be," explained the leader. "But in some you're Arthur's son, in others his brother, in three or four you actually run off with Guinevere and lead a successful war against Arthur, in one you're even a greater magician than Merlin. And since the definitive history hasn't been written yet, why take chances?"

"Well, I admire your honesty, if not your choice of words," replied Raven. "And while we're at it, which knight are you?"

"Sir Agravaine," was the response.

"You certainly are," said Raven. "Okay, let's go see the king."

"Right," said Sir Agravaine. He paused and stared at Raven. "I suspect he doesn't like you any better."

"If he can help me, he'll never have to see me again."

"You're going to blind him, you sly little traitor?" asked Sir Agravaine with far more curiosity than hostility.

"No, of course not," said Raven. "I'm just trying to get home, and I hope he can help me."

"You've forgotten where you live?"

"Don't understand me so fast," said Raven. He considered explaining his situation, realized he was going to have to do it again for King Arthur and that Sir Agravaine would almost certainly be present, and simply grimaced. "Just take me to Arthur."

"You're the boss," said Sir Agravaine with a shrug. "Well, not really. Arthur's the boss, or on some days it's Guinevere, and word on the street—well, on the dirt walkway—is that Galahad is destined to be the boss. But you're my assignment, so I'll be happy to take you to Arthur. Well, not happy, exactly, but willing. After all, it's my duty, and in all immodesty I'm one of Nature's noblemen, or one of Camelot's, anyway."

"Do you plan to talk for another hour, or do you think we might go visit Arthur now?" asked Raven.

"Right," said Sir Agravaine, finally starting to walk again. "Follow me—and I hope you're either Arthur's son or a greater magician than Merlin, or preferably both."

"Oh?" said Raven, falling into step behind him. "Why?"

"Because I would hate to be serving the self-centered failure you appear to be," answered Sir Agravaine.

"Let's just walk and not speak," said Raven.

"Suits me," said Sir Agravaine. "Maybe if I don't listen to you anymore the urge to run you through with my sword will diminish, at least a bit."

"And maybe I won't turn you into an undersize toad and stomp on you," replied Raven.

"Hah!" said Sir Agravaine triumphantly. "I *knew* it!"

They proceeded in silence, and another ninety seconds found them at a huge, magnificently carved door.

"The throne room," announced Sir Agravaine. "Open up!" he snapped, raising his voice. "I have the intruder with me."

"How thoughtful," commented Raven.

"Well, he did throw you out the last time you tried to usurp the throne," said Sir Agravaine.

"I was probably having a bad hair day," said Raven, stepping through as the door opened.

The throne room was exquisitely paneled, and on the walls hung almost a dozen tapestries of Arthur, one as a child, one a young man, one at his wedding ceremony, one pulling Excalibur out of the stone, others depicting other moments that were central to his life and reign.

Arthur himself sat on a cushion that resided upon an ornate golden throne. He wore no armor, obviously feeling safe in his own castle. His beard, a reddish brown, was beautifully trimmed, and his hair was coiffed to within an inch of its life. He wore a large diamond ring on the small finger of his right hand, and an even more impressive one on the ring finger. He stared at Raven for a long moment, then stood up.

"So, Mordred, what brings you to my castle?"

"Merlin's aerodynamically sound raft," answered Raven.

"Be not clever with me, Mordred," said Arthur. "Why are you here?"

"It's a long story," said Raven.

"Dinner's almost ready," said Arthur. "Shorten it."

Raven emitted a deep sigh. "I am not who you think I am," he began.

"*That's* a relief," said Arthur. "Which of Merlin's creatures are you, and why does he think this is amusing?"

"Don't understand me so fast," said Raven. "I come from another world, or at least a variation of this one, and I am trying to return to the time and place where I belong."

"You mean that?" asked Arthur, leaning forward with interest.

"Absolutely."

"So if I help you get home, I'll never have to see or deal with you again?"

Raven decided not to explain that there was almost certainly one more Mordred wandering about the countryside. "That's right."

"What do you need?" asked Arthur. "Other than the queen, that is."

"I'm not sure."

"Will you know it when you see it?"

Raven decided that if he said no Arthur would either throw

him in prison for wasting the king's time or throw him back into the wilderness, neither of which were acceptable alternatives, so he merely muttered a vigorous "Absolutely!" and was glad he was in a world where his nose didn't grow six or seven inches when he uttered the word.

"How do you plan to search for this undefined something?" asked Arthur.

"I'll just throw myself into court life for a few days, and when I spot it, I'll take my leave of you."

"I don't know," said Arthur, rubbing his chin thoughtfully. "The last four times you threw yourself into court life you left, usually under a black cloud, but like a bad shilling you keep coming back."

"This time I won't."

"I admire your certainty," said Arthur. "So tell me, Mordred, what have you been doing with yourself since last we were together—other than plotting my downfall, that is?"

"Why would I plot your downfall?" asked Raven.

"Why would anyone?" responded Arthur. "For the power and the glory." He paused thoughtfully. "And for the queen, of course."

"Is she around?" asked Raven.

"Aha!" said Arthur with a triumphant smile. "I knew it! You *did* come for her!"

"Not so," said Raven. "But she *is* my queen. I just think it would be proper and fitting to pay my respects."

"That's what they all say," muttered Arthur.

Raven felt a need to change the subject. "So who are you going to war with next?"

"Well, I've conquered, or at least pacified, most of Britain. I suppose the next thing is to look east across the Channel, and go to war with France or Spain or one of those other totally unimportant little kingdoms."

"Uh . . . they're more than unimportant little kingdoms," noted Raven.

"Not when my Knights of the Round Table get done with them," replied Arthur confidently. "We've never lost."

"I admire your confidence," said Raven. "But has it occurred to you that no reigning monarch has ever lost a war?"

Arthur frowned. "I hate it when you bring up facts like that." He glared at Raven. "I'm remembering all the reasons I don't enjoy your company."

"Believe me, I want to go home even more than you want me to."

Arthur shrugged and pointed a lean forefinger. "There's the door." Suddenly he burst out laughing. "There's the door!" he repeated. "Oh, that's a good one! I must remember it and use it again!"

"Hilarious," said Raven without the trace of a smile.

"So where are you living these days?" asked Arthur.

"I've been moving around quite a bit," said Raven truthfully. "But my permanent home is in Manhattan."

"Manhattan?" repeated Arthur, frowning. "That's in northern Scotland, right?"

"Close enough," said Raven, who didn't feel like explaining it.

"Well, I could provide you with an armed guard to get you there," said Arthur. "Or at least to the edge of Camelot."

"I thank you for the offer, but the route I travel can only accommodate one, or at most two."

"Must be very narrow," offered Arthur.

"It's very difficult to find," acknowledged Raven.

"Ask Merlin. He knows everything."

"He can't help," replied Raven.

"Really?" said Arthur, surprised. "Then ask Morgan le Fay. She knows everything he doesn't know."

"I probably will," admitted Raven. "But I thought I might find some answers right here."

"I've already offered you an armed guard."

Raven shook his head. "No, I need to know how to find the proper route, where to enter it."

"Then you want a magician," said Arthur.

"Probably," agreed Raven.

A guard entered the throne room, walked up to Arthur, and whispered in his ear. He nodded, waved the guard away, and got to his feet.

"It seems I have a meeting with this new Sir Galahad before dinner," he announced, walking to the door. "I'll see you at the feast."

"Is there anyplace I should go in the meantime?" asked Raven.

"The throne room's as good a place as any," answered Arthur. He grimaced. "I have this feeling you won't be alone for long."

And with that, he walked out into the corridor.

28

Raven spent a minute walking around the room again, looking at the tapestries on the walls and the artwork on the shining shields beneath them, then decided to sit down and wait for the queen—and since there was only one chair in the room, he seated himself on the throne. There was the pillow he had seen, it was cushioned with leather that somehow looked like wood, it was on a platform a couple of feet above ground level, and it gave him a clear view of all the doors. He decided that one could get very used to sitting there.

Then a door opened, and a woman wearing a golden crown entered. Raven leaned forward, staring intently at her, then grimaced and sat back. Guinevere was definitely not Lisa.

"Hello," she said, approaching him.

"Hello," he replied.

"You look very comfortable and at home on the throne," she said. "Have you killed my husband?"

"Certainly not!"

"Oh," she said with no show of emotion. "It's been awhile, Mordred. How have you fared?"

"I'm still alive," he replied.

"Did you learn much during your wanderings?"

"A bit."

"About women?"

"Almost nothing," he said promptly, having no desire to encourage her.

"What a shame," she said. "Perhaps I should teach you a few things."

"They say ignorance is bliss," replied Raven.

She frowned. "What do they know about bliss?"

Raven stared at her. "So who do you like in the fifth at Aqueduct?" he said.

"What nonsense are you speaking, Mordred?" said Guinevere.

"Just making conversation until dinnertime."

"Arthur is busy talking to the new kid," she said. "He could be an hour."

"Anything's possible," agreed Raven.

"I'm so glad you agree," she said, moving closer to him and laying a hand on his shoulder.

"I misspoke," said Raven. "Some things are impossible."

"Oh?" she said. "What, for example?"

I can't be too blunt. She's royalty too, and with Arthur elsewhere she could summon a guard and have him kill me if I get her mad enough.

"Oh, flying," he said.

"That's not so," she said, drawing even closer to him. "I'm told that *you* flew here."

"Actually, Merlin flew here. I was just a passenger, along with Sir Pellinore and Champion."

Her face lit up. "There's a new knight named Champion?"

"He's Sir Pellinore's horse."

Her face darkened. "That ugly beast? Why, he's almost as old as Pellinore."

"All God's creatures can't be beautiful, your highness," said Raven.

"True," she purred. "And how fortunate for some of you that I don't give a damn."

"Have you read any good books lately?" he asked quickly.

"Certainly not."

"Well, then," he continued, "have you read any exceptionally bad books lately?"

"I have queenly things to do with my time," she said harshly. Suddenly her face and tone softened. "Feminine queenly things," she amended.

"Perhaps you'd better go do some of them before we're called to dinner," said Raven.

"I'm doing some of them," she shot back. "I'm greeting a visitor to the court, and questioning his motives."

"I have no motives," he said.

"I don't know that for a fact," she said. "For all I know, you have a dagger concealed on your person, and are just waiting for the proper moment to plunge it into my heart."

She reached out and began examining him for the dagger.

"I'm unarmed!" he yelled, trying to pull back and realizing that he was already pressed against the throne.

"Perhaps," she said, running her hand down to his waist. "But if you're here to kill Arthur or myself, that's exactly what I'd expect you to say."

"I tell you, I am unarmed!" he said.

"Prove it," said Guinevere.

He frowned. "How?"

"Strip to the buff. Then I'll believe you."

"And if someone comes in, they'll cut my head off," said Raven.

She smiled. "If someone comes in, that's *not* what they'll cut off."

He stared at her, resisted the urge to cover his groin with his hands, and got to his feet.

"I'm hungry now," he said. "Let's go."

"Dinner won't be served until Arthur arrives in the dining hall."

"Then let's go and get good seats now."

"I'm the queen," said Guinevere. "I can sit anywhere I want."

"Well, I feel the urge to stretch my legs, so let's walk over."

"You don't have to be standing to stretch your legs, or all kinds of things," she replied with a grin.

He stared long and hard at her. "Somehow I don't think Ava Gardner quite captured you. And Julie Andrews and Vanessa Redgrave didn't even come close."

"What are you talking about?"

"Oh, nothing," said Raven.

"Then back to the subject at hand," said Guinevere.

"Dinner?"

"Getting to know each other better."

She took a step toward him, and he backed away quickly. As she approached he kept backing away until he came up against the wall. He looked around desperately, and suddenly saw an ornate sword hanging just to his left. He turned, grabbed it, removed it from the wall, and turned to face her.

"That was the sword of Uther Pendragon," said Guinevere.

"Arthur's father, right?" said Raven.

"Yes. Now put it down and come over here."

"I like the heft and feel of it," said Raven.

"It's the sword of a great warrior," she said. "It doesn't become a little wimp like you, Mordred."

"Even little wimps can have an occasional moment of glory," replied Raven. "I wonder what the history books will say if I should run you through with your father-in-law's sword?"

"Stop being silly, come over here, and kiss me!" she demanded. "Time is getting short."

"Time may be short," said Raven, "but this sword is quite long enough." He swung it through the air in a figure eight. "Wouldn't you say so?"

"I am fast losing interest in you, Mordred," she said harshly.

"I'm shattered."

"Last chance," she said. "Put that silly thing down and come to me."

"No, you come to me," said Raven. "Preferably with your neck exposed."

"That's it!" she snapped. "We're going off to dinner!"

"If we must," said Raven, placing the sword back on the wall.

"Would you really have used it?" she asked as they walked to the door.

Beats the hell out of me, thought Raven. Aloud, still aware of her proximity, he said, "Only if I had to."

"Let's go, then," she said, walking out into the corridor. "Is there anyone you'd like me to foist you off on . . . um, introduce you to? It's the least I can do to thank you for sparing my life, or at least the embarrassment of calling for help?"

"Well, there's one person I'd like to meet."

"Oh?" said Guinevere. "Who?"

"Morgan le Fay."

She frowned. "You'd really rather be with that ugly little—?"

"It's a weakness of mine," said Raven. "I love stabbing women."

Her eyes widened. "Then I shall be more than happy to introduce you to that ravishing sorceress!"

29

They walked together, though not arm in arm, to the vast dining hall, which was still relatively empty. A few of the castle staff were scurrying about, arranging the place settings, and a couple of knights standing in one corner were conferring in low voices.

"You're sure she's coming?" asked Raven, looking around for some old woman, the female version of Merlin, perhaps even wearing the same conical magician's cap.

"She was invited," replied Guinevere as they seated themselves. "And believe me, when my husband invites you, you come."

"He seemed pleasant enough to me," remarked Raven.

"You present no threat to him."

"Why would he invite threatening people to the castle for a meal?" asked Raven.

"To keep an eye on some, to poison others, to be amused or entertained by a few," answered Guinevere.

"Ah, yes," said Raven. "Uneasy lies the head, and all that."

"I wouldn't know," replied Guinevere. "It's been years since I lay next to the head, or any other part, of the king."

"Do they have marriage counselors in Camelot?"

"I have no idea what that is," she answered. "Therefore, I

assume we don't have it." She sighed deeply. "We could go from now until midnight just making a list of all the things we don't have in Camelot."

"Yet you stay," noted Raven.

"Well, I *am* the queen," said Guinevere. "Besides, whatever we don't have here, they don't have even more of it everywhere else."

A few knights and their ladies entered the room.

"I wonder what's keeping Arthur?" mused Guinevere. "I do hope this Galahad character isn't trying to kill him." She frowned at the thought, then suddenly smiled. "Of course, if he *does* kill him, I'd be the supreme ruler, wouldn't I?"

"As well as a grieving widow," said Raven.

"Oh, *that*," she said with a dismissive shrug. "Oh, look—your date has arrived."

"My date?"

"Morgan le Fay."

Raven turned to look at the doorway, and saw a slim, black-clad woman enter the room. She wore no witch's hat, carried no wand or other magical paraphernalia, but it was obvious by the deference that was shown her, much the same as Merlin received, that she was a powerful person and that everyone was aware of it.

There was something very familiar about the way she carried herself, the way she walked and moved, and then, as she turned in his direction, Raven was able to see her face.

"Lisa!" he whispered.

"Come on, get up," said Guinevere, getting to her feet. "I'll introduce you."

Raven was up instantly, and followed the queen as she

made her way through the growing crowd of knights and ladies until the pair of them stood directly in front of the newcomer.

"Morgan le Fay, I have someone here who is very anxious
to meet you. May I present the occasionally famous and occasionally infamous Mordred?"

Raven bowed, as he'd seen various of the knights do, and
gently extended his hand, which she took.

"You seem . . . *different* . . . somehow," said Morgan with
Lisa's voice.

"I hope the change is an improvement," said Raven.

"It could hardly fail to be," said Guinevere before Morgan
could answer. "I'll leave you two to transact your business,
whatever it may be, and busy myself greeting guests—especially
Galahad, when he's finally through boring the king."

"Have we business to transact?" asked Morgan.

"I hope so," answered Raven.

"Now, or shall we dine first?"

"Whichever you prefer."

"It's been a long day," she replied. "Let's have dinner. You
can tell me what you want while we're eating."

"I don't think so," said Raven.

"Oh?"

"Anyone who overhears will think I've gone mad."

She smiled.

"Have I said something funny?" he asked.

"That is precisely the kind of business that interests me."
She paused. "I'm told you arrived with Merlin. I assume he
couldn't be of any help to you?"

Raven shook his head. "No."

"Of course," she replied. "He's good at the normal stuff—conjuring, raising the dead, protecting cities—but when you get down to the really interesting stuff. . . . well, he just never did his homework. He was always cutting classes."

"How would you know?" asked Raven curiously. "I mean, he's got to be forty or fifty years older than you."

"That proves my point," she said with a smile. "He was off practicing swordsmanship (as if he would ever need that talent) on the day we learned our rejuvenation spells."

"You mean you're as old as he is?" asked Raven.

She shook her head. "Actually, he's almost a year older."

"Remarkable."

Suddenly the room fell silent, and Arthur entered in the company of the most handsome, most physically perfect man anyone in the assemblage had ever seen.

"Knights and ladies," said the king, "allow me to present the newest member of the Round Table: Sir Galahad."

There was polite applause, and Galahad inclined his head slightly to acknowledge it.

"And now, to dinner," said Arthur.

The meal began with a thick soup, followed by roast beef. Raven toyed with his meat, but barely ate any.

"Don't you like it?" asked Morgan.

"Where I come from, we add onions and ketchup and other things to our meat."

"Let me see what I can do," said Morgan, pointing a forefinger at Raven's beef and uttering a brief spell. "Try it now."

Raven took a bite, chewed it thoughtfully, and smiled. "I don't know what you did to it, but it's better than any roast beef I've ever had."

"If you don't like anything else, you know who to ask about it," she replied, matching his smile.

Dinner took about an hour, and then Arthur rose to make a brief speech. Like most speeches Raven had heard under similar circumstances—which is to say, political dinners—it was carefully crafted, used impressive words and phrases, and left the audience no more enlightened or informed than when he'd stood up to talk.

This was followed by three more speeches from various knights, none of them memorable in the least, and finally Arthur rose again and suggested that since it was a lovely night, or at least not raining yet, that everyone adjourn to the courtyard.

The room emptied out until there was no one left in it except Raven and Morgan le Fay.

"Now, what did you want to speak to me in private about?" she said.

He nodded his head. "I have serious and urgent need of your services."

"What can I do for you?"

"This is going to seem odd," he said, "but I am not Mordred. My name is Eddie Raven, and I am not from Camelot."

"I knew that already," she replied, flashing him a smile.

"You did?" he said, surprised.

"Am I not Morgan le Fay?"

"Anyway, I need to get back to when I came from," said Raven. "I have a feeling that only a sorcerer—a powerful one—can transport me there."

"I can try," she said.

"Thank you."

"Close your eyes, Eddie Raven," she said, laying a hand on his forehead. "Try to make your mind a blank."

He did as she asked, and was motionless for a full minute.

"Oh, my goodness!" said Morgan. "What a strange place you come from. Machines racing around without horses, even more flying in the air, women wearing the most immoral clothing, noises and music everywhere, endless people. I don't know how you stand it!"

"It grows on you," said Raven.

"Like a fungus," she opined. Suddenly she froze. "What am *I* doing there?"

He shook his head. "It's not you. It's a girl—a woman—named Lisa."

"You're sure?"

He nodded. "There's a Morgan lookalike in every world I've been to—Casablanca, Oz, Manhattan . . ."

"I've never heard of any of them." She was silent another moment, and then frowned. "If I interpret your mind correctly, you did not *choose* to visit Camelot or these other worlds, but were *sent* here."

"That's right. And all I want to do is get back to *my* world."

"That shouldn't be too difficult," said Morgan.

"I don't know the stellar coordinates or anything like that," he said.

"I am a sorceress, not a scientist," she said with a smile. "I don't need any of that."

He sighed deeply. "*That's* a relief," he muttered.

"Well," said Morgan, "the room is empty, there's no one to bother us or affect my concentration, Merlin's not around to write down every one of my spells, so we might as well get on with it. Unless you'd rather stay here." She smiled. "I can always use an assistant."

"That's a more attractive offer than I think you can imagine," said Raven. "But I really need to go home."

"All right," she said, laying her hand on his. "Now close your eyes, and don't speak until I finish casting the spell."

She began uttering the spell in an unfamiliar tongue, and finally stopped and opened her eyes. "As I suspected," she said.

"I beg your pardon?"

"The spell to take you back to your time and place is inscribed on Excalibur. I need only read it, and the rest can be accomplished in seconds."

"Then what are we waiting for?" said Raven, getting to his feet. "Arthur had it with him at dinner. I'm sure it's still in his scabbard."

Suddenly a strong, familiar voice rang out: *Stop!*

"Was that you?" asked Morgan, frowning.

"No," answered Raven.

"Then who—?"

"It's Rofocale," said Raven. Since he couldn't see Rofocale, he turned to where he imagined Rofocale's essence must be. "Why are you interfering?" he demanded.

You don't want to return to your world, Eddie Raven, said Rofocale's voice, and Raven could tell that Morgan could hear it too.

"Why the hell not?" demanded Raven.

Because that is what the Master of Dreams wants! thundered Rofocale. *He is waiting for you.*

"Who or what is the Master of Dreams?"

He is your archenemy, Eddie. He takes different forms in

different worlds. In Casablanca he was Colonel Massovitch, in Oz he was the Wicked Witch, in other worlds he's other things. Surely you have realized that you are beyond the realm of the possible and have entered the realm of the magical.

"Why is he my archenemy?" demanded Raven. "What did I ever do to him? I didn't even know he existed until I met you."

"Eddie," said Morgan, laying her hand on his, "I intuit that he's telling the truth. You mustn't go back to your world. Not yet, anyway."

"So I just stay here until he kills me?" demanded Raven.

"No," she replied. "We will use all my magic and all the disparate bits of knowledge you have acquired during your adventures, and together we will seek him out and defeat him."

"We don't even know what he looks like or where to find him," said Raven.

"We will find him," she said with certainty. She stared at a fixed spot halfway across the room. "Will you help us?"

When I can, answered Rofocale.

She frowned. "When you can?" she repeated.

"He took a bullet that was meant for me," explained Raven. "A number of bullets. My guess is that he's spending most of his time sleeping, or unconscious."

"All right," she said. "We might as well get busy preparing for our eventual confrontation with this Dream Master."

Master of Dreams, said Rofocale's voice, suddenly weak and hoarse.

"Right now?" asked Raven.

"Your life, and at least two worlds—yours and mine—depend upon it," answered Morgan. "Have you really got something more important to do?"

30

"I think," said Morgan after considering the problem, "that we'd best repair to my castle while we devise a plan of attack."

"Attack?" repeated Raven. "We don't even know where he is."

"That's why we need a plan," she said. "Are you ready?"

"I don't know," said Raven. "Do we ride double on a broom?"

"I'm a sorceress, not a witch," she said with a smile. "Hold my hand."

He reached out for her hand, found that it felt as good here as in Manhattan, heard her whisper a spell, and suddenly, with no sense of movement at all, he found himself inside a totally different castle, smaller and more tastefully decorated than Arthur's or Merlin's.

"Would you like something to drink?" she asked him.

"Have you got any coffee?" said Raven.

She frowned, then laid a hand on his forehead as if reading it. "Not for centuries, yet."

"Then I'll have whatever you've got—or just water."

"Water it is," she said, and a goblet of it magically appeared in his hand.

"That's magic!" he exclaimed.

"I *am* a sorceress," she said. "Now to business. Can you describe the Master of Dreams for me?"

Raven shook his head. "I didn't even know he existed until recently."

She frowned. "All right, we do it the hard way."

"The hard way?" he repeated.

"We observe other worlds, worlds that coexist with this time and place, and see if we can spot him, or at least his work."

"I don't know," said Raven. "A couple of the worlds in which I found myself don't really exist."

She sighed deeply. "How little you know, Mordred. They *all* exist."

"By the way, I'm Eddie Raven, not Mordred."

"I know," she said.

"Then why did you call me Mordred?"

"You're wearing Mordred's face and figure," answered Morgan, "so I assume that's the way you wanted to be addressed."

"Definitely not," said Raven. "But I don't know how *not* to look like this."

She uttered a few words that made no sense to him, looked at him, and smiled. "So *this* is the real you! I approve."

He wished there was a mirror handy, but he settled for taking her word for it.

"Thank you," he said. "I feel more competent already."

"Then set your mind to work, Eddie Raven," she said. "We have to figure out where the Master of Dreams will appear next."

"I haven't been here long enough to be truly threatened. Merlin's the most powerful person I've met—prior to you, anyway—but Arthur is king, and he's got an army ready to do anything he demands. Got to be one or the other."

"And do these manifestations have anything in common?" asked Morgan.

"Not that I can tell."

She sighed. "Well, we've got to start somewhere. Hopefully by dawn I'll have eliminated a number of possibilities."

He smiled. "You always were a bright one."

"Always?" she repeated. "We've only known each other for maybe half an hour."

"I've known you for a couple of years," said Raven. "Back in my world your name is Lisa."

"Lisa," she said, and then repeated it. "A very pleasant name. Not bold and forceful like Morgan." She considered the name for a moment. "I *like* it."

"Shall I start calling you Lisa, then?" he asked.

She shook her head. "I'd better be bold and forceful a little longer, until we confront the Master of Dreams."

"You're the boss." He sipped his water, put the goblet down, and stared at her. "What do we do now?"

She lowered her head in thought. "The trick is to figure out where he'll appear next."

"Is that a problem?" asked Raven. "I mean, I haven't *chosen* any of the worlds I've been to, and surely *they* didn't choose *me*—so I assume it was the Master of Dreams' doing, and that he'll whisk me off to the next world when he's ready."

She shook her head. "In the first three worlds you didn't have a protector, Eddie—or at least, not a healthy one. But I'm with you now, and he doubtless knows it, so he'll want time to prepare whatever traps he's got in mind for you. So it's up to us—to me, really—to see if Rofocale's right about his location, and if so, to transport us there before he's totally ready for us."

"And how do you do that?" asked Raven.

"I read your memories, your hopes and dreams, and see where he's most likely to be waiting for us."

"You can do that?" asked Raven. "I mean, right here, in like an hour or two?"

She shot him a confident smile. "Am I not Morgan le Fay?"

"Well, that's the problem, isn't it?" said Raven. "Because in *my* world you're *not* Morgan le Fay, you're a girl named Lisa who I'm pretty sure I'm in love with."

"But we are not *in* your world, Eddie Raven," she replied.

"All right," he said with a sigh. "What do I do?"

"As I said, relax."

"This is about as relaxed as I'm likely to get after what Rofocale told us."

She held out a hand. "Here," she said, grasping his hand, "come with me."

She led him down a broad corridor to a large room, a library with two walls of books and scrolls, and had him sit in a chair that was more comfortable than it appeared.

"Now lean back, close your eyes, and let your mind just drift gently on the night air," said Morgan.

He relaxed and closed his eyes.

"And if you *must* think of me, try to imagine me with my clothes on," she said, frowning.

"Sorry," said Raven, trying to order his thoughts.

"Just let your mind drift," she said. "Think of the worlds, real and imaginary, that you've always been fascinated by."

She was silent for a long minute, then sighed deeply.

"Is something wrong?" asked Raven.

"I don't know where you read about them, or why they interested you, but we really don't want to visit a world peopled by Zeus and Hera and Apollo and the rest of the Greek gods."

"We don't?" asked Raven. "I've always found them fascinating."

"Oh, they are, no doubt about it," replied Morgan. "But the least powerful of them is still more powerful than Merlin and myself combined, and I don't think our quarry wants any part of a world where he's among the weaklings."

"Makes sense, I suppose," agreed Raven. "What now?"

"Just keep relaxing," she said. "You've got hundreds of real and imaginary worlds stacked up in there." She frowned. "I wish you hadn't read so much science fiction."

"I preferred fantasy," he said.

"Same thing," she said—and suddenly froze. "No, I take it back. It's not the same thing at all!"

"What have you found in here?" he asked, tapping his head with a forefinger.

"A world that seems perfect for him," she said. "A world of fantasy and magic and powerful evil figures, a world where very little could present a threat to him." She paused. "Rofocale said he was on Earth, so we can pick the world where we meet him, and he'll show up there."

"So that's where he'll be—this world, whatever it is—that you're talking about?"

"In all likelihood," she said. "Let me just check to make sure." She closed her eyes and concentrated again. "Damn!" she snapped.

"Something wrong?"

She flashed him a self-deprecating smile. "I found a world I wish he'd gone to, but when I examined it I had to admit he wasn't there."

"What kind of world?"

"A world where you and I would be Nick and Nora Charles," she replied.

"The world of *The Thin Man*?" he said, frowning.

"We'd have made a great team," she said bitterly. "Oh, well, it wasn't to be. At least not this time." She paused. "Are you ready?"

Probably not, he thought as he truthfully answered, "As ready as I'll ever be."

"Then hold my hand," she said. "We don't want to get separated while I cast the spell."

He gripped her hand, heard her chant the first few words, and then he was . . . well . . . *elsewhere.*

31

"Look down!" said Raven. "We're flying! We're a mile in the air!"

"Do you recognize this world?" she asked.

"From up here?" he replied. "Hell no! You're the one who transported us. Where are we?"

"It doesn't work like that, Eddie," she said. "I found it in *your* mind and memory."

"Let me think," said Raven. "I mean, how the hell many worlds can we fly in?"

"There's a lovely green glade down there," said Morgan, pointing to it. "Let's land there and figure out where we are and what we need to do next."

They spiraled down and finally landed gently on a lush green field.

"Anything look familiar?" she asked.

He shook his head. "Not yet. But I'm sure it will sooner or later. All the others did eventually."

"I didn't see anything resembling a city as we were flying," said Morgan. "I wonder if there are any people on this world at all."

"Of course there are," replied Raven. "The Master of Dreams wouldn't waste his time on an empty world."

She nodded her head. "Makes sense," she admitted.

Raven heard a melodic tinkling sound off to his right. "What the hell was *that*?" he said.

"What was *what*?" replied Morgan.

He frowned. "I'm not sure. Kind of a very tiny melody."

"Oh?" she said, scanning their surroundings. "How far away?"

He shrugged. "I don't know."

"I don't see anything. What kind of instrument was it? Certainly nothing as big as a piano, or it couldn't stay hidden."

"No, it wasn't piano music," replied Raven. "It was more like tiny little chimes." He frowned. "And they weren't playing a melody, at least not one that I could identify."

She sighed. "Well, we've only been here a few minutes. Eventually things will start making sense."

He shot her a wry smile. "You have more confidence in the logic of the universe than I do." Suddenly he blinked his eyes very rapidly and shook his head. "Damn! There it goes again."

She smiled at him, and then chuckled. "Yes indeed," she said. "There it goes again."

"You heard it?" he asked.

She shook her head. "No," she replied. "But I can see it."

"What and where is it?" he demanded.

She smiled again and pointed. "Hovering about an inch above your right shoulder."

He turned his head, saw something colorful and glittering where she had indicated, quickly took a step back, and stared.

"Son of a bitch!" he said.

"I hate to correct you, but it does not look like any puppy I have ever seen," responded Morgan.

"Just an expression," answered Raven. "But I know who and where we are now."

"You do?"

"You didn't read enough fairy tales when you were a kid," said Raven with a smile. "And to be honest, you probably pre-date this one by a millennium or more."

"Could you explain, please?" said Morgan.

"Certainly," he said, turning to the tiny, glittering winged fairy. "Tinker Bell, say hello to Morgan, who we will call Wendy for the duration of our stay in this world. Wendy, this is Tinker Bell."

"That means nothing to me," said Morgan. "Can you give me any more details?"

"Yeah," replied Raven. "For as long as we're on this dirt-ball, my name is Peter Pan, and the name of the world is Neverland."

"Neverland?" she repeated with a smile. "How evocative and romantic."

"It's evocative, all right," said Raven. "And it'll be a lot more romantic after we find the Master of Dreams and kick his ass."

"Ask Tinker Bell where he is," suggested Morgan.

Raven grinned. "I don't have to."

"Oh?"

"I don't know his exact position, but I know where we'll find him."

"Would you care to enlighten me?" said Morgan.

"He'll be on a pirate ship, and his name will be Captain Hook."

"What makes you so sure?"

"Because he's the one guy in this world who wants to kill me, the one guy in all of Neverland I consider my enemy." He turned to Tinker Bell and smiled. "And I bet I know somebody who can lead us right to him."

The glittering crystalline girl, all five inches of her, smiled and nodded her head vigorously.

"Okay," said Raven. "No sense waiting."

They took off and began flying—he loved the feel of it—and soon saw a large body of water. They headed directly toward it.

"You seem to know something about this world, Eddie," said Morgan.

"What I can remember from when I was eight or ten years old, yes," Raven confirmed.

"So you know if they have any weapons with greater range than a sword?"

He frowned. "Damn! I *don't* remember that. But if it's a pirate ship, I suppose they've got to have a cannon or two."

"We'll be sitting ducks—well, flying ducks—as we approach them," she said.

"Not if we do it in the dark," replied Raven. Then: "I think."

"It's not a safe approach, but at least it's a minimally safer one," said Morgan. She looked up. "We've got about two hours of daylight."

"I don't feel any strain from flying," said Raven. "How long can we stay aloft?"

"No wings, nothing to get tired," she answered. "Besides, it could take us hours to find this ship."

Tinker Bell began chiming furiously, and they both turned

to look at her. She shook her tiny head, then pointed to a spot
a few miles distant.

"Do you see a ship?" asked Morgan.

"No," replied Raven.

"Neither do I," she said.

"But Tinker Bell does," said Raven. "Let's slow down a bit
and make our leisurely way there. We could be over it just
about the time the sun sets."

Morgan nodded her agreement. "Makes sense."

They slowed down, literally drifted on the wind, and found
themselves hovering above the ship just as night fell.

"Ready?" asked Raven.

"Of course."

"Hook—well, the Master—is mine," he said.

"Why is he Hook?" she asked.

"Got a hook in place of one of his hands. If you land and
he's still standing, don't get within reach of him."

"Oh, I'm not without some offensive and defensive magic,"
she replied with a smile.

"Shit!" he exclaimed. "Of course you are! What have you
got that can set the damned boat on fire?"

She reached into a pocket and withdrew a handful of small
pellets. "Good thinking," she said.

"Can I have a couple, or do they just work for you?" asked
Raven.

"You can use them too," she replied. "Just say 'Flame!' when
you want them to activate."

"Just 'flame'?" he said.

"Well, you *could* say 'magnesium/Teflon/Viton fluoropoly-
mer' if you prefer."

"'Flame' will do just fine," he assured her. He looked down. "Okay, let's go to work."

They spiraled lower and lower until they hovered some twenty feet above the ship. Then Raven nodded to Morgan, and she tossed a handful of the pellets onto the ship, shouting "Flame!" half a dozen times, and instantly the wooden decks were ablaze.

A tall man with a mean-looking hook at the end of his left arm burst from the captain's cabin, spotted Raven flying above the deck, and shook the fist of his real hand at him.

"I know you, Eddie Raven!" he growled. "Come down and meet your death like a man!"

Raven floated slowly to the deck. "Come meet your death like a roast turkey," he said, tossing all his pellets at the Master of Dreams and gently saying "Flame."

The Master's robes went up in flames, and as his hair caught fire and began burning brightly, he pointed a finger toward Raven.

"You were lucky this time, as you were in the last three worlds, but you haven't seen the last of me!"

And with that he was gone.

"What happened?" said Raven. "He couldn't have burned up that quickly."

"He left before he *could* become a pile of ashes," answered Morgan.

"Then we won!" said Raven exultantly.

She shook her head. "It's not that easy, Eddie," she said. "It just means he's moved to another world."

"Where?"

She shrugged. "I don't know yet," she answered. "All I know

is that he found it in your memories. Let's fly to shore where I can go through your subconscious and try to figure out where he'll be."

He agreed, and ten minutes later they were sitting on a log on the beach, while she laid her hands gently on his head. "My goodness, but you have a lot of scantily clad women in there!"

"Sorry," he said.

"The strange thing is, they all look like me." Suddenly she tensed. "I think I see where we'll be meeting him next—pardner."

32

"Where the hell are we?" said Raven, looking around at the barren, dusty street.

"I have no idea," replied Morgan. "These are *your* memories, not mine."

"But we're in the middle of some dusty shantytown, and I come from midtown Manhattan, which has about two million people per square mile."

She stared at him. "What do people in Manhattan wear?"

"Suits, ties, sports jackets, sports shirts, slacks, shoes—the usual," was Raven's reply.

"You're not wearing any of them, except by the most elastic definition," said Morgan.

He frowned and looked down.

"Blue jeans?" he muttered. "I haven't worn blue jeans since I was in grammar school. And boots? There's no snow on the ground. It's got to be eighty-five degrees out."

"Not just boots," she noted.

He looked again. "Spurs?" he said, frowning.

"And a broad-brimmed hat to keep the sun out of your eyes," said Morgan. "Who wears that?"

He shrugged. "A cowboy, I guess. The only thing I'm missing is . . ." He froze as his hand slid down to his hip and came in contact with the six-gun. He withdrew it, held it up in front of him, and stared at it.

"Goddamn!" he muttered.

"What does this mean?"

"That I'm a gunslinger."

Morgan frowned. "You throw guns?"

He shook his head. "Just a slang expression. It means that I'm a gunfighter." He stared at the handle. "And I must be pretty damned good at it. That's a *lot* of notches."

"Notches?" she asked.

"It's traditional to carve a notch onto the handle every time you kill a man." He frowned again. "But am I a good guy or a bad guy?"

She pointed at his chest. "Does this help?"

He looked down. "A star," he said. "Yeah, that helps. It means I'm a lawman."

He patted the star, and realized there was something in his pocket behind it. He reached in, and pulled out the fixings for a cigarette, rolled it, and studied it. "No filter."

"What is it?"

"A cigarette," he answered. "Tobacco. You light one end and inhale the other."

"It sounds terribly unhealthy."

"It is," he replied. "Killed a few million people just during my lifetime. Very addictive," he added. "Government has made them harder to get, as well as more expensive." He shook his head. "Hasn't stopped everybody, but it's helped a bit."

"That's interesting," noted Morgan. "You kill people and you have a habit that kills you."

"But it doesn't answer any questions, such as: Who am I?"

"Maybe that gentleman who's emerging from the building down the street can tell us," suggested Morgan, pointing at a young man who walked out onto the wooden sidewalk carrying a canvas sack over his shoulder.

"It's worth a try," agreed Raven, as the man climbed down from the sidewalk onto the dusty street. He raised his voice. "Hold on for a minute, fella. I want to talk to you."

"That's what they all say, Marshal," said the young man. "I got no beef against you, so just let me pass and no one'll get hurt."

"I just want to ask you a question or two."

"You and ten other sheriffs and marshals," he said. "You'd think that Billy the Kid had killed enough of you that you'd start leaving him alone."

"That's got to be him," Raven whispered to Morgan. "Stand aside."

"I just read your mind. I know who Billy the Kid is or was. He'll kill you."

"He might kill Eddie Raven," answered Raven. "But he ain't gonna kill the Duke."

She frowned and stared at him as if he was crazy. "Duke?" she repeated. "You're a nineteenth-century cowboy, not British royalty."

"I'm Duke Wayne," said Raven, gently brushing her aside with his left arm while his right hand lay poised above his holster. "Now step away."

"I don't want any trouble, Marshal," said the Kid.

"That's too bad," answered Raven, "because you got a little more trouble than I think you can handle."

"I've killed twenty-one men," said the Kid. "You'll make twenty-two."

I hope you can read my mind, Morgan, because we're going to come through this okay. Billy the Kid killed twenty-one men in his brief life. That means he's not going to kill me.

"Just put the bag down, turn around, and walk out of town," said Raven.

"Can't do it, Marshal," said the Kid. "That's more than you'll earn in a lifetime."

Raven reached into a pocket, withdrew a nickel, and held it up. "See this nickel?" he said. "That's more than *you'll* earn or even see in a lifetime if you don't drop the bag and walk away."

"Can't do it, Marshal."

"Sure you can, Pilgrim, when you consider the alternative," replied Raven.

"I *tried* to let you live," said the Kid with a sigh.

"And I'm trying to return the favor," said Raven.

"Okay, Marshal," said the Kid. "Hit leather!"

And before the Kid's gun was out of its holster, Raven had pumped two bullets into his shoulder and another into his thigh.

The Kid groaned, and his pistol went flying into the street.

"We can stop right here," said Raven, as the Kid's hand began reaching for another gun that he'd tucked inside his belt.

"Not a chance, Marshal," grated the Kid.

"Your choice," said Raven with a shrug. He aimed his pistol at the Kid's head. "Hope you know a short prayer. You ain't got time for a long one."

"Damn!" screamed the Kid. "You've been lucky so far, Eddie Raven, but I promise you won't survive our next encounter!"

And with that, he and the town were gone.

33

"**D**amn!" muttered Raven, who looked a lot more like himself and a lot less like John Wayne. "He can't get away *every* time."

"No," agreed Morgan. "One of these times *he'll* kill *you*."

"You're the one who picked the venues," said Raven. "Go through my mind and pick one where he can't win, or even survive."

She grimaced. "It's not that easy, Eddie. He can manipulate your dreams as easily as you can. Why do you think people have nightmares?"

"Then we're just going to have to move a little faster, be a little meaner. I mean, hell, there's a zillion dreams and alternate realities out there. Even if he hasn't been able to beat me, we haven't been able to finish him off. One of these times I'm going to get careless or he's going to get lucky or it's simply going to be his turn to win."

"That's why we can't waste opportunities," she said.

"We set Captain Hook on fire, and I shot Billy the Kid. How was that wasted?"

"He lived through them," she said bluntly. "You set fire to Hook while he was on the water, and you put three nonfatal bullets into Billy the Kid. Wherever we go next time, we have to be more careful, more thorough." Her expression softened, and she gently stroked his cheek with her hand. "I'm getting very fond of you, Eddie. I'd hate to see that monster win."

"So would I," agreed Raven, placing his hand over hers. "I have a hard time thinking of him as a monster. A villain, sure. But a monster?"

"In this case, is there a difference?" she asked.

He considered it, and then shrugged. "Probably only academic," he said.

"Well, we'd better prepare for our next meeting," said Morgan.

"He seems to thrive on fantasies and movies," replied Raven. "See if we can track him down in a real historical venue."

"All I can do is see where he's most likely to appear," she said, laying her hand on his forehead.

"Why the hell doesn't he invade someone else's memories and subconscious," said Raven. "Why mine?"

"I have no idea," said Morgan. "I think you'll have to get the answer to that from your friend Rofocale."

"He's not my friend," answered Raven. "I've known him for one night."

"Well, next time you're in contact with him, just ask," she said. "And . . . wait a minute . . . yes, I've found the Master of Dreams—and this time he's not in an imaginary locale."

"Where is he?" said Raven.

"You'll see," she said, as dizziness overwhelmed him. "We're already in transit."

A moment later his head cleared. The first thing he saw was Morgan, not as she had been dressed, but clothed in a white gown, a golden crown, elegant sandals, and a jeweled dagger strapped around her waist and residing in a matching sheath.

"Where are we?" he asked.

"That should be easy for you to deduce," she said. "I'm dressed like an Egyptian queen, and you're wearing a toga."

"A toga?" he repeated, looking down as his bare legs. "You know, I *felt* a little flimsy." He considered their clothing and their surroundings. "Caesar and Cleopatra?" he suggested.

She nodded. "It certainly looks like it."

"I assume Cassius still has a lean and hungry look."

"Perhaps," she said.

"Perhaps?"

"That was Shakespeare, not necessarily history."

"J. M. Barrie wasn't history, and neither was L. Frank Baum, but the son of a bitch damned near killed me in Neverland and Oz."

"Point taken," she said.

"What now?" he asked, looking around at his surroundings. "We seem to be in some large building."

"Probably the Senate," she said.

"Damn!" muttered Raven. "He doesn't waste any time, does he?"

"You want to confront him, Eddie," she said. "It wouldn't make much sense to put you on a ship crossing the Mediterranean, or at some army encampment where you're reading dispatches or perhaps writing orders."

Raven shrugged. "What the hell," he said. "When you're right, you're right."

"Thank you."

"So what now?"

"Now we wait," said Morgan. "The Master of Dreams surely knows you're here. I expect he'll be along any minute."

Raven's hands went down to his hips. "I'm not wearing a sword!"

"Do you know how to use one?"

"You pull it out of its sheath and swing it," he said.

She shook her head. "That won't do you much good against men who have spent their whole lives honing their military skills, Eddie."

"Fine," he said. "Give me a gun."

"They don't exist in this era."

"I saw a lot of stuff that didn't exist in Neverland," said Raven.

"That was a just a starting point, Eddie," answered Morgan. "Dreams and fantasies evolve, and whatever you saw was consistent with what the author originally put there." She paused. "But this is history, and handguns didn't exist two millennia ago."

"So we just wait until we can figure out what the Master of Dreams has in store for us?" he said bitterly.

"Uh . . . I don't think you'll have to wait very long," she said, turning toward the door, where almost a dozen men entered the room. When the last was inside, they closed the door and stared at him.

"What happened to 'Hail, Caesar'?" said Raven.

"That is what we have to talk about," said the closest of them, starting to walk across the room toward Raven.

"Keep your distance," said Raven.

"Or what will you do?" said the man with a contemptuous smile.

"Chop you into little pieces and feed you to the dogs," said Raven.

"You are welcome to try, Caesar," said the man, still approaching.

Raven whispered to Morgan without ever taking his eyes off the approaching warrior: "Is this him?"

"No," she said, frowning.

"He's not Cassius?"

"He *is* Cassius," she replied. "But he's not the Master of Dreams."

"Shit!" muttered Raven. "I am not enjoying this."

"Maybe I can help," she said, waving her hand at the floor between Raven and Cassius and uttering a brief spell—and suddenly they were separated by a wall of flame.

Cassius screamed and jumped back. "What magic is this?" he demanded.

"The same magic you will encounter every time you threaten me or the illustrious Cleopatra," answered Raven.

Suddenly Morgan handed him a small sphere, about the size of a golf ball.

"What's this for?"

"You'll know when you need it," she said.

The fire died down, and a different warrior approached. "I apologize for Cassius," said the man. "He is an ignorant man. Everyone knows that Caesar is protected by the gods."

"Just keep telling yourself that," said Raven, watching Cassius out of the corner of his eye. "And now, what can I do for my loyal followers."

The man looked around. "There are spies everywhere," he said. "I must whisper it to you."

"What the hell, why not?" replied Raven.

The man approached, and Raven, who was half a foot taller, inclined his head. "As I said, what can I do for you?"

The man suddenly had a knife in his hand.

"You can die!" he cried.

"Oh, shit!" muttered Raven. "You too, Brutus?"

Suddenly he remembered the sphere Morgan had given him. It looked too big to stuff down Brutus's throat, so he smashed it against the man's head—and like an egg, it cracked open and a foul-smelling blue fluid began running down Brutus's skull and into his face. He screamed once, turned on his heel, and raced out the door.

His last words before he vanished from sight were, "Damn you, Eddie Raven!"

The others, impressed by her magic, followed him, and Raven turned to Morgan.

"Well, I guess we know who the Master of Dreams was."

She smiled and nodded her head.

"Fighting him to a draw beats the hell out of losing," said Raven, "but one of these times I'd like to win and get it over with."

"I know," said Morgan.

"I want to go back to my life, and a girl who looks like you but is called Lisa and doesn't perform magic, and where people aren't trying to kill me every time I walk into a restaurant or a bookstore."

"You *did* encounter him in your old life, Eddie," she pointed out. "Lisa was shot, Rofocale was shot, the store owner was killed, and I don't think it's unreasonable to assume he knows where you live and what your habits are in your former life."

"Don't call it my *former* life," said Raven irritably. "It's the one I'm going back to if I ever send this bastard back to *his* former life."

She made no reply, and after a minute he shrugged.

"I apologize," he said. "This is just a little more than I bargained for."

"I know."

"All right," he said with a sigh. "Go look between my ears and pick the next venue."

"We came close to beating him in Neverland," she mused.

"Can we go back there and try it again?"

She shook her head. "But I've found a world with a similar name. We keep fighting to a draw. Maybe just the name will give us the advantage we need."

"You really think so?"

"Anything is possible," she admitted. "One can always hope."

"Okay," said Raven. "What's the name?"

She told him.

Raven grimaced just as ancient Rome began vanishing around him. "I think you're clutching at straws."

34

"Well?" she asked him.

Raven examined his new body. "Could've been worse," he said, then added, "I suppose." He stared at her. "You look fine, though. A little young, but definitely Morgan, which is to say definitely Lisa."

"Well, in this world I *am* a young girl."

"I know," he said. "And I'm a white rabbit. I suppose I should keep looking at my watch to keep in character."

"Not necessary," she said. "Hopefully you won't be a rabbit much longer."

"I'll be somebody's lunch?"

She shook her head. "Of course not. But you're only a rabbit and I'm only a little girl called Alice because those are the first two entities anyone encounters in Wonderland."

"The rules seem to change in every world," he complained.

"Of course they do," she answered. "After all, every world is different."

"Well," he said, looking around, "we're here. And so, I assume, is the Master of Dreams. What do we do next?"

"Try to figure out who he is," answered Morgan. "And then dope out a strategy to totally defeat and destroy him."

"*Can* he be destroyed?" asked Raven. "After the last few worlds, I'm starting to have my doubts."

"Absolutely."

"You say that with a comforting degree of certainty," remarked Raven. "Would you care to explain it to me?"

"You've defeated him in every world where you've encountered him, and yet he theoretically had all the advantages. He knew who you were, he knew you were after him, he knew I was helping you—and yet you beat him every time. And believe me, Eddie, if he didn't *know* he could be destroyed, he wouldn't have run. He'd have stayed and done battle with you, mano a mano, or at least mano a thingo."

"It sounds logical when you say it," agreed Raven. "But he keeps getting away."

She shook her head. "No, Eddie—he keeps *running* away."

"She makes sense," said a low voice from behind them.

Raven and Morgan turned and found themselves confronting a caterpillar that was longer, top to bottom, than either of them.

"What do you know about it?" demanded Raven.

"Absolutely nothing," replied the caterpillar. "But her nose didn't grow, so she must be telling the truth." It stared at them. "You, of course, are the White Rabbit, though you're more a rusty gray mixed with bits of brown dirt. But who is she?"

"Morgan le Fay," said Raven promptly.

"Pay no attention to him, friend caterpillar," said Morgan. "My name is Alice."

"Ah, Alice!" said the caterpillar. "We've been expecting you."

"You have?" she said, surprised.

"No, not really," replied the caterpillar. "It just seemed an appropriate thing to say. Have you eaten yet, or are you saving him for dinner?"

Morgan put a protective arm around Raven. "He is my friend, and where I come from we do not eat our friends."

"That's strange," said the caterpillar. "Where I come from they make the very best eating of all." It paused thoughtfully. "In fact, for the life of me I cannot figure out why the Queen of Hearts hasn't had the king barbecued."

"Where would one find the queen?" asked Raven.

"On the throne, of course," said the caterpillar. It lifted the nearest of its left legs and peered at a tiny watch on it. "Ah!" it said. "Precisely three twenty-seven. Time to go find my evening meal."

And within seconds it had morphed into a colorful butterfly and flew off into the distance.

"Why did you ask about the queen?" asked Morgan.

"My memory is that she's about as evil as they come," answered Raven. "From what I can recall of Wonderland, she seems the likeliest candidate."

"I don't know," she said. "After all, Caesar was the most powerful man in Rome, but he wasn't the Master of Dreams."

"Yeah, but we knew that he got killed," answered Raven. "I don't remember anyone killing the Queen of Hearts."

She shrugged. "Okay, you've got a point. I suppose we'd best put her at the top of our list."

"I wouldn't," said a voice above them.

They looked up and saw a very strange-looking cat perched on the limb of a tree.

"The Cheshire Cat!" said Raven.

"That's so formal," replied the cat. "Call me Cutie-Pie instead."

"Whatever makes you happy, Cutie-Pie," said Morgan. "Now please tell us why we shouldn't put the Queen of Hearts on the top of our list."

"She's half fat and half muscle," answered Cutie-Pie.

"So what?" said Raven, frowning.

"So you definitely don't want her on the top of your list."

"Who do *you* think should be above her?" said Raven.

"Not *who*, but *what*," replied the Cheshire Cat.

"Okay then, *what* should be above her?"

"Veal parmesan. Shrimp de jonghe. Saganaki. Peanut butter and jelly sandwiches, but made with grape jelly on white bread only."

"We don't want to *eat* her," said Raven. "We just want to talk to her."

"Talk to that madwoman?" said the cat. "You must be as crazy as *she* is. Crazier, since she clearly can't help herself, whereas you can spend the next hour rubbing a charming cat's back if you've a mind to."

"No, thanks."

"Even half a mind will do," persisted the cat.

"We're in a hurry, Cutie-Pie," said Morgan. "Direct us to the queen's castle and we'll scratch you on the way back."

The Cheshire Cat shook its head. "If you go there, you ain't coming back," it said adamantly. "Not no way, not no how."

"You really won't help us?" said Raven.

"Right the first time."

"Then go away, or I'll whistle for the Cheshire Dog."

"There *is* one?" asked the cat nervously.

"Beats me," said Raven. "Shall we find out?"

"NO!" screamed the cat, jumping down to the ground and racing off. "I'm outta here!"

Raven turned to Morgan. "I'm trying to remember if Alice had such a difficult time in the book."

"I've only seen bits and pieces of it in your memories," she replied. "I've never actually read it."

"Well, I know she survived."

"Did the rabbit?"

"Damned if I know," admitted Raven.

"We might as well get started," said Morgan. "The one thing we know is that the queen isn't right here."

"We were walking, or at least facing, to the left when we got here, and the cat ran off to the right, and the butterfly flew that way, so it makes sense that civilization—or whatever passes for it in Wonderland—is to our left."

Morgan nodded her agreement. "Makes sense."

Raven chuckled.

"What is it?" she asked.

"I just hope 'makes sense' isn't a total contradiction in Wonderland," he replied.

They began walking, and after about twenty minutes they came to what alternately appeared to be a narrow river or a wide stream. They strode along it for a few hundred yards, and suddenly heard two voices—one gruff and human, one gruffer and inhuman—singing off to their right. They fought their way through some shrubbery, and in a few minutes came upon a balding man wearing overalls and boots and brandishing a saw, and a mildly humanoid walrus. Both were harmonizing rather badly on a racy bar-room ditty.

"Well, by gad," said the balding man, "we've attracted an audience."

"So we have," agreed the walrus. It turned to Morgan and Raven. "If you'd like to hear an even more obscene song, we've got a million of 'em."

"Not necessary," said Raven. "Allow me to introduce my friend and myself. She is Alice, and I am the White Rabbit."

"The Sort-of White Rabbit, I'd say," replied the walrus. "And we are . . . well, damn it all, I don't know our names. Just call us the Walrus and the Guy with the Saw."

"The Carpenter," corrected his companion.

"Pleased to meet you," said the Walrus. "What an odd co-incidence, too."

"A coincidence?" said Morgan.

"Yes, to learn of two Alices and two White Rabbits in the same day."

"I'm not following you," said Raven. "Two of us, you say?"

"Right," answered the Carpenter. "The ones the queen wants tortured and killed, and you two delightful intruders. I had no idea they were such popular names."

"Uh . . . let me get this straight," said Raven. "Word went out this morning that the queen wants us dead?"

"Possibly."

Raven frowned. "Possibly?"

"Possibly it was this morning. But it might have been a few minutes after noon."

"But she definitely wants us dead."

"Perhaps."

Raven simply stared at the Carpenter. "Perhaps?"

"It all depends how many Alices and White Rabbits are walking about Wonderland today."

The Carpenter held up his saw, as if prepared to do battle.

"At least three of each," said Morgan quickly.

"Ah, well, then," said the Carpenter, lowering his saw, "what ballad may we entertain you with? Have you ever heard 'The Ring Dang Do'?"

"We'll take a rain check," said Raven.

The Walrus looked up at the sky. "It's going to rain, you say? Funny, the clouds must all be in hiding. Well, best we do the same. I'd invite you to our humble bungalow, but we only have one guestroom, and it's filled with baby oysters that we're going to slaughter for dinner."

"We quite understand," said Morgan. "I wonder if I could prevail upon you for one favor first?"

"Probably not," said the Carpenter. "But it can't hurt to ask."

"We want to go to the castle and place ourselves under the queen's protection while she's hunting for that other Alice and Rabbit," she said. "Can you tell us how to get there?"

"Just follow the river until it makes a hard left turn at the foot of a forested hill. Climb the hill until it levels out, and you're there."

"If you've any doubts," added the Walrus, "just stand still and listen."

"For what?" asked Raven.

"For the queen, of course," answered the Walrus. "Her whisper is three times louder than a lion's roar, and a whole lot more frightening."

"Talks a lot in her sleep, too," said the Carpenter. "Mostly she screams 'Off with his head!'"

"Not always," said the Walrus. "She yells 'Off with their heads!' almost as often."

"It must be comforting to hear her and know she's in good health," said Raven.

"Well, that's one way of looking at it," answered the Walrus.

"And now you'd best be on your way," added the Carpenter, "as we have some serious bloodletting to do."

Raven and Morgan thanked them, and recommenced walking along the river.

"He's *got* to be the queen," he said after they'd proceeded almost a mile along the twisting, curving river.

"It certainly seems like it," she replied. "Let's hope we can get to the palace unhindered and without any more delays."

Raven looked ahead and frowned. "We should be so lucky," he said grimly.

35

They walked for another hour, and suddenly heard singing in the distance.

"Sounds like two men," remarked Raven.

"Not very melodic," commented Morgan.

"Well, we just need some information, not a concert," said Raven.

She made a face. "Good. I don't think I could listen to much more of that."

They kept walking, and in a few minutes they saw a path leading inland from the river. The singing seemed to be coming from there, so they followed it and soon came to a clearing where two oddly shaped, not-quite-human creatures were singing a duet.

"Excuse me," said Morgan. "We don't mean to interrupt you, but—"

"Then don't!" said the one on the left.

"We just need some directions," said Morgan.

"Fine," said the one on the right. "Go directly to hell, do not pass go, do not collect two hundred dollars."

"One hundred thirty-six dollars and seventeen cents," said the one on the left. "My partner forgets about inflation."

"We have no money," said the one on the right, "so why should we worry about inflation." He stared at Morgan and Raven. "You're still here."

"Like the lady said, we need some information," said Raven, "and we're not about to let an ill-mannered lout frighten us away."

"*Two* ill-mannered louts, please," said the one on the left.

"You got names?" asked Raven. "Or do I just call you Lout Number One and Lout Number Two?"

"I'm Tweedledee," said the one on the left, "and he's Tweedledum."

"No!" said the other. "It's Pluto Day."

"Right," acknowledged his partner. "Okay, he's Tweedledee and I'm Tweedledum. Now perhaps you'll tell us why you've interrupted our brilliant concert and then go away and leave us to our art."

"We need to see the Queen of Hearts," said Raven.

"You're that close to death?" asked Tweedledum.

Raven frowned. "What are you talking about."

"Most people see her for just a few seconds before they are separated from their heads." He shrugged. "I suppose there are advantages."

"Of course there are," said Tweedledee. "If you no longer have a body, you only have to eat once a day."

"I never thought of that," admitted Tweedledum. He turned back to Raven. "So you both want to lose your heads?"

"No," said Raven. "We just want to know where to find the queen."

"Bullying the king, of course," said Tweedledee. "That's what queens do."

"They do?" said Morgan.

"When they're foul-tempered fiends and they outweigh their husbands three-to-one," replied Tweedledum.

"Four hundred," said Tweedledee. "She's off her diet."

"We just want to know if we're proceeding in the right direction," said Raven.

"Well, you've certainly found the team that'll make everyone forget the . . . ah . . ." said Tweedledee.

"The Stones?" said Tweedledum.

"No," said Tweedledee.

"The Beatles?"

"No."

"The Glenn Miller Orchestra?" asked Tweedledum.

"Right!" exclaimed Tweedledee, giving his partner a grateful hug. "I thought I was going to be another two hours remembering."

"You were right, though," said Tweedledum.

"I was?"

"You've forgotten Glenn Miller already."

"Glenn who?" said Tweedledee with a puzzled expression.

"Uh . . . guys," said Raven. "I hate to interrupt, but—"

"I don't believe you," said Tweedledum. "I think you love to interrupt, or you wouldn't keep doing it."

"What I really love is beating the crap out of ugly little critters who don't answer my questions," said Raven, starting to lose his temper.

"Well, yes, there is that," said Tweedledee. "So tell me, dear friend and esteemed lady, why were you interrupting our magnificent duet in the first place?"

"To make sure we're going in the right direction to get to the palace," said Raven.

Tweedledee frowned. "Does she live in a palace? Or perhaps a castle?"

"What if I told you I didn't give a damn what she lives in, I just want to get there."

"I don't know," replied Tweedledee. "What if you *did* tell me that?"

"It would mean that I am running out of patience," said Raven, "and the next time I didn't get an answer I would punch you as hard as I can."

"Well, thank goodness you haven't told me that."

"Consider it told," said Raven.

Tweedledee turned to Tweedledum. "Are you just going to stand there and let him threaten me like that?"

"Certainly not," said Tweedledum.

"Well, then?"

Tweedledum walked over to a large rock and sat down on it. "I'm not standing there anymore." He turned to Raven. "Okay, do your worst."

"Tell you what," said Tweedledee to Raven. "You definitely have a point, there's no denying it. We've treated you badly. Come back tomorrow, *he'll* be Tweedledee, and you can beat the crap out of him. I'll even hold your coat, if you remember to bring one."

Raven turned to Morgan. "Any ideas?"

She muttered a brief spell and waved her hand at the two creatures, who promptly elevated a few feet above the ground and turned upside down.

"Answer whenever you're ready," she said pleasantly.

"You can't do this!" cried Tweedledee.

"All the blood is rushing from our brains!" added Twee-dledum.

"I'm getting weak . . . dizzy!" said Tweedledee.

"Farewell, occasionally cruel world!" whimpered Tweedledum.

"Oh, come on!" snapped Raven. "You've only been upside down for maybe ten seconds."

"But I've always wanted to say that," replied Tweedledum.

"You said it before I could," growled Tweedledee. "I'm never speaking to you again."

"Never?" asked Tweedledum.

"Well, until the next time," replied Tweedledee.

"I'd like an answer now," said Raven. "I'm running out of patience."

"Doctors run out of patients," said Tweedledum. "You're running out of the milk of human kindness."

"And if you're not running out of it, at least it's turning sour," added Tweedledee.

"Okay," said Raven to Morgan. "Clearly we're never going to get a straight answer out of these two clowns. Let's go."

"Put us down first!" cried Tweedledee.

Raven shook his head. "That's not part of the bargain," he said. "Don't worry, though. It'll probably be dark before all the predatory creatures figure out that you're absolutely helpless." He paused. "If the first one they attack remembers not to scream and attract still more attention, it could be hours before they realize there's a second body just waiting to be torn apart and eaten." He walked over to Morgan. "Shall we continue?"

"Might as well," she said.

"No—wait!" screamed Tweedledee and Tweedledum in unison.

"Sorry," said Raven, "but we have no more time to waste."

"Go south southeast for one and sixty-three hundredths of a mile . . ." began Tweedledee.

"When you come to the tree with the heart carved on it and the inscription 'Oglethorpe Loves Throckmorton,' turn fourteen degrees to the right . . ."

"And when you reach the three stumps in a row—always assuming nobody has chopped down another tree right there— you'll see a trail leading uphill through the woods . . ."

"And when you come to the first branch, bear to the left until . . ."

Raven and Morgan listened until the two creatures were done. Then she uttered a spell and they each fell to the ground while emitting an enormous oof! followed by a dozen smaller versions of the same sound.

"See you around," said Raven over his shoulder as he and Morgan began walking to the southeast.

"Not if we see you first!" they hollered in unison.

As Raven and Morgan continued walking, they could hear the two creatures joining in another duet, and a grin spread across Raven's face.

"What's so amusing, Eddie?" she asked.

"If Glenn Miller were around, he could sue," replied Raven. "They are massacring that piece so badly no one will ever want to listen to it again."

A bespectacled middle-aged man in a suit and tie stepped out from behind a bush.

"Thanks," he said, walking in the direction of the singing. "I think I'll do just that."

Raven did a double-take, then smiled. "Happy to be of service, Glenn."

She turned to him. "Glenn Miller?"

"Of course," he said. "Okay, let's go—and hopefully this time we can go a few miles before we have any more interruptions."

And it was almost as if a disembodied voice whispered in his ear, *You should be so lucky.*

36

"I almost get the feeling he's hiding from us," remarked Raven as they walked along the trail.

"Don't be silly, Eddie," replied Morgan. "This place—all of Wonderland—was established long before we arrived here."

"Maybe he's just worried about assassins."

She shook her head. "You're not thinking clearly, Eddie."

"Oh?"

"The Master of Dreams didn't build this kingdom, and he wasn't worried about assassinations even a few hours ago, because a few hours ago he was busy being Brutus."

Raven shrugged. "The whole thing is just a little confusing."

"Well, try to think your way through it," she said, "because it isn't *me* he's after."

"That's the other thing that puzzles me," said Raven, frowning. "Why me? There's a hundred and fifty million men just in the United States in my era. What draws him to me—or me to him, whichever the case may be?"

"Hopefully we can find out when we finally confront him," said Morgan. "Or *her*, as the case may be."

"Oh, the king may be controlling the queen," replied Raven, "but Rofocale is the one guy who seems to know what's going on, and he keeps referring to the Master of Dreams, not the Mistress."

She shrugged. "Well, hopefully we'll find out soon enough."

Suddenly they heard voices again.

"Tell me they're not singing," muttered Raven.

She smiled. "Just listen. You know they're not."

He sighed deeply. "I also know that nothing's quite what it seems in this damned place."

"They're not singing," she confirmed, closing her eyes and concentrating. "But they certainly are noisy."

"Some kind of outdoor tavern, do you think?" asked Raven.

"How would I know?" she said. "Does Wonderland *have* taverns?"

"I keep forgetting," said Raven. "It's just that you're so like . . . well, I believe I mentioned her . . . that sometimes I assume you *are* her."

"Just remember which of us is a girlfriend and which is a sorceress," said Morgan.

"Don't worry," answered Raven. "I wouldn't put her through this on a bet."

"Thanks a heap, Eddie," she said with a wry smile.

"I mean . . ." he said, and then sighed. "I apologize."

"There's no need to. I understand the situation."

Strange shrill voices came to their ears.

"I'm glad one of us does," he muttered. "Let's go see what the hell they're celebrating."

They proceeded for another quarter mile, and then the path veered and they found themselves in an open area on the banks of the river. There was a long table surrounded by a dozen chairs, all but two of them empty. On one chair sat a strange-looking little man wearing a shirt, vest, pair of pants, and a stovepipe hat. On another chair sat something that could have been a distant relative of the rabbit body in which Raven found himself. Sitting atop the table, between the other two, was a small but elegantly dressed mouse.

"Okay," said Raven. "*This* I know."

"You do?" said Morgan, staring at the trio. "What are they?"

"If memory serves right, they're the Mad Hatter, the March Hare, and the Dormouse."

"You needn't tell me which is which," she said. "Their names or titles are self-explanatory. What are they doing?"

"Unless I miss my guess, they're having an unbirthday party," said Raven.

"An *un*birthday party?" she repeated, frowning.

He nodded. "You get three hundred sixty-four a year. Three hundred sixty-five in leap years."

"Welcome, welcome, welcome," said the Mad Hatter. "Can I perhaps interest you in a hat?"

"You could interest us by pointing to the palace," said Morgan.

"Ah!" said the March Hare. "You're off to see the queen."

"That goes without saying," remarked the Mad Hatter. "Anyone would *have* to be off to see the queen."

"Shhh!" said the Dormouse, holding a finger to its lips. "Even the trees have ears."

"They have?" said the Mad Hatter. "I never noticed them before." He got off his chair and walked over to the nearest tree. "Hey, tree," he said. "Can you hear me?"

"Certainly not," replied the tree. "I don't have any ears."

"Hah!" said the Mad Hatter. "I *knew* it!"

He walked triumphantly back to the table. "So what do you want to see the queen for?" he asked.

"She's so big you can hardly avoid seeing her once you get near the palace," added the March Hare.

"We have business to discuss with her," said Morgan.

"If I were you, I'd discuss it with the king," said the Mad Hatter.

"You would?"

The Mad Hatter nodded. "He's ever so much smaller and less frightening."

"Right," added the March Hare. "When he gets mad, he's much more likely to yell 'Off with his knees!'"

"We'll keep it in mind," said Raven.

"Are you sure I can't sell you a hat?" asked the Mad Hatter. "Guaranteed not to fall off, even after the queen beheads you."

"I haven't even met her," said Raven. "What makes you think she'll want to behead me?"

The Mad Hatter pulled back a sleeve, revealing a glowing wristwatch with a tiny set of chimes hanging down from it. He stared at it for a moment, then looked up. "Oh, she'll want to, all right. It's almost three in the p.m., and she hadn't beheaded anyone since noon."

The Dormouse tugged at his sleeve and whispered something to him.

"All right," said the Mad Hatter. "Since one twenty. But that's still a long time for her to go without a beheading."

"We'll just have to take our chances," said Raven.

"Really?" said the March Hare. "You're a chance-taker, are you?"

"When I have to be."

"Wonderful!" said the March Hare, pulling a printed sheet of paper out from a vest pocket.

"What's that?" asked Raven.

"Today's morning line," answered the March Hare. "Let me see . . . Beheading, even money . . . Run Through with Sword, four-to-one . . . Bear Hug (that's spelled B-e-a-r; the queen is never without her royal robes), six-to-one . . . Feed to elephants, ten-to-one."

"Elephants don't eat meat," noted Raven.

The Mad Hatter smiled. "That's what their last six meals said. Before . . . well, um . . ."

"So where do you want to place your money?" asked the March Hare.

"In my pocket," said Raven.

"That's hardly very sporting," said the March Hare sullenly. "Especially considering that you're going to be dead before sunset."

"We're that close?" said Raven.

"Just over that next ridge," said the Mad Hatter, pointing.

"Is there much of an army guarding the castle?"

"Dear me, no!" said the Mad Hatter. "She can't very well behead you if you can't gain access to the castle."

"So she has no army?"

"Oh, she has a huge one," said the Mad Hatter. "But they're for fighting bloody wars of conquest, and for subjugating entire populations. Believe me, the queen doesn't need anyone or anything to protect her."

"Right," said the March Hare. "You want protection *from* the queen, not *for* her."

"Especially if you're the king," said the Dormouse.

The March Hare sighed and shook his head sadly. "Yeah, he's the only one who ever beat the odds."

"Just over the hill?" said Morgan.

"That's right."

"Then we'd best be going."

"If I can't sell you a bet, how about a funeral plot?" asked the March Hare. "Very reasonably priced, since you won't need the extra room that a head takes up."

"I think I'll pass," answered Raven.

"You certainly will," said the March Hare.

"Away," added the Dormouse.

Raven walked over to where Morgan was standing. "Okay," he said, "let's get the show on the road."

They began walking up the hill.

"He's *got* to be the Queen of Hearts," said Raven. "She's got to be the most bloodthirsty creature, human or otherwise, in any real or imagined world."

"Probably," agreed Morgan.

"We're as prepared as we'll ever be," continued Raven. "Let's make sure we end it in this world."

"We'll do our best," she replied.

"That's not the most positive reinforcement imaginable," he said wryly.

"We're not going up against the weakest enemy I've ever encountered," she said. She reached out, took his hand, and squeezed it with her own. "But together, we just may pull it off."

37

Nobody tried to stop them as they approached the castle. Indeed, most of the guards and soldiers just looked at them with enormous sympathy.

"Well-protected place," remarked Raven. "I wonder if they've ever had a revolt or an insurrection?"

"From what we've heard about the queen," replied Morgan, "I suspect if they *have* had any they were of incredibly short duration."

"Hard to argue with that," said Raven, pointing to two large containers along the side of an outbuilding. One was labeled trash and the other was heads.

A guard approached them, brandishing a sword. "Who are you that invades the palace of the Queen of Hearts?"

"Two travelers from afar," replied Morgan.

"Afar . . . Afar . . ." muttered the guard. "In what direction does Afar lay?"

"That way," said Raven, gesturing behind him with his thumb.

"And what is your purpose here?"

"We'd like to see the queen," answered Raven.

The guard looked stunned. "You *want* to see the queen?"

"Absolutely," said Raven. "If we're going to live here, we

want to meet whoever's in charge." He paused. "Is there a king too?"

"Not so's you'd notice it," answered the guard. He stared at them disbelievingly. "You really want to see her?"

"Yes," said Raven. Then: "What does she look like, so we can tell her apart from her handmaidens."

"She is the most gorgeous creature in the world!" shouted the guard.

"We're not hard of hearing," said Raven.

"I didn't yell for *your* benefit," said the guard.

"So may we meet her?"

The guard shrugged, made a gesture that seemed to say it's your funeral, turned on his heel, and began leading them into the palace.

They passed a number of gold and ivory sculptures, most of them in the shape of hearts, walked past a squad of guards that instantly sprang to attention, saw that the queen wasn't with them, and relaxed again.

They walked down a winding corridor, and finally came to an ornate golden door at the end of it.

"You're absolutely sure?" said the guard softly.

"Absolutely," said Raven.

The guard gently knocked on the door.

"Who the blazes is it?" bellowed a hoarse female voice.

"Two visitors to see the queen," said the guard, unable to keep his voice from shaking.

"Damned lucky for all of you that I just finished my beauty sleep," growled the queen.

"So shall I usher them in, your majesty?" asked the guard.

"First make sure they aren't carrying any concealed weapons," said the queen. "Then make sure they're not smuggling in any vials of poison. Especially chocolate-flavored poison. You know how partial I am to chocolate."

"Yes, your majesty."

"If you miss one, even a tiny one, I'll turn your head into a bowling ball."

"Oh, good!" said a squeaky male voice. "I *like* bowling."

"Of course you do, my dear," said the queen. "It's just about the only thing you're good at."

"Back rubs!" said the voice, which Raven and Morgan now assumed belonged to the king. "I'm very good at back rubs."

"When you remember to trim your fingernails," said the queen. "Okay, show them in."

The guard opened the door, then stood aside while Morgan and Raven entered the throne room. Seated upon an oversize throne was the oversize queen, a good three hundred pounds of fat, wearing a golden gown covered with hundreds of little red hearts.

The king was a full head shorter and wore a robe that was in need of both repairs and cleaning. He had a nondescript little beard, narrow squinting eyes, and a body that could have used a couple of months' worth of rich desserts with every meal just to get to a state of undernourished.

"So who are you?" demanded the queen.

"My name is Eddie Raven . . ." began Raven.

"Nonsense!" bellowed the Queen. "You're a rabbit, not a raven."

"Whatever makes you happy," he said. "My name is Eddie Rabbit, and this is my friend Morgan."

The queen stared at Morgan.

"You are very pleasing to the eyes," she said at last, and then frowned. "I hate that in a woman."

"No problem," said Morgan, uttering a quick spell that made her every bit as fat and almost as ugly as the queen herself.

The queen looked at her and smiled. "I like you already!" she growled.

"Thank you, your highness," said Morgan.

"So what are you and the bunny doing in my kingdom?"

"We were wondering if it's a nice place to live," replied Morgan.

"Well, it's certainly a nice place to die," said the queen. "Living is another matter."

"What is life like here?" asked Raven.

"Brief," said the king, and the queen threw back her head and laughed.

"Do the arts flourish here?" continued Raven.

"Not really," answered the queen. "But once we invent the crayon, the sky's the limit."

"The sciences?"

"Such as they are," said the queen. Suddenly she kicked the king, who uttered a startled groan, flew back ten feet, and fell to the ground with a thud. "You kick 'em, they fall down. Cause and effect. *That's* science."

Eddie, can you read/hear/feel this?

Raven frowned at the voice in his head.

Well, Eddie—can you?

I don't know how to reply.

Just think.

Okay, I read you and I'm thinking. What now?

Something's strange here.

You can say that again.

No, I mean really *strange. I can read some of their thoughts too. She didn't know she was going to kick the king—it was just instinct, because she* likes *kicking defenseless things.*

Okay, she didn't know.

But he *did.*

Oh?

He didn't duck or try to defend himself, and it had to hurt. Why wouldn't he protect himself?

Son of a bitch! It's because it would spoil the illusion that she calls all the shots and he's just the little wimp who married her!

I can think of no other reason.

We're only going to have one shot at this, so let's wait a couple of minutes and make sure.

Okay, Eddie.

"So if we decide to settle here, what kind of rent are we looking at?" asked Raven aloud.

The queen reached down her neckline and withdrew a wicked-looking dagger. "I can rend you in any of a dozen ways. What's your preference?"

"Hilarious," said Raven grimly. "Can I ask what may, on the face of it, seem an unwise question?" said Raven.

"You can," said the queen. "Of course, I reserve the right to respond brutally if I don't approve of it."

"My question is this: If you keep beheading everyone, who is left to pay the taxes that support your lavish lifestyle?"

She looked puzzled, and turned to the king. "Who is left, my love?" she said.

"We don't kill all the rich ones," replied the king.

She turned to Raven. "There you have it," she said. "Good sound economics."

"Just the way they teach it in college," said Raven.

Suddenly the queen's face contorted in rage. "In *college*?" she bellowed. "We don't allow an educated class in Wonderland! How do you think I remain on the throne?"

"Through brutality, violence, and luck," answered Raven.

Not smart, Eddie.

"Off with his head!" screamed the queen.

Suddenly a dozen guards entered the room and surrounded the king.

"Not *him*, you idiots!" yelled the queen. She pointed at Raven. *"Him!"*

Bribe her, Eddie. Make her an offer no one would refuse.

You're kidding.

Just do it.

"I'll give you one hundred diamonds, rubies, and sapphires if you'll just forgive me and forget the whole thing," said Raven. "I'll even toss in a few emeralds."

The queen stared at him as if considering. Then suddenly she shook her whole body, like a dog shedding water, and signaled one of the warriors to pull out his sword.

Okay, Morgan, we tried. I don't blame you. What happens next isn't your fault.

Shut up, Eddie! I have to concentrate.

On what?

She *wanted* to take the offer. He *ordered* her not to. *She's not the Master of Dreams, Eddie—he is!*

At least I'll go to my grave knowing we came close, he thought bitterly.

Shut up, Eddie!

I'm not speaking.

Stop thinking. I've got to concentrate!

"All right," said the queen, stepping back to give the swordsman more room. "Off—"

I've never done this before. I hope it works.

"With—"

Whatever it is, you're not the only one who hopes so.

Quiet!

"His—"

NOW!

"Head!" screamed the queen.

Raven braced himself for the feel of the blade slicing through his neck. Instead he heard a thud as a head fell to the floor and rolled up to his feet.

Raven looked down at himself, and realized he was wearing the king's robe. He touched his head, and came in contact with the crown. He then took a good look at the head on the floor, and realized that it belonged to the White Rabbit.

You did it!

Let's get out of here while they still think you're the king.

And they did, while the queen was preoccupied with singing a victory song and doing a happy, if awkward, little dance around the White Rabbit's corpse.

Once outside she stopped and turned to him. "I have one last adjustment to make before I leave you, Eddie."

"Leave me?" he repeated. "What are you talking about?"

"I belong in my own time and place, Eddie," said Morgan. "Even as we speak I'm being drawn back there. But first . . ."

She placed her hand atop his head and uttered one last

spell. Suddenly he was taller and slimmer again, and the crown had vanished.

"You're Eddie Raven again," she said, leaning forward and kissing him lightly on the cheek.

He reached out to hug her, but she had vanished.

And, a moment later, so did he.

EPILOGUE

———◆———

Raven overcame a brief spell of dizziness, blinked his eyes a few times, and saw that it was evening and he was back in his Manhattan apartment. He looked around for something—*any*thing—to convince himself he hadn't just been hallucinating for the past few days, but everything seemed absolutely normal. The chairs, the books, the clothes, not a thing was out of place, not a thing spoke of the places he had been and the things he had done.

He pulled out his cell phone, began calling local hospitals, and was just about to give up when he found Lisa on the fifth try. A nurse explained that she was asleep—it was, after all, well past midnight—and he determined to visit her the next morning.

He walked to the dining area, pulled a bottle of bourbon out of the beat-up cabinet, poured himself a tall, stiff drink, downed it, and poured another.

"Well, real or imaginary, at least *that's* over with," he muttered.

No, Eddie, said a familiar voice inside his head.

"Rofocale?"

Yes.

"What the hell is going on?" demanded Raven. "Why is this happening to me? I'm nothing special. I'm no hero. Hell, I'm just a guy from Manhattan."

No, Eddie. You are far more than that, far more than you can currently imagine or comprehend.

"What the hell are you talking about?"

You must find the answer for yourself—and you'd better hurry, because the Master of Dreams was just a stalking horse for a far worse enemy who awaits you.

"To hell with it—and you!" growled Raven. "I've had it with Dream Masters and fantasy worlds and having the girl I love used for target practice. Count me out!"

I wish I could, said Rofocale's voice within his head, *but this is not a burden that you can share, or ignore, or simply wish away. The future of this and all other realms depends solely upon you.*

And with that, Eddie Raven was left alone with his memories—and his challenges—once again.